Anonymous

Household Puzzles

Anonymous

Household Puzzles

ISBN/EAN: 9783337403621

Printed in Europe, USA, Canada, Australia, Japan

Cover: Foto ©Andreas Hilbeck / pixelio.de

More available books at **www.hansebooks.com**

'We're comming to meet you, Uncle Randolph, Baby and I."

p. 201

HOUSEHOLD PUZZLES

BY

PANSY (Mrs. G. R. Alden)

Author of "Wanted," "Stephen Mitchell's Journey,"
"Twenty Minutes Late," "Ester Ried," Etc.

❋

BOSTON
LOTHROP PUBLISHING COMPANY

CONTENTS.

1

CHAPTER XII.

CHAPTER XIII.

CHAPTER XIV.

CHAPTER XV.

CHAPTER XVI.

CHAPTER XVII.

CHAPTER XVIII.

CHAPTER XIX.

CHAPTER XX.

CHAPTER XXI.

CHAPTER XXII.

CHAPTER XXIII.

Contents.

HOUSEHOLD PUZZLES.

CHAPTER I.

"SPLIT THINGS."

ERMINA RANDOLPH drummed listlessly yet gloomily on the window pane; she
was watching the snow as it came down
in wandering flakes. "Spitting snow,"
Maria called it. Maria was in the
kitchen, making cookies. They mostly used
cookies in the Randolph family, in preference to
other kinds of cake; not that they preferred them
either, but they *wore* better. You could "split
them thinner," Maria said, and "work in plenty
of flour, and flour cost less than butter and
eggs." This was the genius of the Randolph
family — at least it was the necessity — to "split
things thin," and "wear" them as long as possible.

Helen came in from the white world outside, bringing flakes of snow on her cloak and sodden lumps of it on her rubbers.

"One rubber leaks," was her announcement; "one foot is as wet as water. I do wish I had a new pair."

"Of feet?" queried Ermina, turning from the outside snow. "Now, I should like a new pair of almost anything conceivable, except feet; I am very well satisfied with the ones I have."

A glance at her trim, well-shapen foot would not have led you to feel surprise at this conclusion.

"Why don't you have a better fire?" was Helen's only answer to this sentence.

"Coal is dear," Ermina said, with a shrug of her shapely shoulders.

"What *isn't?*" Helen answered, and there was a little spice of tartness in her voice; "I'm not going to freeze to death to accommodate the price of coal."

Then she put forth her wet foot and slipped back the under slide with decision; the dingy leaden mass of coal instantly glowed at the change and the air seemed to feel warmer. Helen dropped her bundles on an empty chair, herself into another, and sighed forlornly as she held up both hands to view her finger ends gaping from each separate glove finger.

" Isn't that an elegant pair of gloves for one's best to wear in making morning calls?" she said, with quiet sarcasm.

" Especially when you have the baker and the butcher and other *elite* of the town to call on," Ermina answered, in the same tone. " What arrangement did you make about bills, Helen?"

" Don't ask me!" said Helen, in a tone of disgust. " For pity's sake let me forget for five minutes that there is such a thing as unpaid bills in the world. I made the only arrangement I could, of course. Got them all to wait another month; though I felt tempted to ask them what earthly good they thought that would do them. Unless some of this horrid mud turns to money or some equally wild thing happens, I don't know how they are ever to get their pay."

" They always do, though," Ermina said, thoughtfully. " Father brings it about somehow."

" I know he does, after puzzling and twisting and borrowing, until he doesn't know which way to turn next. Such work as we have! I'm sick of living, Ermina!"

" Well," said Ermina, " you had better shut that damper, because the coal bill is increasing with every lump that falls, and I'm afraid you'll be sicker of living before it is paid. Come into the kitchen; Maria is baking cookies, and I presume it will be hot enough there for you to bake your foot if you want to."

This Randolph family belonged to a representative class. I think when you have made their acquaintance you will be on familiar terms with perhaps one-third of our American race. Families who live in well appointed houses, with very neat and appropriate parlor furniture, somewhat the worse for wear, it is true, yet whose defects are skillfully concealed — families who are on terms of intimacy with half the neighborhood, who are invited to tea at Mrs. Harvey Smith's who keeps a second girl, and lives in serene indifference to her kitchen expenses — families who exchange bows with Mrs. B. Lawrence Livermore, who lives on Belton Avenue, and hardly so much as knows that she has a kitchen attached to her house — yet these same families live in a state of perpetual unrest and unhappiness, their occupation a frantic stretch at the family purse to make it meet the necessities, to say nothing of the comforts of life. Of this class were the Randolphs — people who sat down in utter despair on Saturday nights, who brooded over ways and means during all the long Sabbath day between faint efforts "not to think their own thoughts," and who rose up to the burden of life again on Monday morning with its problem all unsolved. Mr. Randolph was a merchant — at

least he had been — one of the unfortunate,
struggling, disappointed ones, borrowing of this
friend to-day to meet the demands of yesterday's
lender.   With him there had hardly been a yesterday to look back upon when he was free and
fearless of to-morrow's claims ; not at least since
he was a boy, and that he thought must have
been a hundred years before.   He commenced life
too early, did Mr. Joseph Randolph, just as many
a hot headed young American will do after him.
It had not always been thus with his family ;
they had not known of his struggles ; pity they
had not.   It is not entirely the fault of the
women that they are, many of them, the helpless extravagant mortals that society has made
them.   The Randolph household had eaten and
drank, and slept and dressed, in blissful indifference as to how the bills were paid.   Economical they were to a certain extent, at least they
thought so ; though in these latter days they
would have smiled over their former ideas of
economy.   They had never considered themselves wealthy, indeed they always spoke of
themselves as poor ; but a new dress a-piece
when they needed it, and fresh hats and bonnets
when the seasons changed, and fresh gloves and
ribbons and laces at their pleasure, this was
economy ; as for the butter and sugar and meat,
those three awful whirlpools into which so much

capital is sunken, Bridget the maid of all work,
attended to them, unmolested by any of the feminine heads of the household. Ermina was only
sixteen when the change came; first a long,
serious illness on the father's part; then months
of invalidism for the mother: then Tom came
home from college in disgrace and untold difficulty, requiring among other things much money
to be raised, and suddenly it came to their
knowledge what the father had known for a
long time, that he could not pay that money nor
any other. It was a very quietly managed matter. Mr. Randolph could not even fail on a
great scale; the failure must be third rate, as
his business had always been. There was no
red flag or immense sacrifice of goods; the family had not even the excitement of a great change
outwardly to involve and interest them. Mr.
Randolph merely slipped quietly and meekly
from his position of master to that of subordi-
nate. His principal creditor took the business
entire, and the former owner as his clerk, at
a fair enough salary for a clerk, but not one
equal to supporting a family of seven. This,
then, was the problem for the family brain, how
to make a hundred dollars do five times as much
as a hundred dollars *will* do, and have a surplus
for incidentals — unceasingly worked at it was,
but not as yet solved. Mrs. Randolph helped

feebly at it sometimes, but Mrs. Randolph had
no head for figures, never *had* had even when
she was " parlor border in Madame La Blanc's
seminary." When she said this she always
sighed. Mrs. Randolph was one of those unfortunate beings who had come down. Now *that*
is a very difficult thing to do. You may talk of
the impossibility of making a graceful *ascent*
in the social scale, but unless you are a very remarkable woman you will find a graceful *descent*
at least equally difficult. Mrs. Randolph, for instance, had no real conception of what economy
meant. In a general way it meant to use as
little point lace as could be reasonably got along
with, and to buy no new jewelry for awhile;
but when one *never* bought point lace and jewelry, how were these rules to be reduced to practical use? To Mrs. Randolph her daughters were
absolute wonders; nothing that had happened to
her girlhood, sheltered as it was in the home of a
New York millionnaire, where she reigned an
only daughter, could be used to help her household in their troubles. The millionnaire indeed
had gone to absolute ruin years ago, but not until he had carefully finished his daughter's education in the art of spending millions, and
married her to a man who had no millions for
her, which, by the way, is one of our American
puzzles. Meantime she looked on in helpless

bewilderment, while the young ladies turned and and darned and colored, remarking now and then in a helpless, dazed sort of way,—

" There's my lavender silk, girls; it is trimmed with thread lace. You might do something with it. You do such wonderful things, all of you."

And Ermina would respond good-naturedly,—

" Spare us that affliction, mother, I beg, in addition to all our other trials. Don't send us up and down the earth in a frantic hunt after something that will do to wear with lavender silks and thread lace."

The young ladies were very unlike in characacter. Who ever saw four young ladies, children of the same parentage though they be, who looked or acted alike in any but minor points? Helen was the nominal head of the party, being one of those persons who are prompt to express an opinion and act upon it, and who get the name of being quick in their conclusions, nothing generally being said about the amount of time they have to spend in repenting afterwards. So Helen did a good deal of the talking; she could do it well. She fretted a good deal about the state of things; was sorely tried over the rips in her gloves, yet mended them faithfully, and made them last just as long as possible, and made every one aware that she did. When Helen sacrificed her own convenience you were

sure to know it; and as she was in a continual
state of doing without things that she did *not*
want, there was an uncomfortable sense of martyrdom about her. Ermina took things philosophically; the ragged glove-fingers, and faded
ribbons, and mended collars, might try her soul
as fully as they did Helen's, but it was natural
for her to be gravely comical over them all.
Surfacely you would have supposed Ermina to
be perfectly indifferent to existing troubles, that
is, as a general thing. There came, however,
to her horrible days when life was worse than
leaden, absolutely black. Wretched days were
these in the Randolph household — days to be
remembered and shivered over. There was one
comfort, they came rarely, and between their
coming Ermina tugged at the family snarl and
was good-natured over it. Grace was a little
past seventeen, was the family beauty, had the
name of being utterly thoughtless and light-
hearted, was merry and bright, and the least bit
hoydenish from morning to night, day after day,
and week after week. " It was a wonder,"
Helen said sometimes "that she didn't think a
little. I'm sure I had a great deal of thinking
and planning to do at her age." But on the
whole they seemed willing that Grace should do
the laughing and merry-making, and let thinking
alone; nor ever noticed that Grace's gloves had

a way of lasting longer than other people's, at
least she applied less often than the others for
shillings from the carefully guarded fund; that
the fashion of arranging her hair was changed
whimsically often they were apt to discover.   It
required closer sight to find that when the
brown hair ribbon was hopelessly soiled, a plain
black velvet band became the style, and when
the black velvet grew rusty, severe simplicity
suddenly became her best, and her hair was
combed back straight and plain without band
or bow.   Little sacrifices, very trifles in their
way, nobody thought of noticing them.   She
herself did not name them sacrifices, but she
was very steady about them, and if she had been
one who ever did any thinking they would have
had the appearance of being premeditated and
systematic.

The other daughter was Maria.

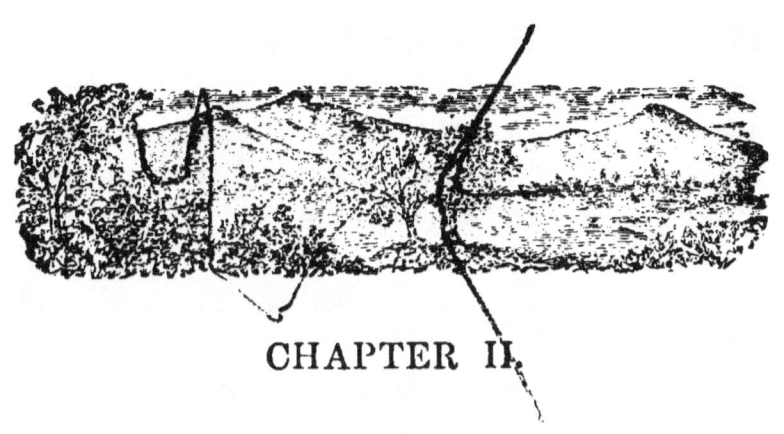

CHAPTER II.

RAISINS.

OW we will go to the kitchen and see Maria. You think you know all about her. Confess, oh, most wise and far-sighted reader, that between the time of closing the last chapter and opening this you have said something after this wise: "I know what sort of person Maria will be. She will be an old maid — real old — with a crooked nose, cross-eyed very likely, and sour — oh, as sour as vinegar, but gifted with all the excellencies in the calender." Yes! Well, Maria is just exactly fifteen, this happening to be her birthday. She is engaged in making cookies, perhaps you remember, for while we have been going back over the history of the Randolph family for a period of forty years or so, Helen and Ermina have made their transit from sitting-room to kitchen. Maria has her head in the oven, her curls are gathered into a net, and the net is

dusted with flour. "Maria always flours everything, from her net to her shoes," Ermina says,
"and that is why the barrel is forever empty."

"How nice and warm it is here," Helen said,
shivering and squeezing between the wall and
the stove.

"Cookies take a fearful amount of warming
material," Maria said, emerging from the oven
with very glowing cheeks. "That and their
rapid disappearance are the two faults they
have. Girls, don't you think that heartless flour
barrel is empty!"

"Oh, for pity's sake!" Helen said, in dismay.
Ermina laughed.

"You ought not to have told her," she said.
"She has the blues now, and she's cold. This
fire just suits her. She has been wasting coal in
a reckless manner. As many as three pieces
fell into the grate while we were there."

Maria turned toward the shivering woman behind the stove.

"Now, Helen Randolph!" she said, in tragic
tones, "you *haven't* been and opened that slide!"

"After all, it's not so bad as your making
cookies out of an empty flour barrel," laughed
Ermina, as Helen vouchsafed neither word nor
smile.

"I didn't," said Maria. "I have that mira-
cle yet to perform over the bread."

The outer door opened, and with much stamping and kicking of snow the son of the house came in. A tall, finely-formed, fair-faced, curly-headed young man — *quite* young he was, hardly nineteen, and looking even younger. You couldn't help being attracted by his face despite a certain look of recklessness that it had about it. It was one of those faces that are picked out in a crowd, and a student of human nature would find himself wondering whether its owner was going to be prominent for his good or evil life — prominent in some way he was pretty likely to be.

"A woman's rights convention," he said, tossing his cap on a chair and taking a corner of the wood-box for a seat. "What's the subject under discussion, feathers or flounces? Let me have the bearings of the question and I'll make a telling speech on the popular side."

"We have so many of either to discuss," Helen said, sarcastically. "We are much more interested in hearing whether you have secured that situation."

"Never a sign of a situation has this fellow."

"Didn't you *apply* for it?"

"I did, ma'am," rising, and making her a profound bow, probably out of consideration for the sharpness of her tones.

"Then what was in the way?"

2

" Well, several things. I might have been too tall, for instance. He undoubtedly observed that it took an unusually large pattern to make me a pair of pants."

" I wish we could ever secure a sensible answer from you on any subject." Helen said this with increasing irritation, and Ermina spoke eagerly,—

"Tom, do tell us what was the matter. We were so certain that you would succeed this time."

Thus appealed to, Tom answered with great apparent seriousness,—

" The main difficulty was that he did not seem to appreciate the peculiar cultivation of my tastes and appetites, and insisted on a style of article to which I am not accustomed."

" What on earth does he mean?" said wondering Ermina.

" It is very plainly to be seen, I should think." This from Helen, in her loftiest tone. " He objected to a clerk with an everlasting cigar in his mouth, just as any sensible man would. It has turned out just as I expected."

Tom seemed immensely amused. He laughed until the wood-box beneath him shook in sympathy.

" Upon my word, Helen," he said, when he could speak, "your name ought to have been

'Just As I Expected' instead of 'Helen.' What a vivid imagination you have!"

"If I had to depend on a salary for a living I wouldn't smoke it up."

"Not until you had one at least. Never was a fellow less likely to smoke up a salary than I am, so far as I can see at present."

"It's too bad, anyway." began Helen again. "Poor father has the burden of us all resting upon him. I wish *I* were a young man."

"Just be the *wife* of a young man, Helen; that will help father immensely. I might speak to Horace about the occasion for haste if you would like to have me."

Whereupon Ermina laughed. That girl always had to laugh at things which seemed to her laughable, no matter what the consequences. The consequences at this present time were that Helen flushed angrily, and darted sharp glances at her from her very black eyes as she said to her brother,—

"If I were reduced to the condition of hanger-on, supported by my father, I would at least try to be a little less insulting to my sister."

Tom opened his mouth to speak, but Maria came to the rescue with a change of topic.

"Tom, have a cookie?" And Tom filled his mouth with cookie, and was necessarily silent.

"That's economical!" Helen said, with energy

Whereupon Tom laughed until he choked. The conversation had suddenly taken a ludicrous form.

Mrs. Randolph's voice was heard in the distance calling Ermina, and as she went to answer the summons, Helen quietly departed by way of the hall door. Tom swallowed his cookie and seemed lost in a reverie.

" I did try for the situation, Maria," he said at length.

"I know it," said Maria, with her head in the oven, from whence she presently emerged with the last tin of cookies. " What was it all about, Tom ? "

" Why," said Tom, brushing the crumbs of his cookie into the wood-box. " the horrid old fellow wanted me to sell wormy raisins. I did get the place, you see, and set to work as large as life : and about the second thing that happened was Horace Webster coming after raisins — those small, sticky, seedless things, you know, Maria, that look just like a mess of gum that somebody has chewed. Well, there were worms in them, the horridest little wretches that ever squirmed and I told Horace about it, you know, just as any decent fellow would. I thought the box had been left open, and so the raisins got spoiled ; so I opened another box and there were some more of the vile little kickers ! So Horace went away

without the raisins, and old Colby was in a tremendous rage. So we had a worm and raisin
talk just then and there, and the upshot of it all
was that I came away without my situation.
Now don't you see. I ought to be put in a Sunday-school book for a good boy who was a martyr
to my principles!"

"I see," Maria said, laughing merrily. "But,
Tom, why couldn't you have told the girls about
it just as you have me, instead of talking such
nonsense?"

"There's a difference between you and the
girls, you see. Did you believe the nonsense
that I told them?"

"No, of course I didn't."

"But they did, you see; and therein lies the
difference between you. There is no use in ex-
plaining things to them, when people think you
are the worst fellow in town. Let them think, *I*
say, if it's such a comfort to 'em."

"They don't think anything of the kind; and
you were rude to Helen, you know."

"Not till she was rude to me, though; besides, she ought to be as good as gold, no matter
what I was — she professes to be so good, you
see, and I don't."

"Because she isn't always what she professes
is no reason why you should be as wicked as you
can."

"Look here, Maria, don't you take up preach
ing; two of that profession are enough in one
family. Helen and Ermina are equal to all that
is needed in that line."

Maria laughed good-naturedly.

"I'm not preaching," she said, "I'm talking
common sense. You make too much of what
Helen says. I don't mind her in the least. She
is tired this morning. She has been out on very
ugly business, trying to pay bills without any
money; and besides, Tom, the flour barrel *is*
empty, and naturally enough, she is worried as
to how it is going to be filled."

"Why don't she have faith?" Tom said, with
sober face and a gleam of mischief in his bright
brown eyes; "she believes that all things work
together for her good, and, unless she considers
it for her personal advantage to be starved, she
must think that the barrel will be filled somehow."

"Of course it will be filled; but it's not very
pleasant to think that Mr. Hammond will never
be paid for it; and I don't see any way to pay
him."

"I don't know about that," Tom said, meditatively; "if it's for his good to be paid — why,
he *will* be, won't he? Isn't that the doctrine?
And if it *isn't* for his good, ought we to wish
him to receive evil? Isn't it a delicious muddle,
Maria? I declare it is just ludicrous."

" One would think that you had a very different father from the one that you have," said Maria, with great gravity. " You don't suppose his religion is all pretense, do you? "

"One would think you were my grandmother, at the very least," Tom said, half in mockery and half testily. " I don't pretend to think that any of it is pretense. I only say that you and I have said a hundred times, that it is a contradiction and confusion, so far as my brain can follow it. There's Helen, and Ermina, and Grace, and you. Now, suppose you ask father which ones are helps and comforts to him. You are not so lowly-minded but that you see for yourself that father depends on you to manage things, and to help generally, and that Grace is comfortable to have around him. As for Helen and Ermina, the sooner they are married and settled the more comfortable father will be; and yet those two profess to have something to help them in their every-day affairs, and you and Grace have to help yourselves. A fellow can't help thinking that things are mixed."

" My cookies are — and baked," was Maria's prompt response; " for which I am duly thankful. It's time for potatoes and onions now, and you know you hate the smell of onions, though I think myself they are superior to tobacco; but on the whole, I would advise you to leave.

Don't go to supposing that I don't understand and appreciate your harangue, and I don't see through things any better than you do — the only difference is, that I don't see any use in trying to see what I can't see. Only I do think that you are hard on Helen. She tries to help, and she economizes; and she has been out in all this snow, looking for drawing scholars."

Tom whistled.

" Why didn't you go out and look for French scholars and let the cookies slide," he said, solemnly.

"Now, Tom, what's the use of talking so. Helen *can't* make cookies, nor peel onions; she just doesn't know how. There are things that she *could* do if she had the opportunity."

"So there are things that I could do. I could take a sleigh ride, or go skating, or eat a turkey — a good share of one, anyhow; all I lack is opportunity. Yet Helen wanted me to leave these things that I know I *can* do, and try to sell tobacco and things."

"You are too absurd," laughed Maria. "You know very well that Helen *could* teach drawing if she only had some scholars. How can she help it if there are none to be found?"

" How much shoe leather is she going to waste hunting after them? One would think she might have decided about a year ago that they were not available material. I know a few things that you could do if you had a chance. You could walk through algebra and geometry and Latin with great pleasure. Why don't you sit down behind the stove and glower because you can't devote yourself to such pursuits instead of to onions? Oh, how they smell."

"It just resolves itself into this, Tom; if you can't get the situation in the bank that you wanted — why, you are willing to sell tobacco."

"But not worms," Tom interrupted.

"Well, since you can't get an opportunity to sell tobacco without worms, why don't you try for a job at wood-sawing, for instance?"

Whereupon Tom whistled a little, and then was silent. After a little either the argument or the onions were too much for him, and he left Maria in solitary possession of the kitchen.

CHAPTER III.

TWO PETERS.

A T family worship that evening the Randolph household were all together. They had a very pleasant custom of coming together for this service, immediately after tea. Mrs. Randolph sat in the low rocker in front of the stove, with her feet on the hearth, and around her shoulders a small bright shawl. She nearly always sat with her feet on the hearth and a shawl around her. She shivered occasionally, which was also a habit of hers. She was a frail, fair little woman; a few lines were on her forehead and about her mouth, brought there by her hopeless attempts to assist at the family problem; her pretty gray hair waved gracefully above the low forehead; her collar was a bit of rare lace, remains of her early grandeur; and her alpaca wrapper was faced with pretty plaid silk — this, also, was a remnant of early days. Altogether

she seemed a dainty, well preserved picture
of an effeminate, loving, lovable woman. How
it happened that she was mother to five hearty,
strong-limbed, strong-willed beings was a puzzle
to some people. It spoke well for the heart
of the Randolph juniors that they had, every
one, a petting, protective care over this mother.
Tom might be rude to Helen, and wild with
every one of them, yet his voice invariably put
on a caress when it addressed the little mother.
Father Randolph sat apart from the others and
took up the family Bible immediately, as if he
either had no time to tarry, or else no heart to
bring to the household reunion. He was a tall,
thin, pale man, with deep-set, earnest eyes, and
a sensitive, finely cut mouth. He had not hand-
led the problem with gloved fingers; he had
tugged at it, wrestled with it, sometimes with
fierce and determined energy, and yet it had con-
quered him; and there was that in the sunken
eyes which said, "I am vanquished; the battle
was too fierce for me. I have failed." Grace
sat at the piano. The young ladies of this
family played the piano—as well educated young
ladies should—that is, they played at it. None
of them had that beautiful gift for it which we
call genius. Helen, in her childhood, had either
to be driven or coaxed to her practice hour. Ermina had gone through the ordeal more bravely,

simply because of her talent for yielding to the
inevitable. Later in life — in their early young
ladyhood — they had been comparatively faithful, because "everybody played," and of course
they must; and their father, so long as they had
the money to do it with, had unflinchingly paid
Professor Fero's awful bills, because he had been
educated to believe that "they" would think it
strange if his daughters did not take lessons.
Grace had never accomplished much with Professor Fero. They did not get on well together,
and, by means best known to her father and herself, she early escaped from his tuition. Yet
Grace was the only one who could play, at
family worship, the sweet and tender hymns that
her father invariably selected. I said the young
ladies played. Perhaps at fifteen Maria is not to
be counted under that term. Maria did not play
at all. Great was the little mother's consternation
when she announced her determination never to
take a music lesson. What would "they" think?
she plaintively asked her daughter; but *that*
daughter being hopelessly indifferent to "*their*"
opinion, persisted in her headstrong course, af-
firming that there wasn't even any "*drumative*"
powers in her; and her father, taking secret
pride in his youngest daughter's determined spirit,
recognizing a something akin to one-half of his
own nature, upheld her in her decision, and

thereby several hundred dollars were saved. Grace waited at the piano while her father read aloud one of his favorite hymns.

"When gloomy clouds across the sky
   Cast shadows o'er the land,
  Bright scenes of bliss illume my path,
  For Jesus holds my hand.
    Safe will be my rest,
    With his presence blest,
    If on sea or land
    Jesus holds my hand."

Tom, meantime, with his chair tilted back against the wall, listened and made his mental observations. There was one other person, who for the time being, belonged to the household: young Peter Armstrong, who was errand-boy in general in Mr. Freeman's factory; and it suited Mr. Freeman's convenience to have Peter boarded at his neighbor Mr. Randolph's. "Just as a matter of accommodation," Helen was wont to explain, not with intentional untruthfulness, but with that long-cultivated habit of smoothing over family matters. "Just because we like the money that he pays regularly every Saturday night," the more strictly truthful Maria would add when opportunity offered.

Peter Armstrong wore his pants tucked inside his boots, and his jacket was patched at the elbows; also, he never had his hair parted evenly, and often forgot to part it at all. He was one of Helen's trials. She considered it very queer in him to want to come in the parlor to prayers. It was certainly rather awkward; suppose somebody should call!

However, Peter did most decidedly like to come in to prayers, and it suited Mr. Randolph to have him come, and he sat, on this particular evening, near Maria, who was his firm friend and ally, and joined a very low voice to the singing. After which, Mr. Randolph read, in subdued, sad tone, the psalm commencing, "He that dwelleth in the secret place of the Most High shall abide under the shadow of the Almighty. I will say of the Lord, He is my refuge and my fortress: my God; in him will I trust." On through the blessed triumph of faith and truth embodied in the psalm read Mr. Randolph. There was no change in the sadness of his voice, and if the lines on his face became less drawn, the change was too slight for Tom to discover it. He looked at his mother. She was yawning behind her thin hand and looked too sleepy to heed what was being read. Helen had discovered a rip in her best gaiter, and was looking down at it with frowning face. "I'll wager a box of cigars that she hasn't heard a word father has said," was his mental comment, and he turned his attention to Ermina. That young lady was stretching her neck out of the window to look after the movements of Sarah Freeman, who was passing on the other side of the street. A wicked laugh shone all over Tom's face, his eyes danced, and it was with difficulty that he could restrain himself from whistling, so certain was he that four who professed to be guided by the words of inspiration were totally indifferent to their import now; and then he chanced to glance at the rough-looking boy who sat next to Maria. There was an air of reverent attention about his face, and withal such deep and solemn appreciation of the holy words, that Tom's face instantly sobered. "That fellow thinks he knows what all that is about. I wonder if he really does? I declare his face fairly shines, and he's a dull sort of fellow, too, I always thought. I just wonder, now, if he does get something from the reading that I don't?"

"'He shall call upon me, and I will answer him; I will be with him in trouble; I will deliver him, and honor him,'" read Mr. Randolph. "That is a precious promise," he said, and Tom turning suddenly to him found that the heavy lines were smoother, and something in his prayer made his son think that he, too, had gotten hold of the inner meaning, if there was one. There was always that troublesome "if" coming in to perplex Tom Randolph.

They scattered their various ways directly

after the prayer. Tom, intent upon the thought that Peter had suggested to his mind, followed him through the kitchen.

"What are you going to do?" he queried of Peter, in the absence of any thing better to say.

"Nothing particular. I've got it all done for to-night," was Peter's somewhat ungrammatical reply. "I'll help fix the kindlings and things, if you like."

This last was a very satisfactory sentence to Maria, for Tom was so much given to waiting for convenient seasons for preparing kindlings that it often fell to her lot to split a bit of board for herself as best she could. Thus admonished Tom repaired to the woodshed and commenced a vigorous attack on the woodpile, preparing, meantime, to attack Peter Armstrong and find the meaning of that reverent face.

"Did you notice the words that father read this evening?" he asked, at last, plunging into the midst of the subject.

"Did I notice them?" repeated Peter, driving his axe into a knotty stick. "I reckon I did."

"What did you think of them?"

"Thought they were true."

This answer Tom revolved for some minutes in surprised silence, it was such a strange thing to hear a simple expression of belief in *anything*. His college bred ears were unused to it.

" Do you mean to say that you feel just as that expressed," he said at last, returning to the charge. " Like, for instance, that verse, ' There shall be no evil befall thee ' — and — well, something else. I don't remember the rest. But do you pretend to say that you are not afraid of anything happening to you any more ? "

" Not that exactly," Peter said, slowly and thoughtfully. " I meant, I believed that people could feel so ; could be sure, you know, that everything was just right. If I was as good, now, as the man who wrote that verse I could feel it."

" Pooh ! " said Tom, contemptuously, " he wasn't very good. I happen to know something about *him*. He did several things that weren't exactly perfect."

" Most people do," Peter said, splitting a stick into delightful kindling wood.

" Then nobody is good, it seems. So what does your explanation amount to ? "

" It amounts to their trying after it pretty hard."

" And never getting there," said Tom, pausing in his splitting. " I should think that was pretty stupid business, always trying after a thing and never getting it ; never being satisfied

3

with one's self, even after one had tried. What is the use ? "

" They *do* get satisfied," Peter said, earnestly. "There's a verse your father read yesterday morning, 'I shall be satisfied when I awake with thy likeness.' Then's when it is."

Tom whistled.

" That's a long time to wait," he said, with a queer little laugh.

" Maybe not."

" Anyhow, a fellow is perfectly willing to wait; that's a time that a body don't like to think about."

" I do," Peter said, splitting vigorously. " I like it first rate. It is my opinion it will be a splendid time."

Tom laughed immoderately, and then sat down on a stick of wood to meditate.

" Peter," said he, presently, " it's my opinion that you are not much like your namesake."

" My namesake! Who is he? I don't know another Peter anywhere around."

" He isn't 'around,' but he was once, considerably."

" Peter who ? "

" Ah! there you have me. I'll be hanged if I ever even heard of his other name."

" And you knew him ? "

" Well, not intimately, except by reputation.

You see, he was rather before my time. I'm talking about the individual who had so much to say in Bible times."

" Is there a Peter in the Bible?" queried Pe-.er Armstrong, pausing in his work and speaking with animation. Whereupon Tom laughed louder and longer than before.

" You needn't laugh," his companion said, with gravity. " Though I suppose it is queer not to know things. But I never had a Bible of my own until a few weeks ago, and I don't remember reading anythlng about any Peter in it. I *do* know that there is a book in it named Peter; did *he* write the book ? "

" I think it is altogether likely that he did, though I'm not very well posted."

" Well, I mean to know more about the Bible one of these days. I never went to Sunday-school till I come to this town to live. I never went much of anywhere, I tell you now! A chance is a good deal to a fellow, and I missed mine ; but I'm going to get along without it the best I can."

" I've missed *mine*, too." Tom said it a little bitterly. " You're just as well off without it. Chances ruin fellows, sometimes; mine did me "

" Ain't you rather young to be ruined ? "

This question seemed to amuse Tom immense ly. He went off into another hearty laugh.

" I declare, I don't know but you're like him in some things," he said, when he could speak.

" What about him ? what did he do ? "

" Oh, *my !* Don't ask me. What *didn't* he do ? He was an irrepressible fellow, I tell you ; *always* doing something. I advise you to make his acquaintance."

" I shall," said Peter Armstrong, with a determined thud of his axe into the knotty stick before him ; and Mr. Thomson Randolph knew just about as much what his gay words had accomplished for Peter Armstrong's future life as the most of us know what our words are going to do for us or others.

CHAPTER IV.

THEORY.

THERE was a storm without; a regular
January storm — wind, and snow, and
gloom. The sitting-room was cosy and
bright, or would have been but for the
solemn faces gathered there. The wind
was so high that ordinary comfort absolutely de-
manded the opening of the slide, despite the
frightful waste of coal; so the stove glowed.
So did Helen's face; not because of the warmth
of the room so much as of the fire within. Hel-
en was in absolute ill humor. Some heavy trial
had evidently crossed her path. She sewed
industriously, but with that ominous click of the
needle against her thimble, and an angry snip-
ping of her thread by the pert little scissors, that
plainly indicated a disturbed state of mind.
Ermina sewed too, but in a listless, weary, look-
out-of-the-window manner that did not partic-

ularly advance the hemming. Occasionally she
grumbled at her cruel fate in having to hem
at all. It would look ever so much better
stitched; they stitched everything now-a-days,
anyhow. And everybody that *was anybody*
now-a-days had a machine; even those Paddocks
across the way, poor as church mice, had a Grover & Baker machine.

"But she earned it, Ermina, taking in plain
sewing — the young girl did, I mean; that
one who sits at the end window so much."

This from Grace, in deprecating tone, as
if half ashamed at herself for taking the part
of "those Paddocks."

"You seem to be very familiar with their
affairs. Are the Paddocks supposed to be
friends of yours?"

Helen's tone was sarcasm itself.

"Why, I see Alice Paddock every Sunday in
Bible-class, and occasionally we walk home together. Of course we have to talk a little."

"Where would be the harm, if they were
friends?" Ermina said, being in a belligerent
mood.

"Oh, no *harm*, certainly, if there is a congen-
iality between them   I should imagine that
there might have been some difference in their
education and surroundings."

"Alice Paddock is a real sensible girl."

This was Grace's final sentence, for she turned to the piano and began her drumming.

Helen jerked her thread through the cloth in expressive silence.

" Where is Maria ? " questioned Ermina at last.

" Gone after sugar," Grace said, from the piano.

" It seems to me that Maria is always gone after sugar," said Ermina, with a sharp laugh. " The grocers will think that is the chief of our diet. I wonder where so much sugar goes to ? And we never have much of anything to eat, either."

Mrs. Randolph sighed.

" I never had to go for sugar in my life," she said, plaintively.

" Nor to turn dresses inside out, I presume ? " Helen said, eyeing her work with disdain.

" No, never ! " Mrs. Randolph answered solemnly.

Helen interrupted the musician.

" What do you propose to wear to that absurd party ? "

" Why, my blue skirt and polonaise, I suppose. That is all I have, you know."

" Then I should certainly have sense enough to stay at home. You look like a dowdy in that."

Grace laughed cheerily.

"Now, I think I look very nice," she said, brightly.

"It's well to have a good opinion of one's self."

This Helen said, speaking very sharply. Mrs. Randolph looked distressed, her eldest daughter was a trial and a puzzle to her. *She* never spoke sharply, nor hid covert double meanings inside her words.

Helen had most of the conversation to herself. No one seemed inclined to talk.

"I would have a little respect for my own sisters, if Mrs. Marshall had none," she commenced again, as the tone of Grace's music lulled a little. "If she doesn't know that she is very rude, I would endeavor to teach her something."

"Helen Randolph, what *are* you talking about?"

This from Ermina, spoken somewhat snappishly.

"I was speaking of Mrs. Marshall. I thought I spoke with sufficient distinctness to be understood. Mother, is that your idea of politeness — to invite one daughter, and she almost the youngest, and ignore the existence of the others?"

The distressed look on **Mrs. Randolph's face** deepened.

" Why, I don't know," she said, hesitatingly. "I had no sisters, you remember. But Judge Harlowe's family lived just across from us, and the two young ladies almost never went out together. I have known Carrie to go to a large party and Susie to go to prayer-meeting on the same evening. Yes, Helen, I really think it used to be done by the very first families."

Helen bit off her thread with an impatient jerk. Evidently her mother's lapse into the past disturbed her.

" I shouldn't allow Grace to go out this evening, anyway, if I were you. It storms furiously, and there is every indication that the storm will increase," she said, emphatically.

She had touched the right chord at last. Mrs. Randolph was personally very susceptible to changes in the weather, and imagined all her children to be equally so. She roused into something very like energy and poor Grace's chances for an evening entertainment were diminishing. At this opportune moment there occurred a break in the discussion. Maria came in, fresh from the outside world, with glowing cheeks and energetic movements.

" How warm you are here," she said, and gave the slide a push. " Mother, your cheeks are becomingly rosy. I think you must look just as you did the evening father tells about — the first

time he ever saw you.   Grace, don't thump now,
I want to talk.   Helen, did you know Mrs. Monroe
was going to have company to-night?"

Helen gave a visible start, and her flushed
cheek turned a deeper red, but she controlled her
voice to answer, with dignity,—

"I know nothing about Mrs. Monroe's movements.   She *may* have company every evening in
the week."

"I can't say as to that.   I'm only speaking for
this evening.   I met her in the store.   I told her
I was certain you knew nothing about it, and she
said she was certain you did, for she sent you a
note this morning by little Kate.   But I felt perfectly certain that little Kate had not delivered
it, and told her so; and she entreated me to see
about it the minute I reached home, and assure
you that she was depending on you.   Half a
dozen friends to tea at seven.   That means at
least thirty friends, and tea at nine; but I didn't
tell her that.   I only assured her that I would
do my best to retrieve little Kate's blunders."

"Didn't she say anything about me?" interposed Ermina, quickly.

"Not the first thing."

"How excessively rude!   Helen, if she has no
respect for your sisters, and doesn't know that
she is rude, I would endeavor to teach her."

Helen's face was scarlet.

"At least she had propriety enough to invite the eldest instead of the youngest," she said, coldly.

"Such an awful storm as it is," continued Ermina, "and likely to increase by evening. Mother, you won't think of letting Helen go?"

A rarely good quality had Helen. When the laugh was manifestly against her, if meantime her own prospects had brightened, so that she could afford to laugh too, she made no effort to hold on to and nurse her ill-humor, but joined merrily in the merriment at her own expense; so she made merriment in the household by suddenly joining in the ringing laugh with which Grace greeted Ermina's words, and the little frail mother looked with puzzled face from one to the other of her four daughters, thought for the twentieth time that they were all enigmas to her, then smoothed the wrinkles from her forehead, and laughed pleasantly with the rest. It was in this fortunate mood that the awful puzzle of dress came up. I wonder if there is a woman in America, who, the question of going or not going being settled in the affirmative, does not think next, What shall I wear?

"I've a great mind not to go, after all," Helen said, the gloom returning. "Nothing decent to wear. The rest will be dressed in black silk at the very least."

"You might wear my polonaise if I were not going out." This from Grace, who had given up all attempts at thumping.

"Aren't you afraid she would look like a dowdy in it?" queried Ermina.

"Why, no," laughed Grace. "She didn't say *she* would look like a dowdy. I think myself it is quite becoming to her; and to me too, for that matter."

Meantime Helen had had opportunity to run over the articles in her somewhat limited wardrobe, and was back in the depths of ill humor.

"What's the use of talking such nonsense!" she said, in intense disgust. "You *are* going out, and that settles the whole question. I don't mean to go a step. I haven't the least desire to go out in company, if I can't go without being the subject of remark."

"Isn't *your* black silk suitable, dear?" This in a meek voice from Mrs. Randolph.

"Suitable! I should think not. Why, mother, the overskirt is a third longer than they wear them now. They don't wear overskirts much now, anyway; they make everything into polonaises. It's too ridiculous that Grace should be the only one in the house who has anything that they wear."

"Of all the absurd and ridiculous people in the world, I think '*they*' are a little the worst.

What *earthly* right have 'they' to say what we shall wear and what we shall not?"

Maria's outbursts were greeted by the several members of the family according to their several natures. Mrs. Randolph looked at her in puzzled surprise. Ermina said sharply,—

"I wish 'their' responsibility didn't end there. If they would only agree to furnish the articles *I* would wear them."

Grace laughed, a merry, fun-loving laugh, and Helen said with an air of dignified superiority,—

"Don't be so silly, Maria."

Silence after that for a little, only for Grace's fingers touching the keys softly and lightly here and there. Maria went back to the kitchen or the quiet might not have lasted. Presently Grace spoke her thoughts, at least some of them.

"Helen, you truly may wear my polonaise if you care to. I've decided not to go out this evening. Susie Truesdell is coming in, and we are going to practice for the concert."

"Why!" said Helen, in softened tone, and a little touch of a smile, "that's a sudden resolution, isn't it?"

"Not very," in cheery tones. "I told Susie if I decided not to go I would send her word, and Tom will run in for me after tea."

"Well," Helen said, after a moment's hesitation, "if you have quite decided not to go I will wear it. You know it is more becoming to me, because I wear it with a black silk skirt; and I'm very much obliged to you, I am sure; but I don't want you to stay at home on my account."

"There isn't much time left before the concert," was Grace's relevant answer, and she dashed into the merriest of waltzes.

After tea, while the family waited for Mr. Randolph to come in to prayers, Ermina told over to Tom with great apparent relish the history of the day, with its mistakes and bewiderments as regarded invitations, detailing Helen's share in the conversation with all the more vividness perhaps because her heart was a trifle sore at having been left out of both parties. Also she was just a little vexed at Helen for accepting her sister's pretty little sacrifice. It would not have been Ermina's nature to have done this.

"It all shapes itself beautifully," Tom said, entering into the whole subject with great glee. "Theory and fact agree this time."

"What do you mean, my son?" Mrs. Randolph questioned.

"Why, the 'all-things-work-together' notion, mother. I say they have come out right this time. It isn't often I discover it; but the thing is very plain to me, that if Helen had been invited to Mrs. Marshall's, in all human probability she would have accepted, and then she would have been too late for Mrs. Monroe; and it's twenty-nine times more genteel to be invited to Monroe's mansion than it is to go to Marshall's two-story abode, even leaving Horace Monroe out of the question, and I venture to say he is in it."

"My son!" said Mrs. Randolph, reproof in her voice and an amused smile on her face; but something had jarred exceedingly on Helen. *Her* voice was sharp and indignant.

"Tom, I *would* make an effort not to be quite so irreverent, before my mother at least."

The entrance of Mr. Randolph, Bible in hand, checked the reply that Tom was aching to make.

"How came you to give up your party and your dress, for Helen's benefit to-night?" This was the question Ermina asked as she and Grace went up to their rooms together, the evening being over, the practicing done.

"How came I to? Why, it came itself just as easy."

"No doubt. Things *do* to you, apparently. But *I* mean what was your object?"

Grace laughed.

"Most everything has an object," she said, lightly. "Well, let me see. Helen thinks twice as much of parties as I do. She wouldn't have found any fun in staying at home, and I've managed to have considerable. Then it's a horrid storm, and it's a trouble to dress for a party, you know. Why, dear me! I just happened to think I wouldn't go, so I didn't."

"That child is heedless and indolent even with her pleasures," Ermina said, as Grace bade her good-night, and went on to the room which she shared with Maria.

And Grace opened her drawer and lifted the lid of her collar-box to pat lovingly a dainty white ruffle.

"You're all ready for next time now," she said, brightly. "And very likely there will come a 'next time' in which things don't clash so. Who knows?" Then the thoughtless child went to bed.

"I wonder if it *was* irreverent?" Tom said, lingering in the kitchen while Maria sponged bread. He had just seen Susie Truesdell home through the pelting storm, and was waiting to warm his feet. Some chance word of hers had suggested the conversation early in the evening, that had been so sternly rebuked by Helen. "I wonder if it *was* irreverent? I suppose it was — in me — since I meant it for pure fun. But can't you see how, if you believed it at all, Maria, you would like to have a wholesale belief?"

"Wholesale?" said Maria, pausing in her stirring.

" Yes; go away down to the bottom of things —believe it through and through—things working right for parties as well as for — "

" Bread-making, for instance," suggested Maria, as he hesitated.

" Yes, that's it exactly — bread-making, wood-sawing, *anything.* Nothing too small, you know. I'd believe the whole of it or none of it."

"Do you mean to say you believe none of it?"

" Well, no, not exactly that. I'm not prepared to turn infidel, in theory at least. It's enough for me to practice it. Theory and practice don't agree in this life, Maria, and that's the trouble, except in bread-making. I'm willing to admit it in that instance."

" You may theorize about bread-making, though, till next week, and if I don't get up in the morning and mix it you won't have any bread."

" I know it. That's where they agree, you see. Theory and practice — then you get results. I wonder where the world would be, how far advanced, if people made the two things match everywhere as they do in bread ? "

" For instance, in regard to going to bed," said Maria, tucking her bread up in flannel and setting it behind the stove.

"Yes'm; your instances are striking. I'll

4

practice on that last one." And Tom lighted his lamp and vanished.

"If I had known anything about it myself I might have helped him." This Maria said to the stove just before she left it for the night.

CHAPTER V.

A SERMON.

TO go back to the early hours of that stormy evening. The storm continued, and indeed increased in violence, proving Helen to be a true prophetess. Much debate arose over the projected tea-party, and the propriety of Helen's braving the storm.

"Ladies are curious beings," was Tom's comment. "No *man* would venture out this evening unless he was obliged to do so."

"Nonsense!" Helen said, energetically. "Every gentleman who received an invitation will be present. You'll see if they are not."

Tom's answer was not soothing.

"Bless me! I was speaking of *men*, not of the be-whiskered, perfumed fellows that my lady Marshall gathers about her."

"She moves in the very best society," Helen

said, with quiet dignity. "People consider it an
honor to be invited to her house."

"I'm glad I wasn't considered worthy of
the honor, for the wind is too much even for
me." This from Ermina.

"What a commotion about a little snow!"
Helen said, fretfully. "I've been out worse
evenings than this."

"Not this winter," Mr. Randolph said, speaking on the question for the first time just as
he was about to leave the room. "This is decidedly the most severe storm of the season;
nothing but necessity compels me to face it.
You will do well to think twice, Helen, before
you decide to go out."

"I shall go," said Helen determinately. "I
am not going to waste half the day getting
dressed for nothing."

"*Go!* Of course you will. Who doubts it?
You would go if the snow was piled three
feet above your head, and you had to go through
a tunnel. The fellows *are* tunneling down by
the bridge, anyhow."

Mrs. Randolph looked horrified.

"Is it really so bad as that, Thomson? I
wish you would conclude not to go, Helen. I
shall feel distressed about you."

Helen's voice was more gentle, as it always
was when she addressed her mother, but quite
decided.

"There is nothing to distress yourself about, mother. Only Tom chooses to annoy you. There will be good paths, and they will send me home in the sleigh if it is necessary. Tom, it is unfortunate that you can find no better employment than making mother feel uncomfortable. I really wish you had something to do with yourself in the evening. *Some* boys study, but I suppose we must give up all hopes of you in that direction."

Tom gave a lugubrious sigh.

"I suppose you must," he said, in a solemn, nasal tone. "I *was* the pride and joy of my eldest sister's heart, the very apple of her eye, she lived and breathed only for me; but I have fallen from the high pedestal whereon her high hopes placed me, and now it is sadly to be feared that I shall bring down her brown switch with sorrow to the grave."

Ermina and Maria were convulsed with laughter, but Helen's eyes blazed angrily — ridicule was a thing that she could not meet pleasantly; and Tom, having finished his sentence in a sepulchral voice, saw fit to vanish through the open door. Words sent at random sometimes stayed by that young man. "Something to do" — he heartily wished it for himself. Maria's attempts to stay up the falling fortunes of the family, to economize the very pennies, kept him

from very shame from the many convivial pleasures in which his heart delighted, and which had
been the bane and the cause of the sudden closing of his college life. Fortunately for him such
pleasures cost money, and money he hadn't;
neither was he willing to "join the fellows"
and "trust to luck" to meet his share, as had
been his college habit. Maria was too constant
an example for that. He had failed thus far
in obtaining work of any sort — he had lost
all heart for study. "What was the use of
study?" he asked himself, grumblingly, now
that college doors were closed against him.
There actually seemed to be nothing for Tom to
do but to "lounge around and be a nuisance."
This was what Helen in one of her petulant
moods had said of him. On this particular
evening he "lounged" out to the kitchen.
Maria had left it in neat array but in great loneliness. Tom drummed on the tin pan that
was turned over the bread sponge, and wished
that the sponger thereof would come out so they
might have a talk. That not happening, and
the kindlings having been made ready early in
the evening, there seemed absolutely nothing
to take his attention. He opened the door
and stepped out on the piazza to view the
weather. From the wood-house chamber window there came the rays of a modest light on

the snow. It suggested to Tom an escape from his wearisome self. He would go and visit Peter. Quite delighted at this novel idea, he went three steps at a time up the back stairs, and knocked loudly at Peter's door. Receiving a low-toned preoccupied "come in," he pushed open the door, and the inmate was revealed to him, perched on a high stool, his elbow resting on the little old table, his head in his hands, gazing at an open book. He expressed neither surprise nor bewilderment at seeing his unusual visitor, but glancing up, said, gravely,—

"I've found him."

"Have you, indeed?" Tom answered, briskly. "That's lucky, I suppose. Who might he happen to be?"

"Why, that Peter you told me about. I've looked off and on for him every night since you told me; but as I didn't know in what place to look, it took considerable time to find him. I've got him now, though — the very first of him I guess. It reads as though they hadn't told anything about him before."

Tom sat down on the side of his host's bed and gave himself up to laughter.

"What are you laughing at?" said Peter, in surprise.

"Well," Tom said, quieting a little, "if the

truth must be told, I was laughing at you. You're about the drollest chap I ever heard of. So you've been hunting up Peter ever since?"— and Tom went off into another laugh.

"Well, now," said Peter, gazing at him in undisguised astonishment; "I declare I can't see anything in that to laugh at. I can't, now, to save my life. Why shouldn't I hunt him up? If there was a chap of your name in the Bible, wouldn't you kind of like to know what he did?"

"There is," said Tom, with sudden energy; "I'll be bound if there isn't. Thomas his name is; just what my name was at first, until there were so many of the same name in the family that father changed mine to Thomson. It's just another form of the same name, I presume, though."

"What did Thomas do?"

"I doubt if I know. Some pretty scaly things, if I remember rightly. One of these times we'll hunt him up. Let's hear about the other one now."

Thus invited, Peter turned with alacrity to his Bible, and read, in slow, laborious tone,—

"'And Jesus, walking by the sea of Galilee, saw two brethren, Simon called Peter, and Andrew his brother, casting a net into the sea: for they were fishers.' I tell you I think that's fine," he said, pausing in his reading. "When I read about him walking along and seeing folks, and folks seeing him, seems to me I can't stand it. I want to be along with 'em and have him see me."

"There's undoubtedly a difference in men," Tom said, meditatively.

"What?"

"I was speculating as to what you thought, and what I thought."

"What do you think?"

"Several things. Never mind; go on. Fishermen, were they? I didn't remember that. I suppose it was fine employment in those days. What happened?"

"'And he saith unto them: Follow me, and I will make you fishers of men.' Now, you see," Peter said, speaking mournfully, "he spoke to them. They was nothing but poor fishers, and he stopped in his walk and spoke to them. Where's the sea of Galilee, Tom?"

"Haven't the slightest idea. I can tell you about as little on this subject, I fancy, as anybody you could apply to."

"Well, never mind. I'll find out somehow. Wasn't it fine, though? What would you have done if you'd been one of them fellows?"

"Can't say. What would you?"

"Well," said Peter, meditatively, "I ain't sure. You can't never be *sure*, I suppose. But it's my opinion that I'd have done precisely **what** they did."

" What was that ? "

" Oh, you haven't heard the whole story. Well, I'll read the rest of it. ' And he saith unto them : " Follow me, and I will make you fishers of men. And they straightway left theii nets and followed him.' "

" Now, you see, there's a trouble. I don't un- derstand what that means. I'm bothered a good deal in that way."

" What of it ? " Tom asked, listlessly. " You are not that Peter, you know, so it's of no con- sequence what was said to him, ages ago."

Peter shook his head decisively. " That won't do — it's a thing that came up in the class last Sunday, and it was made pretty clear to *my* mind that there ain't much in the Bible but what was wrote there for us ; it stands to reason, you see. Why would folks want to keep reading the Bible over and over again, if it was all about folks who've been dead and gone a thousand years ago, and didn't mean nothing to us ? It's just what I was anxious to hunt up Peter for, because it's likely enough that the very same things he said to that Peter might mean me too."

" But he called on Peter to follow him, and you can't do that."

" What's the reason I can't ? Ain't it exactly

what I'm trying to do? If there's anything that I'm working at in this world, it's that 'following.'"

"Oh, well," said Tom, "I meant follow him literally, as they did, along the sea-shore of Galilee; they left their nets and followed him."

"No," Peter said, mournfully; "I can't go and follow him as they did. Ain't that exactly what I said? But, then, I can *follow;* folks can do that. He went to heaven, you know, and that's what I'm after. But about that 'fishers of men '— now, that's a poser; I can't take it in, and it's a pity; there's no telling but it means me. I wonder how I'll go to work to find out?"

Tom's conscience smote him; intellectually he understood perfectly what it meant, but it was such a new thing for him to attempt an explanation of Bible language. He leaned against the foot-board, and yawned, and pretended not to have heard; but Peter's grave, troubled face was a reproach.

"What put you into such a strange way of thinking?" he asked, at length.

Peter looked up with a stare of astonishment.

"What way?"

"Why, hunting through the Bible for people and things in a way that no other mortal fellow would think of doing, I'll venture to say."

" Why ? " said Peter, blankly. " The Bible's true, ain't it ? "

" I don't deny it. What has that got to do with the question ? "

" Humph ! a good deal, I should think. If the Bible's true, and it's about me, why shouldn't I want to find out about it ? You fellows study away at arithmetic because it's true, and you want to use what's in it to help yourselves along. What's the reason a body shouldn't work at the Bible for the same reason ? I think it's enough sight interestinger than arithmetic, too — but them ' fishers of men ' is a poser."

Tom laughed uproariously, then yawned, then sat erect, with,—

" Well, now, my beloved Peter, I presume I could read that riddle to you if I tried. Do you know how to fish ? "

His congregation nodded.

" Well, then, you know that there's a thousand different kinds of fish, more or less, and they have to be caught in about as many different ways : some you have to coax, you know, and be very easy with ; and others you have to be very spry over ; and some require entirely different bait from others ; and that's the way with men, I take it ; it requires about as much skill to catch men as it does fish ; and He was going to teach them to be just as skillful. Do you see ? "

Peter drew a long breath, and answered slowly,—

"Yes — I guess I see — yes — I know I do. I take it in. Why, yes — it's plain; and it's grand too. Ain't it now?"

"Jolly! you are worse than St. Peter was to ask questions, I venture to say. Well, sir, I've preached a sermon to-night — the first one in my life — and I must say I had a very attentive audience."

And Tom immediately brought his visit to a close. It was the lingering of this conversation in his brain that suggested that little talk with Maria, of which I told you in the last cha⁻ ⁻

CHAPTER VI.

SMOKE AND BEWILDERMENT.

T was the evening after the party. There was no family worship at the Randolphs' that evening. The head of the household was stretched on the bed in his chamber, his head done up in brown paper, wet in vinegar, of which there was a stifling odor penetrating even to the sitting-room. Maria sat at his feet like a statue, keeping guard just now at the sitting-room door, out of which hovered Mrs. Randolph every five minutes for the purpose of driving the poor victim on the bed half an inch nearer distraction by asking him "How he felt now?" He had the sick headache. The little table at his side held a cup of salt and water, a cup of strong tea without milk or sugar, a cup of soda-water, a cup of brandy and water, and — I don't remember what else; being the result of

62

the united efforts of the family to help "settle his stomach." Of course they did no good. I wish with all my heart I could have been there to whisk his feet into a tub of hot water and wring out a cloth with cold water to lay on the poor abused stomach, covering it closely with two or three layers of flannel — then the Randolph family would have learned two new things; but I wasn't there, neither was any one else possessed of sufficient knowledge or common sense to understand that there is hardly any limit to the power of hot and cold water over nearly every sort of pain. I have often wondered if water were to be procured of the druggist for two dollars a pint whether it would be used occasionally.

The door opened very softly, and Tom, beckoning with his finger, held a low-toned, brief conversation with the statue, and was about departing when Mr. Randolph turned on his pillow.

" Take this vinegar thing off, Maria; it does no good. Is that Thomson ? "

" Yes, father. Will you have a spoonful of the brandy ? "

" No, the spoonfuls don't help me. Tell Thomson to get the envelope addressed to the church treasurer, out of my left hand corner drawer, and send it by one of the girls to the prayer-meeting.

I ought to have been there myself to-night," and Mr. Randolph sighed heavily. "Someway I never seem able to be anywhere when I ought to be."

Tom appeared in the sitting-room ten minutes afterward.

"Here's a paper father wants taken to prayer-meeting to-night. It's addressed to Mr. Prime. Who's going?"

"I'm not," Ermina said, promptly, "are *you*, Helen?"

Helen shivered.

"Dear me! no, I'm not. I feel more like going to bed — ever so much; and it storms dreadfully. Just hear the wind blow."

Ermina laughed.

"Why, Helen! it doesn't begin with last night's storm. *Does* it, Tom?"

"Not by a long shot," said Tom, mercilessly. "But last night there was a party. Don't you know that circumstances alter cases?"

"I know if I had gone to a party in last evening's storm I wouldn't plead the weather against going to a prayer-meeting *this* evening."

"Why don't you go, then?" This from Helen, very snappishly.

"Because I don't want to. No other earthly reason. I'm not afraid of the snow any more than you are, when you want to go to a place.

But I don't feel in prayer-meeting humor to-night; so I stay at home."

"*I* go to prayer-meeting from a sense of duty," Helen said, coldly.

Tom laughed mischievously.

"Ermina stays at home from prayer-meeting because she doesn't want to go; and Helen goes when it is pleasant, and there isn't a party, and she feels like it — from a sense of duty. What is the difference between them, mother?"

Mrs. Randolph looked puzzled and pained, as she always did when any words seeming to be sharp or uncomfortable reached her ears; and Tom hastened to add,—

"Never mind, mother; don't puzzle your brain. ' T-t-that's o-one of the t-t-things t-that no f-f-fellow can f-f-find out,' as the fellow says in the play. I tell you what, Ermina, you'd like to go to the theatre. Well, how is this important document to get into Mr. Prime's hands? I know; I'll send it by Peter."

"Does Peter attend the prayer-meeting?" asked Mrs. Randolph, great surprise in her voice.

"Bless you, yes; as regularly as the minister. I'll deliver this into his hands."

"But perhaps he will not go out this evening, since it is so stormy and —"

"No danger, mother," Helen interrupted. "That class of persons always think that religion consists in going to prayer-meeting, no matter how severe the weather is."

"But people of culture and refinement know enough not to go, except when they feel like it, and there are no parties."

With that sentence Tom wisely closed the door on further conversation, and went off in search of Peter.

The little light was burning over the wood-house chamber. He took note of that before he went stumbling up the dark, steep back stair-case. At the chamber door he paused; there were voices within.

"He's got company," Tom said, hesitating whether to enter. "No; I declare I believe the queer fellow is talking to himself. It's his voice and no other. Reading aloud about his friend Peter, perhaps. It doesn't sound like reading, either."

He stepped nearer the door, then stepped back and instinctively raised his hand to remove his hat. It was the force of habit — for Peter was praying! What there should be strange and bewildering about a young man kneeling in prayer to God I can not pretend to say; but Tom had a very queer feeling come over him as he waited. A curious desire to know what Peter could find to say, or what motive prompted him, mingled with a courteous sense of the impropriety of listening to what was not intended for his ears. He leaned against the stair rail and whistled softly to drown the sound of the earnest words, and waited until the voice ceased and Peter was moving about the room; then he gave a ponderous knock.

"Here's a document to be intrusted to your care — that is if you happen to be going to church. Father wants it given to Mr. Prime. Are you going out?"

"Oh, yes; I'm going to the prayer-meeting. What if you should go along with me, Tom?"

If the invitation had been given under any other circumstances, I feel sure Tom would have been prompt in declining; but in spite of himself he had a feeling of respect for Peter, new and undefinable. Peter had just been praying. Tom was not an idiot. On the contrary, he was an intelligent young man. He sometimes *thought* he could not fail to know that it was a strange honor to be permitted to speak to God. Why he did not avail himself of this honor can not be answered any easier than we can tell why hundreds of young men of intelligence refuse the same privilege. Still he felt the instinctive respect natural to a refined nature for one who had just come from the Holy Presence. He could not quite laugh, even at the idea of his going to prayer-meeting.

"Why should I?" he said, absently.

"Why *shouldn't* you?" Peter asked, quickly; and then Tom laughed.

"Sure enough; one question is as easy of solution as the other, but I suppose the main reason is — I don't want to."

Peter was not a logician. He didn't know there was such a thing as logic. He was not sharp at a retort, or he might have involved Tom in endless bewilderments as to why a being possessed of common sense shouldn't naturally want to go where the King of kings held audience. He was a simple, earnest-hearted boy, his answer was thoroughly simple and undiplomatic, so far as intention was concerned.

"I wish I ever had a fellow to go with me *anywhere,* like other boys. It's awful lonesome to be forever alone."

Tom's brain was equal to any amount of youthful argument. Tom's heart was tender.

"Poor fellow," he said, sympathetically. He understood that feeling. *He* sometimes felt very much alone. "Would you really like to have me go with you, for sort of company, you know?"

"I'd like it *awfully,*" said Peter, with great earnestness.

"Then I'll do it; there's nothing to hinder, and I might as well be there as anywhere else."

Ten minutes later the two appeared in the

Harvard Place Chapel. That chapel was a very pleasant spot under some circumstances. The carpet was bright and neat, the illuminated texts profuse and appropriate and neatly hung, the cane-seated, cane-backed arm-chairs were arranged with regard to comfort and convenience, the gas fixtures were handsome in design and abundant in number. Why the sexton had thought proper to light but three burners for that large room can not be with certainty ascertained. Why the minister, or the Sunday-school Superintendent, or Mr. Prime, or *somebody*, didn't advise him to light more burners does not appear, either; but the consequence was plain — the chapel presented the appearance of a dungeon. To add to the effect, the black hole in the floor, at the northeast corner of the room, emitted more smoke than heat. The other black hole, in the southwest corner, gave neither smoke nor heat, but was hopelessly cold and sullen. The sexton had seen fit to make use of but one furnace.

"We are late," Peter had said, as they ascended the chapel steps.

"Awful!" Tom had answered, with a comical grimace, reserving his answer until they had entered the chapel and discovered three women and one boy partially engulfed in the twilight that reigned.

"Just enough here to play puss in the corner,"

Tom further whispered; "and they have seated themselves as if that were the object in view. I wonder if they could have got farther apart if they had tried?"

Peter shook his head.

"We're late for all that," he said, stoutly. "Mr. Gordon said the meeting begun at seven, and it's pretty near a quarter past."

"And he isn't here himself. My! what a barn this is; a fellow will have to stand on the register to keep from freezing. If I had a match I'd light some more burners. It looks like a jail."

Several more people arrived in the course of the next ten minutes, and Tom, who was industriously counting, reported nineteen in all. Lastly came Mr. Gordon, looking nervous and flurried. He apologized for his tardiness, said a matter of importance had detained him; then the meeting was opened. That is, Mr. Gordon tried to open it. He said, "We will open the meeting this evening by singing the twenty-ninth hymn." It was long metre, and there were five verses. Mr. Gordon read them, then peered anxiously over his spectacles.

"I had hoped that our chorister would be here by this time," he said, in troubled tones. "Is there any one present who will be kind enough to lead our singing? Miss Keller, will you?"

Apparently Miss Keller would neither sing nor

speak. She looked down at her open book, nudged her companion with her elbow, simpered a little, and remained dumb; yet Miss Keller was one of the leading singers in the Harvard Place choir.

"I don't see but we shall have to dispense with singing," Mr. Gordon said, after a distressing silence. "Brother Payne, will you lead us in prayer?"

Tom listened curiously. Mr. Payne was a good man, given to using a large word in place of a small one if a substitute could be found.

"His prayer sounds as if he might be reading it from the dictionary," the wicked fellow whispered to Peter; but Peter's head was bowed and his eyes were closed, the whisper passed by him unheard. Before the prayer was concluded, Tom fidgeted, which was perhaps not strange. Mr. Payne prayed as though he had forgotten all about that duty for weeks, and that nothing of probable or conceivable interest in Church or State must go unnoticed now.

"A very good oration in honor of everything," Tom told Maria afterward; "but as for being a *prayer*, why it *wasn't* any more than the arithmetic is."

Mr. Gordon perhaps being familiar with his material, and expecting little help, then read a psalm, and spoke on each verse earnest, faithful words; but Tom, like all young gentlemen of his age and experience, was a severe critic.

"It was a good sermon, Maria; very good indeed, I should say — what I heard of it; but you see he appointed a *prayer*-meeting."

By this time the chorister had arrived, and the long hymn was sung by the chorister and Miss Keller to a tune unknown by any of the other seventeen, "or anybody else in all creation," Tom said. Mr. Evans prayed after that, ten minutes by the watch of the wicked looker-on. What he said few knew. He had chosen his corner most remote from the others, and his voice was never much above a murmur. A very few prayers and hymns of the length mentioned sufficed to fill an hour, especially when there are long drawn pauses between each prayer. Meantime the room seemed to grow colder, the women shivered and drew their wraps about them, one or two even gained courage to cross the room and stand on the black hole in the floor, thereby monopolizing to a considerable extent what little heat there was. Altogether it was a forlorn, spiritless place. Mr. Gordon struggled hard, both with the memory of something which had detained him, and which still evidently troubled him, and the dispiriting influences which surrounded him. A stranger to earth and earthly prayer-meetings might have imagined that the minister was pressing a great

personal need of his own on the people, so earnestly did he plead with them not to let the time
run to waste.

"I don't wonder at Helen going to prayer-
meeting from a sense of duty, and Ermina not
going because she doesn't want to. I shouldn't
think she would. I'll be hanged if I've been in
such a dreary place before since I used to get shut
up in the wood-closet at school when I was a
youngster. Ugh! I'm chilled through to the
bone. I shan't get warm again to-night. What
upon *earth* do they have it so cold for?" said
Tom, with energy, as soon as he was safely outside the walls.

"It *was* cold," Peter said, thoughtfully.
"Yes," he confessed it was, "*mostly* cold; not so
bad, though, on warmer nights; and one night,
that time it thawed, it was awful hot there, so
they had to open a window."

"I wouldn't have done it," Tom said. "I'd
have bottled it up somehow for future use. Why,
it's abominable expecting people to sit quiet when
they are freezing to death. What do they have
it so dark there for? If anybody wanted to sing
their outlandish tunes they couldn't see to do it.
Nobody will ever want to, though, I presume.
I've heard those words that they sang first sung
ever since I was born, and I never heard them
without Rockingham before. What splendid taste

for two people to yell and screech and growl and thunder through a tune like that in prayer-meeting, chasing each other like a couple of ponies out on a race. I wonder how many times Miss Keller sung that half a line over? I say, Peter, what do they have it so dark there for?"

Peter did not know, he was sure. He confessed that his own opinion was they wanted to save gas.

"Save gas!" Tom repeated, disdainfully. "And they have it like an ice-house for the purpose of saving coal, I presume. It's unfortunate that there are not more men in that church with hundred thousand dollar incomes. I'll tell you what it's for, it's to save paying attention to anything but their precious mills, and stores, and factories, and *selves*. The puzzle is solved. I've often wondered why church-members didn't like to go to prayer-meeting better. I never shall again. The wonder is that they go at all. Such a cold, smoky, dismal old hole. It's a blessed thing that I'm not a minister. If I were I'd kick pretty nearly every man in my church once a year, at least—good hearty kicks, too. Peter, what do *you* go to prayer-meeting for? Did you have a good time to-night?"

"Yes," said Peter, promptly. "You know, Tom, He took a walk with that other Peter down by the sea of Galilee. Peter *saw* Him, and that was about all the difference, I guess; because, you see, I believe He came and stayed by me this evening all the time."

"What do you mean?" said Tom, awe-stricken in spite of himself.

"Why, just that He was there, you know. It is His own house, you see, and He has promised to come."

"It is a puzzle yet," Tom said, this time to his own inner self. "The fellow is talking about something that I don't understand; and yet it is no sham, he feels it and means it. There's Helen and Ermina for one class of Christians, and there's father and Peter for another kind. Mother is like neither of them. I wonder if there's another kind still. What a muddle it is."

CHAPTER VII.

"WHAT IS THE DIFFERENCE?"

THE household had something besides coal
and sugar and parties to think about.
There came an uninvited guest into their
midst. Mr. Randolph had gone to Syra-
cuse on business for the firm, and was to
be absent during the night. At midnight a figure
in long, loose wrapper, and with flowing hair,
knocked loudly at Tom's door, and Grace's voice
summoned him.

"Tom, something is the matter down stairs.
Ermina opened the hall door, and called to me
to tell you to run quick for the doctor. I don't
know who is sick; I just wakened."

"Helen has the toothache, I presume," Tom
muttered; nevertheless, he sprang up, and was
down stairs within three minutes after his summons. Grace met him in the hall.

"It's mother, Tom. Maria heard her groaning away up stairs. She seems very sick."

Wings seemed added to Tom's former speed, his mother was very precious to him. So it was a very little time afterward that Dr. Marley bent over Mrs. Randolph, with grave professional face, questioned as to the earlier symptoms of the attack, and what had been done for her; then turned and addressed Helen as the oldest daughter.

"I will prepare some medicine that may relieve her; keep the warm applications to her feet — that is very proper. I am glad you thought of it. I will step into the dining-room to prepare the medicine. Thomson, you may come with me, if you will."

Arrived in the dining-room, just across the hall, Dr. Marley made no attempt to prepare medicine, but leaned against the long dining-table, set for breakfast, and said, as he looked fixedly at Tom,—

"Medicine will do your mother no good, Thomson; do you realize it?"

"No good!" Tom repeated, dazed and half-stupefied, yet his face grew deadly pale. "What do you mean?"

"I mean that the case is already beyond human aid; your mother is dying, Thomson. It is the final attack of her old disease."

In utter silence, Tom glared for an instant on the speaker, struck dumb with pain; then he turned and rushed to his mother's room. Maria was where she had been since she first hurried down stairs, alarmed by the sounds that reached her from that room — bending over her mother, bathing her forehead, gently fanning her, directing that the hot flannels be wrung out afresh, sending Ermina for Tom and the doctor — using every sense of her alert nature. Helen stood helpless and bewildered. " I don't believe hot water is good," she had said, before the doctor's arrival, when Maria had remarked on the strangeness of their having kept up the kitchen fire on that particular night.

"It stands to reason that when people's feet are ice-cold, they ought to be warmed, if they can be," Maria had answered, determinately, and sent Grace for the water.

She glanced up as Tom entered. "Have you brought — " she said, and then stopped, and for a single instant the fan, which was moving gently back and forth, stopped.

Tom had no need to speak; his blanched face told the awful story.

"What did the doctor say is the matter with her?" Helen began, eagerly.

"He did not say," Tom answered, and the tones of his voice were so strange that both Helen

and Ermina turned to look at him. Whereupon
Ermina staggered back into a chair, and Helen
uttered a stifled groan. "Do something for her
— quick, quick! Why do you waste time?" she
said, turning fiercely to the doctor, who came
back on tiptoe, glass and spoon in hand.

"I have something for her," he said, in low,
soothing tones. "You must be very quiet, my
dear young lady."

"Quiet!" she said, still speaking fiercely.
"How can I be quiet? My mother is suffering,
and you do nothing for her."

From the bedside came a low, clear, decided
voice. "Helen, hush — you disturb mother."
A spoonful of the liquid was almost forced down
the poor mother's throat, and during a moment
of less difficult breathing, she looked pleadingly
up in the doctor's face.

"Am I going to die, Dr. Marley?"

The doctor looked away from the faded eyes,
as he answered, quickly,—

"Oh, we trust not, Mrs. Randolph; don't think
of any such thing. I have given you some medicine which I hope will cure you."

Alas! for the doctors who shrink away from
death as a grim monster, and know nothing about
the Hand of Power that has taken away the
sting. No wonder that the temptation to shirk
or to deliberately deny the truth is too great for
them.

Tom, who stood at the foot of the bed, his face rigid at the attempt at self-control, started and shivered as if a blow had struck him. A lie at such a time seemed awful to him. His mother's eyes turned from the doctor's face to his, and the sweet, soft voice, that had always been so precious to him, spoke directly to him.

" My son, you will tell me the truth. Am I dying ? "

" O mother, mother, *don't !* " It was Helen's voice that answered. " What makes you think of such dreadful things? You are better now, I am sure. Father will be home in the morning, and then you will get well right away."

With a persistence that had been very rare in the gentle mother's life, she said again, " My son, I am sure you will tell me the truth."

Tom trembled as with an ague — his teeth chattered, so that his lips could hardly form the words, but as if each word was a groan wrung from him, he cried out,—

" O mother, I'm afraid you are."

Helen screamed hysterically.

" Tom, that is awful. Oh, you have killed her ! "

Again the firm, controlled tones of the youngest daughter sounded in the room.

" Helen, hush ; your loud voice disturbs her. Doctor, I think she is fainting."

Dr. Marley came forward, and Maria, obeying his directions, deftly and promptly brought back the fluttering pulse once more. Mrs. Randolph's first words were,—

"If my husband were *only* here."

"Mother, he will come early in the morning." Grace had come softly around to the other side of the bed, and spoke these words gently and soothingly.

"Yes, but I am going. Oh, I feel that my boy told me the truth. I am dying, and I am afraid to die — *so afraid;* if my husband were here he would help me; he has always helped me about everything all his life. Oh, what *shall* I do?"

Maria looked around on the different inmates of the room in absolute despair. She could bathe her mother's throbbing temples more skillfully, and lift her more carefully, and fan her more wisely than any of the others. This she knew; but to help her trembling heart to seize hold of the strong Arm ready to sustain her. Ah, how could Maria do that? She knew nothing about that Arm. The feeble, wailing voice continued:

"I don't know what to do. I am afraid of death. I always was. To be buried in the grave seems *so dreadful* to me. I need your father now."

"Mother," Maria said, with trembling lips, "you are a Christian."

6

"Oh, I don't know. I don't even know, Maria, whether I am or not. It is a dreadful thing to be dying and not *know*. Don't you ever come to that place, my daughter, without being *sure* of it. I have never said so much as this to you before. How can I have been a Christian and neglected my children? But we have prayed for you, your father and I, often and often. Oh, is there nobody who will pray for me now?"

Maria looked around again, her face working in agony. The cultivated, courteous, kind-hearted physician leaned against the mantel, ready to use his skill as doctor or nurse, ready to go of errands, ready to do anything, except to *pray*. No hope of his doing that; he had never prayed in his life.

"Helen," Maria said, imploringly.

Helen groaned in agony.

"O Maria, I can't, I can't! I never prayed aloud. I don't know how."

"Then, Ermina, O Ermina, can't you pray for mother?"

Ermina staggered to the bedside and flung herself on her knees, but she burst into such an agony of passionate weeping that Dr. Marley came hastily forward, and whispered her to come away. She was agitating her mother, and he feared she might faint again; and if so they might fail to rally her.

" She should be soothed," he said, in an under-tone to Maria, whom he had recognized as the real head. " This agitation is taking her strength. Is there no friend near at hand who would come to her ? "

Maria shook her head blankly. Their friends near at hand were not such as would be willing to *pray*.

" Mr. Gordon would come," she said. " I can't think of any one else."

" He is much too far away, I fear; still I might send for him. My boy is waiting in the kitchen; it is *possible* he may reach here in time."

" Doctor, is it so *awfully* near ? "

The doctor bowed his head, then went to send his messenger, more than half a mile away, after the minister. Poor Tom, it seemed to him his heart was bursting; he felt as if he would have given up every hope that he possessed in this world if only he had known how to pray for his mother. At this moment a sudden thought, a sudden hope, came to him.

" Peter will pray," he said briskly.

Mrs. Randolph caught at the sentence.

" Go for him," she said pitifully. " Go quick, before it is too late. Oh, I cannot die without somebody to pray. Oh, my children, my chil-dren, *what shall* I do ? "

Even in this moment of supreme anguish Helen

was shocked at the strangeness of the proceedings. "Peter was — well, it looked so singular
— perhaps it was unnecessary — her mother could
not, *could not* be going to die; she had not believed it any of the time. They were all frightened, that was the trouble."

"Tom," she said, whispering as he was passing
through the open door, "the doctor has sent for
Mr. Gordon, and *Peter* cannot help mother; he
is simply an ignorant *boy.* Wouldn't it be better
to wait just a few minutes?"

"Helen," he said, sternly, "mother is *dying*,"
and he went swiftly on his mission.

Helen dropped in a limp heap on the floor and
moaned. She did not believe it, but it was dreadful even to think of for a moment. The unusual
confusion that prevailed in the house had awakened Peter some time before the doctor's boy had
given him the news, and he stood in the kitchen
waiting to be of use. Tom burst in there on his
way to the wood-house chamber.

"Are you here?" he said, stopping. "Peter,
you are the only one in the house who knows how
to pray. Will you come and pray for my mother?
She is dying."

Peter had not been prepared for such useful-
ness. He had his lantern lighted ready to do errands; he had fed the fire and added water to
the kettle against the time that more would be

needed, but this work startled him. Only God had heard Peter pray; but then those three last words, "*she is dying.*" If there was any time when prayer was needed surely it was then.

" I will if I can," he said, simply, and followed Tom swiftly and silently into the chamber of death. He took no notice of any of the faces turned to his, but bowed himself at the bedside. All the others followed his example save the doctor; he leaned decorously against the mantel, and kept his eyes fixed on the face of his patient. Then the Lord himself took the guidance of Peter's lips, for these were the words he uttered:

" Let not your heart be troubled: ye believe in God, believe also in me. In my Father's house are many mansions: if it were not so I would have told you. I go to prepare a place for you. And if I go and prepare a place for you, I will come again, and receive you unto myself; that where I am, there ye may be also. And whither I go ye know, and the way ye know. And whatsoever ye shall ask in my name, that will I do, that the Father may be glorified in the Son. If ye shall ask anything in my name, I will do it. I will not leave you comfortless: I will come to you. Peace I leave with you, my peace I give unto you: not as the world giveth, give I unto you. Let not your heart be troubled, neither let it be afraid."

There was silence in the room as the words of prayer were finished. Mrs. Randolph lay very quiet with closed eyes; they thought she slept. Suddenly she opened them, and her voice was sweet and natural.

"'*My* peace I give unto you.' Thank you — yes, thank you very much; I had forgotten. 'Neither let it be afraid.' No, I will not be afraid, for he says, 'I will come again and receive you unto myself.' I have been a weak, foolish Christian; but *his* promise stands sure. 'I will come again and receive you unto myself.' He has come. 'Peace I leave with you.' Children, tell your father — "

Half an hour afterward came Mr. Gordon, breathless with haste, to speak words of cheer and help to the dying. He found only very fair still clay, the spirit had been received unto *himself.*

Perhaps this is as good an opportunity as any I shall have to record the conversation which took place between Tom and our friend Peter several days after this event.

"Do the words read in connection as you used them in your prayer?" Tom asked.

"It wasn't a prayer," Peter said. "Only as I prayed in my heart, you know, that Jesus Christ would come and speak just such words to her, or maybe more beautiful ones even, if he could find any. I didn't know how to pray words of my own, you know."

" I'm glad you didn't. Are the verses connected as you repeated them ? "

" I don't know. I haven't found them in my Bible yet. These were on a card that Mr. Hammond gave me with a lot of others. This one was named ' Words of Comfort to the Dying,' so I learned it first, 'cause a fellow might have to *die* most any time, you know."

Tom smiled.

" You're queer," he said. " Will you lend me the card ? I would like to learn the words myself, since they were a comfort to my mother."

" Oh, I'll lend it to you and welcome; but they won't do *you* much good, after all. They don't belong to you, you know."

" Why not, pray ? "

" Why, because there's conditions. Promises always have conditions, you know — most al-always; anyway, these have. I asked Mr. Hammond about it. ' If you're my children,' Jesus Christ said, why then ' I'll come again and receive you to myself;' and if you're my children, why you'll do so and so. Well, now, I've met the condition and you haven't, you see — there's the difference."

Tom arched his eyebrows.

" That's taking a pretty high place yourself

and leaving me out in the cold. Rather egotist-
ical, isn't it, as well as selfish?"

Peter looked at him in genuine wonder.

"Why so?" he said. "I don't see how, any
more than it would be if your father should say
to you and me, 'If you do this work I'll give you
each a coat.' I might do the work and get the
coat, and you might let the work alone, and then
you would leave the coat alone too, wouldn't
you? And it wouldn't be my fault because I had
a coat and you hadn't — now *would it?*"

Tom laughed a little.

"You better study law," he said. "Nevertheless, I'll borrow the card; it was my mother's if
it isn't mine, and I want to look at it."

CHAPTER VIII.

MOURNING AND DRESSMAKING.

AS it ever been your desolate fortune to move about a familiar home, doing some very commonplace duty, only a few hours after some crushing calamity has fallen upon the household? Do you know anything of the utter misery of taking up familiar objects associated with your everyday life, feeling that the soul of everyday living has gone from you, and yet that the skeleton of it is left for you to work on at endlessly? Then you can appreciate something of Maria's feelings as she went down in the gray light of that winter morning, to the kitchen to prepare breakfast. Strangely enough, none of the friends who had gathered promptly around them in their sorrow thought to take this care upon themselves. Most of them were those who had hired help in their own

kitchens, and forgot that there were those less
favored in that respect.

Helen remained up stairs in her room, which
was closed on all intruders. Ermina was physically unable to leave her bed, and Grace was
ministering to her needs ; so, of necessity, Maria
went alone to the kitchen. How terrible it
seemed ! Here in the dining-room was everything arranged as she had prepared it herself the
night before — the table set for breakfast, her
mother's place at the head, her mother's chair
placed ready for her.

"Not that chair," she had said to Grace, when
she had been helping her. "Mother doesn't like
any chair but the high one ; she is such a *little*
mother, you know."

Now the little mother was in the room just
across the hall, but she would not come out to sit
in her chair that morning, nor any other. Maria
leaned against the table, dumb with pain. What
a dreadful thing life *was!* Only across the hall
her mother was lying still and white and lifeless,
and here was *she* making coffee and toasting bread
just as usual. If only she could go to her room,
and lock and bolt herself in, and give voice and
expression to her agony ; if she might even be
taking care of some one who was really suffering,
like Ermina ; but then Grace could do that, and
in kitchen work she was a novice, and they must

all eat, even though their hearts were breaking, and dishes must be washed and rooms swept just as if that silent presence across the hall were not all that was left to them of mother. Tom came to the dining-room, and in hoarse tones recalled Maria to outward life.

"Maria, what about father?"

"What about him?" she repeated, in a blank, dazed way. "Yes, the train is due in an hour. Oh!" and that one short, sharp word expressed a volume. For one little minute she had forgotten her father. "Some one must go to meet him."

"Who will go? Can you, Maria?"

Maria shook her head.

"I am not the one, Tom. I can make him a cup of coffee, and coax him to drink it, and have his slippers ready, but for such times as these I am helpless. It seems to me some one who — some *Christian* ought to go."

"Where shall I find one?" Tom asked the question in a tone that at any other time would have savored of sarcasm. "Do you think Helen would be the person to go?"

"Oh, no," Maria said quickly. "She wouldn't go, either; and Ermina is sick. Tom, you must ask Mr. Gordon to go. Mr. Evans is here with his carriage. You get Mr. Gordon to take it and go for father. *He* is the only one to help us now."

"I wish," Tom said, and stopped.

"What do you wish?" Maria asked, drearily, going on with her toasting in an apathetic way.

"I wish father had a child who knew how to be of any comfort to him now."

The muscles of Maria's face worked pitifully She was thinking of that same thing; indeed, she felt the need of some unseen, unknown Arm to lean her own weak heart upon.

"Not but that you always have and always *will* be a comfort to him," Tom hastened to say. "But I meant, Maria, that it seems as if he needed some one who felt as he does about things. You know what I mean."

It was the afternoon of the same day that Maria was summoned from the depths of her pillow in her own room, whither she had crept for a few minutes, to a consultation in the back sitting-room. Helen was standing in the center of the room, Miss Allen beside her; Ermina, looking like a ghost, was propped up among pillows in the great rocking-chair; Grace sat on a low ottoman, but she had moved it away from the green-covered rocker near where it always stood — no one occupied the green rocker to-day. Helen turned as her youngest sister entered.

"Maria," she said, wearily, "what a time you have been in coming. It is necessary to know what you must have made up. Miss Allen is waiting to report to Mrs. Akers."

"Made up!" Maria said. She was not given to repeating words stupidly, but her brain was very dull that day.

"Why, yes. A dress you will need, of course, and a hat, and what about a sack, or would you have a polonaise, and have no outside garment, until we have the heart to think a little?"

Maria began to understand. It was the first dawning of the whole terrible subject of "clothes." She had not given it a thought that day, but she spoke promptly enough now.

"Helen, I don't want anything."

"Don't want anything!" It was Helen's time to repeat now. "Why, what will you wear to — when —" and Helen paused. Maria's face paled, but her voice was steady.

"I suppose you mean to the funeral. I presume I shall wear my empress, as I have nothing else to wear; but I haven't given the momentous question of dress a thought to-day."

"But it is necessary to think. You can't always be a child, Maria. Don't you remember that your empress is brown?"

"Yes, I remember it. I am quite willing to wear brown, just as I always have done."

Helen sat down with a gesture of despair.

"Don't make my task harder than is necessary," she said, wearily. "You cannot think *how* hard it is at best. Of course we will all wear black because it is proper to do so. The question now to be decided is, how much we each need."

"But, Helen, I don't think that is the question to decide. I don't want to put on black at all. If we had plenty of money to waste, which we haven't, it does not seem to me that it is the time to plan and twist and turn about new clothes. But the main objection is that it is expensive, and we have need to economize."

A quickly suppressed exclamation of surprise from Miss Allen did not escape Helen's notice, and her pale cheek flushed. She was deeply sensitive to public opinion.

"Maria, don't be so childish," she said, with an impatient movement. "Of course we are not rich, everybody knows that, and it will be necessary for us to study economy, however trying it may be at such a time; but we will not fail in anything that can in any way show respect to mother. She was too dear a mother for that," and Helen's lip quivered.

Maria only grew paler.

"Mother can not possibly care about such things now," she said, steadily. "I can not see how one color can be considered more respectful than another, and I think we ought not to burden father with any unnecessary expense. He has quite enough to bear now."

"Ermina," said Helen, facing about to her, "had any other idea occurred to you than that of course we would wear mourning?"

"I haven't thought of it to-day only when you spoke of it. I took it for granted that everything was settled. Why, yes, I suppose we will have to."

"Grace, have you thought differently from this?"

Grace confessed that she supposed they would wear black as a matter of course, but she was quite willing not to do it if it was thought best. It had always seemed to her a strange sort of custom.

Helen turned back to Maria.

"You see, Maria, you are the only one who has any desire to do anything strange and out of the ordinary line of common propriety, and as you are the youngest I think you have detained Miss Allen quite long enough; her time is precious, you know. Can you decide now as to what you need?"

No, Maria could not decide further than that she believed the expense to be an unnecessary one, and had quite determined in her own mind to oppose it for the sake of the father who had burdens enough to bear.

"Isn't it rather a trying time in which to propose new measures to your poor father? It would seem hard to intrude questions of dress on him now." It was Miss Allen's decorous, smoothly modulated voice that proposed this question, and Helen promptly answered it.

"Of course it is. Even if we thought of making ourselves conspicuous by unusual proceedings it would be cruel to force father's attention to such a trivial matter *now;* but my sister is young and thoughtless, Miss Allen. Ermina, we must trim with crape, I suppose. Are you particular as to quality?"

Maria's face flushed. It was decided'y not her nature to endure in meekness. She spoke with unusual sharpness.

"Helen, you are *absurd* to talk in that manner. You know father will not even *know* whether our dresses are black or yellow if we don't enlighten him; but he will know all about the enormous bills to be paid; and if you really want to save him trouble you will take care how you lay such an unnecessary burden on him. As for making ourselves conspicuous that is nonsense. Very respectable people get along without burying themselves in crape and bombazine; and I for one shall not consent to any such thing," and Maria walked majestically from the room.

"How old is Miss Maria?" questioned Miss Allen, pointedly, as the door closed after her.

"Just fifteen. She is a spoiled child, Miss

Allen. Poor mother's health has been so frail
that Maria has been allowed to indulge her queer
notions, until she really forgets that she is a
woman. We shall have to leave the question of
her dress until to-morrow. Come in the morning, and I will see that she is reduced to order by
that time."

Poor Maria shed the first tears that had been
wrung from her aching eyes after she went up
from the back sitting-room and the smooth-
tongued dressmaker. In a sense her sister's comment, that she did not hear, was true. She felt
like a woman of forty. It was a long time since
she remembered feeling like a child. Helen had
forgot to mention that the cares and burdens of
life had pressed so heavily on her young sister as
to crush out the youthfulness. That hour spent
on her bed, her face buried in the pillows, herself given over to bitter weeping, was an hour of
work to Helen, the result of which was that Grace
came to know if Maria could go down to father's
room, he wanted to see her.

"What does he want?" she asked, springing
from the bed, bathing her swollen eyes, smoothing her hair, and rapidly arranging her toilet.
Grace didn't know, only as she passed his door
he opened it, and told her to ask Maria to come
to him a few minutes. Maria had seen him for
but a few minutes during that first terrible hour,

7

when the shock was at its heaviest with him. He had grown calm now, but he looked older by ten years than he had two days before. This youngest daughter knew better than did any of the others of the family what the fragile little mother was to him. She longed to throw her arms around his neck, and rain kisses and tears on the worn, haggard face; but such had not been her education, nor indeed was it her nature; self-controlled Maria had been even in her babyhood.

"Will you have a cup of tea now, father?" was all the greeting she gave him.

"Not now, daughter. Sit down a few minutes, I want to talk with you. What is it Helen is trying to explain about this dress question?"

Maria's face flushed. This then was Helen's consideration for father. She hesitated, and looked away from her father's pale face and deep sunken eyes. It seemed very hard to speak of crape and ribbon and the funeral, and mother just across the hall in that cold sleep.

"I don't understand such matters, you know, daughter. Can't it be arranged without me?" There was almost a pleading sound in Mr. Randolph's voice. "*I* think it might have been."

Maria said quickly,—

"But it seems Helen did not. I don't want to wear black, father. It is an unnecessary expense, and I for one haven't the heart to plan *clothes* at such a time."

"But Helen thinks it will be a great impropriety not to. We want to do everything decently and without unnecessary talk. I wouldn't want to do anything that would appear in the least like disrespect to your dear mother."

"Do you think it makes any difference to mother *now* what colored clothes we wear? Doesn't she know that I love her just as much, and mourn her just as sincerely this evening in my brown wrapper as I should to-morrow in black bombazine?"

Mr. Randolph moved restlessly in his chair.

"I don't doubt that you are right, daughter. These things are of no consequence to me. They are trifles in your mother's eyes at this moment. I have no doubt but Helen feels differently, and she says that Ermina and Grace agree with her, and Helen is the oldest, you know; she is in your mother's place now. Let us have no trouble that we can avoid. We must learn to yield our own wishes, you and I."

"But, father, about the bills. Do you know that it will involve a great expense, especially if it is all left to Helen's management. Her taste is highly cultivated in that direction. How will we ever pay the bills?"

A spasm as of pain crossed the pale, worn face, but Mr. Randolph spoke quickly,—

"We shall manage in some way. Life is very hard. A few more bills more or less can not make it much harder. I do not mean to murmur, though. Let us have peace, Maria, at any price."

CHAPTER IX.

DEBTS AND DOUBTS.

"THERE certainly must be people in this world who can not afford to die!"

She did not say it recklessly, nor with even the semblance of carelessness; on the contrary her face expressed intense and painful feeling. She stood in the back parlor by the table which was half covered with sheets of paper in various stages of fold and crumple. It was Maria, of course; no one in the Randolph family besides Maria ever made such startling remarks.

The funeral was over; indeed, two weeks had passed since they laid their mother away. It had been a solemn funeral, and Mrs. Jenkins, the undertaker's wife, had pronounced the details unobjectionable. What Mrs. Jenkins meant by

that may be obscure to the minds of some, but
Helen Randolph understood her perfectly. That
young lady had an eye for details; she had meant
them to be unobjectionable. An unskilled looker-
on would have said that everything was very neat
and plain and appropriate. Ah! to be very neat
and plain and appropriate at funerals means to pay
somebody a good deal of money. The four daughters were shrouded in long crape vails, and about
the details of their dress everything was appropriate also, from the perfect-fitting Alexandre
kids to the wide black bordered cambric hand-
kerchiefs. The velvet-covered casket which was
their mother's last resting-place was literally covered over with rare and beautiful white flowers,
such as blossom in January, only for money.
Some of them were love tokens from outside
friends; others of them were of Helen's own
ordering and selection. "Dear mother loved
flowers *so* much," she had said. From the main
entrance door floated the long crape signals of
death; the arm of each bearer was festooned
with crape; the hands of each bearer were covered with decorous black kids, furnished by the
family.

"*Everybody* does it," Helen had said, when
Maria protested. The carriages were numerous
and costly; the hearse with its solemn black
plumes was the new several thousand dollar one,

that had only been used twice before, for Mrs. Judge Westervelt and General Wallace Thorpe. Certainly the most uncharitable and censorious looker-on of them all could not say that every possible and conceivable token of respect had not been paid to that fair piece of clay which they finally covered with its native dust.

Now it was two weeks afterward, and Maria had been looking over and summing up the bills. Do you wonder at her utterly dismayed exclamation, " There *must* be some people in this world who cannot afford to *die!* "

Ermina came presently into the back room, paused a moment irresolute as she saw her sister's occupation, then slowly advanced. Ermina would have preferred to shirk that business if she could. " How are we ever to pay them? "

This was the one tremendous thought weighing on Maria's heart, and she spoke it.

" Father will probably attend to that." Ermina tried to look and speak with indifference.

" Ermina, that is nonsense," Maria said, sharply. " Don't play Helen, and pretend not to know that father has nothing to pay with and no strength to bestow on them. They are enormous."

" I know it," said Ermina, taking up her own character again. " I am quite as much appalled as you can possibly desire. I don't see our way out of this labyrinth. I have wondered a hundred times within the last two weeks what was to become of us all."

"Ermina, it is late in the day to ask you about this, but I *do* want to know, since you really saw the danger ahead, why you didn't protest against all this needless waste of money?"

Ermina opened her eyes very wide. "I am sure I don't know what you mean," she said, gravely. "I didn't know there had been any needless expense, or at least very little, none to signify."

"There isn't fifty dollars' worth in all these bills that would come under the head of necessary expenses."

Ermina smiled grimly. "Your idea of 'necessary' and Helen's would differ, I presume. You have some queer fancies, you know. Now, I hate bills as much as you possibly can, but I don't see how, in our position, we could avoid wearing mourning without making an outrageous talk."

"What *is* our position, Ermina?"

Ermina laughed.

"It might be hard to define," she said, with sarcasm. "Helen wants us to be considered as belonging to the first society, and so long as Mrs. Monroe and the Conklings invite her to their parties I suppose we are."

"*I* can define our position. It is a continuous scramble after something to eat and wear, without defrauding people out of their just dues. Under such circumstances to have worn brown or gray, or any color that we happened to have, would be infinitely more respectable, and make less talk, than to live on the charity, or at least the forbearance of our friends. I tell you I don't see how we are to live at all."

"We might go to the poor-house," Ermina suggested, gravely. It was evidently all the counsel that she had to offer, and Maria turned away, only saying in the same cold, half-indifferent tone that her sister had used,—

"It would make an 'outrageous' talk, you would find; and, besides, 'they' don't wear crape and bombazine at the poor-house."

"You are sharp," said Ermina. "In fact, you are almost cross. I wish you would leave that part of the programme to Helen, she excels in it; and since you are the youngest you certainly won't have to be responsible for the bills, so I wouldn't worry myself into a fever if I were you." And Ermina left the room and the bills and went away up stairs to brood over the state of affairs, and exhibit more sympathy to the four walls of her room than she would have dreamed of showing to her sister. It was one of the miseries of this Randolph family that they lived in shells.

Maria sat down again and pondered the pitiless staring figures in dumb dismay; the sum total was so much more than even she, who had tried to keep a sharp lookout, had imagined. She knew it was much more than her father had even dreamed of. "If there was only some one to go to for counsel or even for pity," she said, wearily. "What *do* the girls think, I wonder? People must *think*, it seems to me, even though they were not willing to let any one know it. I just wonder what Helen would say to all these? I mean to go and ask her. She certainly ought to know the result of her management." She gathered up an army of bills and went up to Helen's room. That young lady was engaged in retrimming her hat, and as the plume she attempted to fasten showed all the obstinacy and depravity belonging to plumes, the owner of it was not in a pleasant mood to confront. Maria did not wait for moods; she marched without preface into her subject.

"Helen, what is to be done about all these bills?"

"They are to be left on the library table, I presume. That is where bills are generally kept."

"But I mean how are they to be paid?"

"With money, I should imagine."

"Helen, I wish you wouldn't be so very sharp. I have come for suggestions if you have any to offer. If you really have no interest in the matter I may as well go back."

"I have an interest just now in my hat. I wish it was back in the shop where it came from. It is the most unbecoming thing I ever had on my head."

"*I* wish it was paid for. Have you any idea how much it cost?"

"Not the slightest, and I don't care. It is just as plain and simple as anything I could get, and therefore my conscience is clear. People will have to be decent in this world."

"But, Helen, will it be considered decent not to pay for it?"

The plume stood straight up now, one end poking slightly forward; besides, Helen had pricked her finger; her patience was utterly exhausted; she spoke angrily.

"Do, Maria, *hush.* You are perfectly insane over affairs that in no way belong to you. It is ridiculous that the youngest in the house should take us all to task in the way you do. Let the bills alone, and all other matters that don't in the least concern you. That is my suggestion, if you really want one from me."

Maria gathered up her papers, and walked with steady step and burning cheek out of the room.

"If there is anything earthly that I want it is a friend." This she said with dry eyes, but with a strange choking in her voice.

Poor, foolish child! There was a Friend

greater than any earthly, who was waiting for a chance to suggest, to sympathize, to shield, but she passed Him by and struggled on alone.

Grace came through the hall humming a tune. It was a sweet, tender little tune, and Grace hummed it a great deal; and Maria with the rest had imagined that this daughter sang because she was by nature lighter hearted, and grief touched her more gently than it did the rest.

"I wonder if it has so much as occurred to Grace that there is such a thing as a debt to be paid?" Maria said, listening to the song. "I mean to ask her." She went to the door and called.

"Have you any idea how these are all to be paid?" she questioned, as Grace came up to the table, with the tune still hovering around her lips.

"Have you counted them? How much is it? Does father know?"

"You always ask three questions at once, Grace. Yes, I *have* counted them, and they amount to *enough*. I dread to tell father anything about it. If there were only some way in which *I* could help him to pay them."

Grace ceased her humming, but she drummed the notes of the song on the green baize of the table. It annoyed Maria. A good deal had occurred to annoy her that day.

"You never think of anything but music" she said, irritably.

"I'm thinking of it now to some purpose." Grace spoke lightly. "Thinking of giving it up — the lessons, you know. Spring isn't a pleasant time for practicing, and I have several other things that I want to do. The new term opens to-morrow, but I have quite decided not to enter my name at present. What do you think of it?"

"I think it has very little to do with the question before us, as to the paying of these bills," Maria said, coldly.

"Why, yes it has, just a little. Music lessons are expensive articles, and the money I have in my purse ready for the 'payment invariably in advance' that is always required, will make one bill *smaller* at least."

"It would be but a drop in the bucket," Maria said, forlornly.

"I know; but one drop helps to fill the bucket after all. Here's Madame La Farge's bill. Milliners' accounts are always the most disagreeable to let stand. I can pay that and have a part of a drop left, and father need not be troubled with anything about it. As for the others, they will have their day somehow. Don't be worried, Maria."

"So Helen's bonnet is paid for after all," thus soliloquized Maria. Grace's voice reached her from the upper stair; she was trilling the notes of the same tender song.

"She is as light-hearted as a butterfly," continued this youngest sister. "I'm sure I wish I could be like her and let care alone. I thought she was devoted to her music lessons, but it seems she is tired of them, which is a fortunate thing for Madame La Farge."

The words of the song that Grace sang, over and over again, were,—

> "It may not be *my* way,
> It may not be *thy* way,
> But yet in *His* own way,
> The Lord will provide."

There *are* matters wherein sharp, quick-witted girls like Maria Randolph show themselves to be utterly stupid.

There was just one more member of the family to consult. That was Tom. It was while Maria was clearing away the tea things that the subject of her anxious thought came to light again.

"Tom, do you know the amount of the bills?"

"Not in exact figures; but I know they must be stunning. When Helen is at the helm look out for bills."

"Well, have you any idea what we shall do about paying them? You see our necessary expenses take up every bit of the salary, and more, too; and where these extras are to come in, i can't imagine."

"I know," he said, gloomily. "I don't see what is to become of our family, anyway. You can't imagine how much I envy Peter and his regular employment, whereby he earns his board and clothing. I don't see a_y way out of it. I *can't* get anything to do. I've tried all this week. I really am not lying idle of choice, though Helen is kind enough to insinuate it pretty often."

Maria was not wont to be silent, especially when she and Tom were together; but on this particular evening she rattled the tea-cups more than seemed at all necessary, at least to Tom, but as far as words were concerned was dumb.

Tom looked steadily at her for a few minutes, then at the cups and saucers, and inwardly wished they were in Jericho. Presently he spoke again.

"Now, Maria, on your word and honor, what do you think you would do if you were in my place?"

"I may be mistaken," Maria began, with unusual meekness. "I dare say I am; because I know that *not* being in your place alters the case wonderfully; but I *think* that if I were in your place I would saw wood for Mr. Evans, or, failing in that, drive the cows for Mr. Thornton, or turn the grindstone for old Pete."

"Or wear the oilcloth coat that Messrs. Cook

& Co. provide for that industrious employe who
marches up and down the street exhibiting himself, to announce that T & KofE R sold here,"
interrupted Tom, with a little sharpness in the
voice that was trying to be steady. "That's
what the coat says, Maria — in red letters, just
in this style," and he held up to her view
the slip of paper on which he had been printing.
"I saw the chap who wears it to-day, and I
couldn't help admiring his industry. Thank
you for your advice, I'll take it into consideration."

"I didn't mean to be sharp, Tom," Maria said
in dismay. "But I do feel so troubled about
everything. There doesn't seem to be anything
that anybody can do." ·

"Yes, there is; we can all worry with all our
might, and that helps matters along amazingly,
makes home pleasant, you know. Don't imagine
I'm blaming you. I'm a worthless, useless fellow; no one knows it better than I do myself.
Your suggestions are not practical after all, because Peter saws Mr. Evans' wood at odd hours,
and they don't drive cows to pasture in February
in this climate, and old Pete has tumbled on his
grindstone and broken his leg. I've been considering all these avenues to employment, you
see; but they are like the rest, closed to me."

Tom was evidently hurt. He went out at

once, and Maria saw him no more that evening. This, then, was all that her planning had accomplished. She shed some bitter tears over her troubles that night, but they only served to make her eyes red and give her a headache for the next day, and she could not help feeling that her life, too, was out of joint.

8

CHAPTER X.

LIGHT WITHOUT LOGIC.

OM did not appear at breakfast the next morning. Grace had seen him go down Chauncy Street quite early.

"My window overlooks Chauncy Street, you know," she said, in explanation, to her father.

"What can take him to that part of the town I wonder," Mr. Randolph said; and in Maria's heart there was a vague unrest.

"What can take him *anywhere* at this hour of the day?" Helen said. "Tom isn't given to early morning walks."

He came in just before Mr. Randolph was ready to leave, a little flushed, with a sort of triumph in his eyes that Maria did not understand and did not like.

"What will happen next, I wonder? I am

prepared for *anything*, now that you have taken to early rising."

This was Helen's greeting.

"Perhaps the next wonder will be that you will take to doing something useful." He said it good-naturedly enough, but with the usual undertone of sarcasm. "*I* have, at least. Father, I have secured a situation at last."

Mr. Randolph's eyes brightened.

"*Have* you?" he said, heartily. "That is very cheering in these depressing times. What have you found?"

"I heard, last evening, that there was a vacancy in Harter & Wicks' store, and I rushed after it this morning the first thing. There were several ahead of me, but I proved to be the favored one." He addressed his father, but his dancing, wicked eyes were fixed on Maria's face.

The information he gave was variously received. Helen exclaimed in dismay or disgust, it was impossible to tell which; Ermina laughed; Grace looked distressed; while Maria, with cheeks flaming, and eyes that filled with angry tears, looked only on her plate, and was utterly silent. Mr. Randolph's voice was full of distress.

"Thomson, how could you do anything so rash? Times are hard enough; but we are not in actual need. And if we were, we would rather all starve together than to have you descend to this."

"And father an officer in the State **Temper-** ance Society!" Ermina said laughing.

"It's an absolute disgrace," Helen said, with flashing eyes.

"I don't know," Tom said, composedly breaking his egg. "Is it much worse to sell the stuff than it is to drink it? There's your friend, Horace Monroe, patronizes the establishment. He was even out this morning. Now, if he drinks wine somebody must sell it to him, and why not I as well as any other? Father, I couldn't help it. I had to do something. *You* know how hard I have tried to secure something decent to do. Everything failed me, and I was goaded on, partly by my own conscience and partly by the consciences of other people."

Even at this Maria did not raise her head.

"I would rather have lived on bread and water," Mr. Randolph said, pitifully.

"Now that's pretty hard on a fellow, isn't it? — especially when he has done the best that he could. It must be an honest, respectable business, or the law wouldn't permit it, and respectable Christian people wouldn't vote for it nor patronize it. Things are *mixed*, father, I'm willing to admit that."

"*I* don't vote for it, nor patronize it," Mr. Randolph said, firmly.

"I know it, sir," Tom said, and his voice was

almost tender. " I know that very well; and if there were more men like you it wouldn't be voted for, and there would be no chance for me to sell it; but you see men are not modeled after your pattern. Dr. Evans votes for it, you know, and Mr. Wheeler, and Mr. Harris, and a host of others too numerous to mention — every one of them members of your own church - to say nothing of the large company who have it in their cellars, and closets, and medicine cases. Don't you see things are horribly mixed ? "

The sentence commenced in respectful tenderness ended in good-humored mockery; but Mr. Randolph's face retained the pained, grieved look as he answered,—

"You and I, Thomson, have nothing to do with any one but you and me in this matter. God doesn't require us to keep the consciences of other men; and I would rather live all my life on bread and water than to have my son sell rum," and Mr. Randolph went with slow and feeble step from the room.

"It is too bad!" Ermina said, indignantly. "Father has quite enough to bear without this."

"I think as much!" This from Helen. "Tom, if you have no self-respect left, nor a particle of regard for your sisters, one would have supposed that you might have remembered your father.'

"I did remember him, Lady Helen, and therefore concluded to relieve him of my support. That is considerate, certainly; at least you ought to think so, for the times that you have hinted something of the sort to me can not be numbered."

How long this interesting conversation would have continued, had there been no interruption, it is impossible to say. Fortunately the door-bell summoned both Helen and Ermina to a conference in the hall, and the family party broke up.

Tom lingered in the dining-room, while Maria cleared the table. He drummed thoughtfully on the window-pane and wished his solemn-faced sister would speak. He had told the truth at the breakfast table, but not the whole truth The situation was his, provided he choose to accept it. Pecuniarily, the offer was a tempting one. Messrs. Harter & Wicks had been liberal and persuasive. Mr. Randolph, senior, had been all his life an earnest temperance man; in his prosperous days he had been a very influential one. To secure his son as clerk in an establishment whose main business was selling liquor would be a delightful triumph over the temperance movement. But Tom Randolph, though by no means a temperance man from principle still hated the business of rum selling with a cor dial hatred, and was by no means decided, even in his desperate state, to accept the only position offered him. Maria's words had jarred on his nature — all the more, perhaps, because originally his lack of employment was his own fault. Months before this he might have secured respectable places, and many a parley did he hold with his pride over them; but, latterly, when pride was utterly vanquished by the need that he saw pressed sorely, every avenue had seemed closed. It was hard, he said to himself, "That a fellow must be witted with laziness, when he stood ready to pick stones for a living, if only he could find any to pick." He left out of consideration the fact that no one but himself knew that he had made any attempt at stone-picking, and so he nursed his wrath until Messrs. Harter & Wicks' place of business had seemed a sweet revenge. Still he had left himself an hour in which to escape. "If I am not here by nine o'clock," he had said to Mr. Harter, "you may understand that I have changed my mind." It wanted fifteen minutes to nine. His mind was almost changed. He had not remembered that besides shocking the girls, which he rather enjoyed, he would also shock his father. That was another thing.

"It won't pay, I guess," he said to himself, thinking of his father's worn, troubled face. "I'll take another look." If only that solemn-faced Maria would say something. Why couldn't she have known what an influence her sayings had over this brother of hers?

"You don't congratulate me on my success," he said at last, resolved to make her speak, which however, she didn't do. Maria rattled the knives and dropped a teaspoon, but she kept her tongue entirely still. "I should think you might be more agreeable to a fellow after I've taken your latest advice and found something to do at all hazards. Can't you even wish me success as salesman?"

"I have nothing whatever to say," Maria said at last, and she said it with dignity. "If I cannot speak a word to you about finding employment, when you know as well as I do the need for it, and when you asked me for my opinion, without your getting angry and doing something directly to disgrace the entire family, why, the more I keep my opinions to myself the better it will be for you, and I intend to do it after this."

"All right," Tom said, and he seized his hat and rushed off to Messrs. Harter & Wicks' place of business. It was five minutes of nine. "I'll do it!" he said to himself on the way. "They're all cross together; it's impossible to please them, and I may as well not try. I'll earn some money anyway."

As for Maria she cried during the greater part

of the morning, making her nose red and swollen, and ⌐ʰ   orgot to put the soda in her bread, so the family ate sour bread for three days ; but all this did not keep her brother from selling whiskey at the corner store, and she *might* have done it. Maria Randolph had made two mistakes. She thought that what *she saw* in a person's life was all that there was to see, and reasoned accordingly ; also she knew nothing of the practical working of that grand old "whatsoever," therefore she worked without it. "Put yourself in his place," a writer has chosen for a title, and no doubt he thinks it a strikingly original idea. Maria Randolph has never read the book, and I trust she never will; to my mind she is much better off without it; but both she and the aforesaid author must have heard of the wonderful words, "Whatsoever ye would that men should do to you, do ye even so to them."

All this happened on Saturday. On Sabbath, Tom wandered listlessly from room to room. Maria was still on her dignity, and the only conversation Tom attempted with her was to wish that the saloon was kept open on Sunday, to which she made no answer. His wanderings finally took him to the back kitchen, where Peter Armstrong had the privilege of sitting of a Sabbath afternoon.

"Well," he said, halting before that young

man, "how's Peter Bible? I see you have his
life there. I haven't heard anything about him
for some time. Have you discovered what the
fellow's other name is?"

"No," Peter said, "I haven't thought anything about that since. I've found him, though,
again. There's a spell where nothing is said
about him, and I was most afraid that he had
stopped following, but they speak of him again
just as though he had been on hand most of the
time, and I guess he was."

"What is he up to?" Tom asked, taking his
favorite seat on the wood-box.

"He's been having company," Peter said,
meditatively.

"Company!" and Tom's tones were derisive.
"I didn't know he was given to that sort of
thing. Seems to me it was rather frivolous in
him, just like people now days."

"It depends some on the company you happen
to have, I reckon."

Tom laughed.

"Oh, well, as to that, Peter wasn't aristocratic
in those days, I fancy. I presume he had those
brother fishermen to dinner. Very likely he gave
them a clam-bake, though I suppose that isn't
mentioned in the Bible, is it?"

"No," Peter said, gravely. "But the company
is by name."

" Who were they ? "

" Jesus Christ." Peter spoke the name slowly and reverently. The effect on Tom was curious. He started from the wood-box with a half-shocked face, and stared in silence at his companion for a full minute before his surprise found vent in words.

" You *are certainly* a queer chap," he said, at length. " I wonder if it is superior innocence or unusual depth that is at the bottom of it all ? "

" What are you talking about ? " Peter asked the question with an air of unmistakable innocence.

" Where did you get that queer way of talking about things of this sort as though they happened yesterday, or last week, and as if the people were acquaintances of yours ? "

" What's the difference *when* things happened if they truly *happened?* " questioned Peter, with puzzled face. " And as for being acquainted, why I *am* acquainted with Jesus Christ, you know. You can't think how nice it is to think that he went to Peter's house visiting. It speaks of it as though it was just a common enough thing to do. ' And when Jesus was come into Peter's house,' it says, just as though he often went, maybe. I like it ever so much. It makes you remember that he truly was a man, you know. A fellow thinks queer things sometimes.

When you come out I sat here thinking that he, maybe, goes visiting sometimes in heaven — they have houses there, you know; and perhaps he will actually come to my house in heaven some day. Why not? What's the use of laughing at a fellow? It *may* be so, I tell you. Anyhow it don't matter whether it is or not, because he comes down into our hearts now, and stays if we want him."

"I'd like to see some heart where he stayed." Tom stopped laughing and spoke almost bitterly. " It strikes me they must be different kinds of hearts from any that I know. How much of that do you honestly believe, my boy? If the spirit of Jesus Christ actually looks after people now days, why don't he come and look after me?"

" Maybe he don't like the company you keep." Peter spoke gravely enough, but his words set Tom into another laugh.

" There's another of your odd notions," he said. " Where do you get them?"

" It isn't my notion at all. Mr. Gordon said so in his sermon this morning. Didn't you hear him?"

" Can't say that I did."

" Well, you couldn't have been listening then, for he said it, and I thought of you down there in that saloon, and what kind of company you had gone to keeping. He doesn't like *that,* you may depend."

For some reason that was mysterious to him
self, the boy's simple words irritated Tom Randolph.

"See here," he said, sharply, "since you have
studied my case so thoroughly, perhaps you can
tell me why I wasn't better looked after, and employment found for me that was respectable, if
this is not?"

"Perhaps you didn't ask Him to help?"

Tom's good humor returned. He seemed
amused at the childishness of the reply.

"Oh, that's it," he said, carelessly. "It's a
queer kind of reason, isn't it? If He cares anything about me, why doesn't He see that I go
straight, and keep the right sort of company,
whether I ask His help or not. How is that?"

Peter's answer was ready.

"I don't know," he said, simply. "I've
thought about that myself, and wondered why
He didn't. There must be a good reason for it,
or He wouldn't have fixed it so. He just *chooses*
that we should ask for His help if we want it;
and that's all fair and square enough, as far as I
see. If we don't want a thing bad enough to ask
for it, after it's been promised for the asking, why
don't that go to show that we can't be awful
anxious to have it at all? As to why He fixed
it that way I'm sure I don't know, and it don't

make no kind of difference whether I know the *why* of a thing or not, if I know the thing itself."

Thomson Randolph was puzzled. How was he going to answer this simple boy's simple, "I don't know?" This wasn't logic nor argument, and yet it was unanswerable sure enough. Who did know? God had a *right* certainly to do as he pleased. Very likely he had reasons for his plans. There used to be a great deal to be said on this subject when the boys in college discussed theology; but before Peter Armstrong's ignorance discussion fled away and left the college boy speechless.

CHAPTER XI.

MISTAKES — GREAT AND SMALL.

ARVARD PLACE CHURCH was large and handsome, frescoed, upholstered, carpeted, organed, in the latest and most approved style. The congregation was in keeping with the church, large, well-dressed, cultivated. In fact, the Harvard Place Church was the fashion. Into this church, on the evening of which I write, sauntered Thompson Randolph, not from any special desire to be in church, but because it was customary to go, and he didn't know what else to do with himself. His sisters, Helen and Ermina, occupied prominent seats in the choir, and were very beautiful singers. Tom watched them as they fidgeted through the opening prayer, settling their over-skirts and buttoning each other's gloves, and afterward finding, with some rustle of leaves, their places in the note-books.

"I wonder what they will do next?" he whispered to his friend Germain Wilcox, whose seat he occupied. "How much prayer do they fancy they have heard?"

"They are getting ready to perform," whispered Germain behind his glove. "They can't be expected to be interested in anything so commonplace as a prayer. They are going to have a stunning anthem to-night. Sis has been squealing it all the afternoon."

Sis Wilcox was one of the leading sopranos. The anthem was very beautiful, tender, and sweet. Whether some of the effect of its sweetness was destroyed by the previous fidgets in which the choir had indulged can not perhaps be ascertained with certainty. Tom Randolph very rarely paid close attention to the sermon. "Sermons were not his forte," he was wont to say; but on this particular evening something in Mr. Gordon's manner arrested his attention. "Ye *will* not come unto me." This was the text, and the sermon fitted it—a simple, solemn, earnest setting forth of the strangeness of the sinner's position before God. There had been much prayer spent on that sermon. I might almost say that Mr. Gordon had written it on his knees, so anxious had he been to say just the right thing in the most straightforward way. A good and earnest man was Mr. Gordon, whose heart was at times utterly weighed down with a sense of the responsibilities of his position and his longing for the salvation of souls. Early in the evening Tom ceased his running comments on everything that was said and done, and sat erect with eyes fixed on the preacher's face. The style of sermon was one particularly calculated to arrest the attention of a sensible young man, there was such a calm, close, direct appeal to common sense.

"There is no getting around some of his positions. The world is made of fools anyhow, and it looks as though I might be one of the number." These were some of Tom's mental comments. However, during the closing prayer he allowed his thoughts to rove over the church and the village, and succeeded in a measure in shaking off the sense of personality. In the closing hymn he joined with unusual energy, partly because the tune was a particular favorite, and partly because he was aware that the choir preferred to do their own singing without assistance from the congregation. This was a view of matters that always exasperated Tom, and having a powerful voice he did his best to express his opinion.

> "How happy every child of grace,
>   Who knows his sins forgiven;
> This earth, he cries, is not my place,
>   I seek my place 'n heaven."

9

Such was one of the verses, put in striking
contrast with the main idea of the hymn, the
contrast between the state of those who have
"come" and accepted of the promised "life,"
and those who *will not* come.   Very little attention did Tom Randolph pay to the *words;* he
did not discover their appropriateness to the sermon; the tune was the main point with him.
Catching at the words a line at a time, and
while he sang it letting his eyes rove through
the church, it is no wonder that the words
became confused in his brain, and his voice rang
out loud and clear, "I seek *no* place in heaven."

Germain Wilcox laughed.

"That's true enough," he whispered.   "But
it's not quite the idea that Parson Gordon wants
sung.   Can't you read?"

Not another line sang Tom.   It was not embarrassment; few, if any, besides Germain would
be likely to notice the mistake, if they did Tom
was naturally too unconcerned to care; but
there came to him a sudden overwhelming sense
of the truth of the sentiment as he had sung it.
"I seek *no* place in heaven."   It was one thing
for a young man morally, nay, Christianly
brought up, to quietly ignore the facts of death
and hereafter; it was quite another to boldly
declare that he *sought* no future home.   If the
line had read as he imagined, "I seek no place

but heaven," his tongue would have glided smoothly over the poetic falsehood without a thought, but the *true* sentence that he had unwittingly sung filled him with a feeling almost like dismay. He did not saunter home with Germain as he had at first intended, but left him immediately and turned his steps homeward. Peter Armstrong was just ahead; he halted as he recognized Tom.

"Going home?" was all he said; and it chimed in with Tom's thoughts, "I seek *no home.*"

"No," he answered, with a sharp laugh, "I'm going to destruction."

Peter was silent and astonished; he was not quick-witted; he did not quite take Tom's meaning; he would not have known what answer to make if he had, so he made none; but presently said over the two lines of the hymn that had stayed with him:

> "This earth, he cries, is not my place,
> I seek my place in heaven."

The truth of the rendering this time struck Tom forcible. Undoubtedly Peter *was* seeking a place there; no one who came in daily contact with him could doubt it.

"I made a new version of those lines to suit my own case," he said, with an attempt at a laugh, and then he repeated them as he sang them.

"Well," said Peter, gravely, "that's so, ain't it?"

"Nothing could be truer; only a fellow don't enjoy singing it out before a congregation, you know."

"Might as well sing it as live it," Peter answered, speaking very gravely. "It's a dreadful mean way to live. I wouldn't do it if I was you."

Tom laughed.

"You come to the root of things almost as promptly as Mr. Gordon does," he said carelessly. But I am about as well satisfied with the way in which I live as I am with the most lives I see."

This sentence was the embodiment of Tom's hobby; it had in it the great beam behind which he hid while he pointed his finger at the motes in other people's eyes; but Peter did not know this — he knew nothing about hobbies anyway — so he continued his own train of thought.

"It's queer how folks live, ain't it now?" he said. "Knowing that some things are true — there's that line, 'This earth, he cried, is not my place.' Now, everybody can say that. Who ever heard of a man finding a place to stay here on earth? He goes off somewhere, that's plain enough; he's *sure* to die, and he knows he will. Now for them that sing the next line as you did, and there's lots of 'em, where *are* they going to live?—no place on *earth*, and they won't have one in heaven. Now wouldn't you think it would be kind of natural for them to wonder where they *would* stay?"

"I wish Charles Wesley had found some other place to live in before he wrote that hymn," muttered Tom, "I never *was* so haunted."

Then he and Peter both went in the front way to the parlor to wait for family worship. Mr. Randolph had gone to his room, would be ready in a little while, Grace said, so the family lounged in various attitudes awaiting his coming.

"What a *very* long sermon Mr. Gordon had to-night!" Helen said, folding her crape vail. "I got *so* tired. I wonder if it wasn't an old sermon? Someway it sounded like one to me."

"I'm sure *I* don't know. He might preach an old sermon every month and I should be none the wiser. I can't remember Mr. Gordon's sermons; they don't interest me." This from Ermina.

"I think this one was interesting; there were a good many illustrations." This was Grace's timid protest

"I'm tired of his illustrations," Helen said, wearily. "He has about twenty for every sermon. I don't see the use in a minister telling stories all the while, as if his congregation were a parcel of children."

"Nevertheless it is generally considered the most acceptable style of sermonizing," Tom said, as he stretched his handsome self on the lounge, and laid his curly head on Grace's lap.

Helen turned and looked at him in cool surprise.

"Who ever imagined that *you* had any idea concerning the most acceptable styles of sermonizing? I didn't know it was in your line."

"It has been in my line to hear Beecher and Talmadge and John Hall, perhaps you know; and I heard several illustrations used, I can assure you."

"Oh, well, I've no objection to illustrations where they are needed to explain truth to those who can not understand it without. I only wish you had profited by all those you have heard."

"I wish I had, with all my heart," Tom said, gloomily. "I think, myself, that *patterns* are needed as well as illustrations."

Maria here took up the conversation.

"I wish Mr. Gordon would leave his handkerchief at home; how nervous that man does make me, winding it around his hand and twisting it in all sorts of shapes. I'm always afraid he will forget where he is and make an out-and-out rabbit, as I presume he does at home for the children."

"His handkerchief doesn't trouble me as much as his continual fidgeting," Ermina said. "Squeaking boots, too. If I were Mrs. Gordon I'd soak them in grease for a month; and he shrugs his shoulders worse than ever. Helen, did you notice him to-night? It's for all the world just as his baby does, when it wants something it can't have."

"He is so wretchedly nervous, anyway, that it is a trial to watch him. Sis Wilcox says he gives her the fidgets."

"She has them, anyway," Maria said. "She acts like a simpleton. If I were going to whisper and laugh as much as she does, I should choose some less conspicuous place than the choir."

"Well," Ermina said, "she *is* a simpleton; why shouldn't she act like one?"

"She is a member of the same church with yourself," Tom said, pointedly; and Helen made emphatic response,—

"What if she is? That doesn't insure perfection."

"So I perceive. I was simply interested in observing how you all loved each other."

" I wonder who pretends to love her? I'm sure *I* never did."

" But I thought that was one of the articles of your creed? "

" That only helps to show how limited your knowledge of church matters is. Maria, how *many* colors had Laura Fox about her this evening? "

" I'm sure I dont know. I haven't an eye for colors. Besides, my post of observation is not as extended as yours and Ermina's. I listened to the sermon this evening."

" That's a wonder. It was less worthy of attention than usual. I don't like such sermons."

" I don't either," Tom said, laconically. " I never heard a sermon in my life that I thought was more of a nuisance."

" That's a strange word to apply to a sermon, Tom. I thought it was very solemn." It was Grace's soft voice that now interposed.

" I think so, too," Tom answered, quickly. " It is solemn sermons that Helen and I don't like."

" I didn't say any such thing," Helen said, sharply. " Tom, what is the use of making fun of everything? You don't know anything about sermons, and therefore you ought not to criticise them."

Tom laughed sarcastically.

"Perhaps I don't know anything about church-members, and therefore ought not to criticise them."

"No, you ought not. People do not profess to be perfect because they are members of the church."

"That's fortunate; because they are so far removed from it that no one would believe them if they did. I'll tell you what I believe," and he sat erect and spoke excitedly. "I believe the whole thing is a humbug. Here you girls have been to church this evening, listening to what, if it is true, is as solemn as death itself; and you come home and discuss the preacher's handkerchief, and boots, and gestures. Part of you profess to be on the safe side of the line, and to think that the other part of us are on the very brink of destruction; and neither you nor we appear to care. Now how is a fellow to believe there is any truth in any of it?"

"Tom Randolph!" Helen said, in dismay. "I *didn't* know you were an infidel."

"A fiddlestick! If I'm *not*, it is not the fault of the burning and shining lights that I see around me. Take your own case, Helen. Do you believe your own doctrine?"

"Of course I believe it, or I wouldn't profess to."

"Then you believe that Maria, here, is in danger of everlasting destruction; and yet, in the face of such a sermon as Mr. Gordon preached to-night you ask her about the colors that Laura Fox wears. If your doctrine means anything, you ought to be begging and pleading with her to escape for her life."

"I'm not a fanatic," Helen said, coldy.

"No, you are not. I'll answer for that. But you are either self-deceived, or the whole thing is a humbug. If there is religion at all, it must be something different from this milk-and-water stuff, that consists in dressing up in one's best and doing the praising for the rest of the con gregation, and then coming home and picking to pieces what sounded like a solemn sermon. I don't believe in any of it, and I think I'm justified in my conclusion. I tell you I think—"

The sitting-room door opened and Mr. Randolph came in. He went directly toward his accustomed seat, took up the family Bible, and there sounded in the room, on the very breath of the sharp sentences that had filled the air, these words: "Wherefore, laying aside all malice, and all guile, and hypocrisies, and envies, and all evil speakings, as new-born babes, desire the sincere milk of the word, that ye may grow thereby: if so be that ye have tasted that the Lord is gracious. To whom coming, as unto a living stone, disallowed indeed of men, but chosen of God, and precious."

Then Mr. Randolph prayed; and he prayed for his daughters and his son in such a manner that Tom Randolph was left no chance for believing that to his father, at least, this thing was a humbug. He laughed a little as he met Peter's earnest look half an hour afterward as he went to the kitchen for some water.

"It's a great muddle, Peter," he said. "I don't know how to put it. My father means it, I guess, and I think very likely you do; but as for the rest —"

"I know one other who means it," Peter said, interrupting him.

"Who is that?"

"The Lord Jesus Christ."

CHAPTER XII.

WEIGHTY MATTERS IN SMALL SCALES.

WONDER if things are becoming serious in that quarter?" This Maria Randolph said, nodding her head toward the closed parlor door.

"Nonsense!" Ermina said.

"Well, this is the second evening this week, and I think that looks like more than common courtesy. I'm naturally anxious, for if there is one thing more to be dreaded than another in this family it's a wedding; financially speaking, *that* would just about ruin us."

Meantime the closed parlor doors screened from view Helen Randolph and the object of Maria's solicitude, Mr. Horace Munroe. They were standing by the table near the door, she nervously fingering the contents of the card-basket, he looking at her earnestly, searchingly as though he would give much to know exactly what she was thinking.

"Then you need time to consider this matter?" he said at last; and Helen lifted her drooping eyes to his and spoke quickly:

"I *must* take time, Horace; it is so sudden, so very unexpected."

"That seems strange to me," he said, smiling a little, "when I have thought of it so much and so long. Don't you know your own mind, Helen?"

But Helen turned quickly away from his searching look.

"Indeed I can not answer your questions tonight, Horace; my mind is in a whirl of bewilderment. You must give me time. To-morrow evening I will talk with you."

Then she went directly to her own room without joining the family party in the sitting-room.

"It was rather a short call," Maria said. "I guess I needn't groan over the wedding-cake yet."

But there was wedding-cake in prospect; at least Horace Munroe meant to have some if he could bring it about. This was the important question for Helen to settle, and she worked hard at the problem most of the night, and awoke in the morning heavy-eyed, the question still unsettled. There were important difficulties in the way. In the first place, did she love Mr. Munroe well enough to marry him? She liked him very well indeed, enjoyed his society, but Helen Randolph, in common with every well-trained, pure-hearted young lady, had exalted ideas of the love that justify marriage. To enjoy spending an occasional evening with a gentleman, and to have that feeling for him that would make his failures and shortcomings endurable for a lifetime, were two different things. Helen Randolph had grave doubts; they were very unlike in their views and feelings; some of his ideas thoroughly exasperated her; she had come from his society feeling that she never wanted to see him again. How would it be, she wondered, if it came to spending weeks and months and years in his society. She shrank from it. "Leaving all others, cleave only to him." So ran the marriage service. Helen knew it and thought about it. "Of *course* I should do that if I were his wife," she said; yet even as she said it she was conscious of feeling that it would be a trial to spend no more pleasant evenings with Mr. Harper. If Mr. Harper should come to her with such a question — and her face flushed as she realized that there were points about *that* coming that she should not hesitate over. But then he never *would* come; he was nothing to her; had never been. Why in the world should his image come before her now? "Helen Harper," she said, dreamily. "It is a very pretty sounding name. but it will never be *my* name, and the question to be settled is, whether I shall be Helen Munroe. Oh, me! I wish things didn't have to be settled, or could be unsettled again in a lifetime if one happened to make a mistake. What a horrid thing a divorce would be. I should never do that, anyway." Does any lady reading this have the least doubt as to Helen Randolph's duty in the matter? There were other points. As her eye rested on her dust-covered Bible, certain old-fashioned directions found therein came to mind. "Be ye not unequally yoked together with unbelievers." She remembered it. Now Horace Munroe actually made light of all religious beliefs. Not in a coarse, offensive way, but with a good-natured sarcasm, putting things so aptly that she had more than half laughed at things that should make a Christian blush. "But he isn't an infidel," she argued. "Not so much of a one as our Tom is, I verily believe. He goes to church quite regularly evenings; and he would go mornings with *me* of course. Yet, after all, what a strange way it would be to live — for a Randolph; no family worship, no blessing asked at table. Dear me!

I don't believe I *could* live so. Perhaps he
might be different if I were his wife. I might
lead him. He isn't easy to lead, though, and it
isn't my nature to do things of that sort. I
never was designed for a missionary. I suppose
I need help myself rather than to be planning to
help other people. It would be nice to have a
strong, good man to look up to constantly."
And again visions of Mr. Harper, a "strong,
good man," stole over her thoughts. "Horace
is strong enough about some things," she mused,
"and he is good hearted. Very likely I might
coax him into almost anything, only he would
change his mind as soon as he was out of my
sight. He is very fond of me." And a very
tender feeling came into her heart as she thought
of the tremulous earnestness of his usually gay,
careless voice as he urged his claim. "I hope 1
think enough of him so that he wont be disappointed in me — that is, if 1 decide not to disap-
point him. Dear me! I'm tired of thinking it
all over and over. I wish I could go to sleep.
I wonder what the girls will say? It will be
nice to live in a handsome house and have what
one wants without counting the pennies ten
times over before making any purchases. Horace is as generous with his money as any man
can be; that feature of it is absolutely bewitch-
ing."

In this delightful fashion Helen Randolph
spent the night, tossing and tumbling, dragging
the clothes from Ermina's side of the bed, and
being impatiently requested to "for pity's *sake*
lie still," turning her pillow and thumping it
into one corner of the case to get a cool, high
spot for her throbbing head. It wasn't often
that Helen Randolph's cool, calculating head
was caught in such a whirl. It was in the
morning when she was dressed and nearly ready
to go down stairs that she suddenly sought
counsel, or at least sympathy. She drummed
on the window-pane and watched Tom hurrying
down town, as she said, abruptly,—

"Ermina, Horace Munroe has asked me to be
Mrs. Horace Munroe."

"My patience!" Ermina said, pausing in the
hurried arrangement of her hair. "Maria was
right then, after all."

"Maria! What on earth does she know about
it?"

"Why, she was fretting over the expense of
wedding-cake, in view of his numerous calls.
Well, Helen, are you going to marry him?"

Helen laughed a little.

"How you do pitch into things," she said,
as she turned one blushing cheek a little toward her sister. "What *is* the use of being so
blunt?"

10

"Blunt?" said Ermina, going on with her brushing. "I don't see anything very blunt about that. I suppose you know whether you want to marry him or not, and I just asked for your decision."

This was precisely what Helen did *not* know, but she did not choose to say so to her sister.

"I haven't given it yet," she said, quietly. "I took time for consideration; and then, of course, I shouldn't give a positive answer without consulting father."

"Father won't like it," Ermina said, positively.

"Why not, pray?" and the ready flush of indignation mounted on Helen's cheek.

"Because he thinks Mr. Munroe is dissipated."

"Oh, nonsense! father musn't expect young men in these days to be made after the pattern of a generation back. Horace is as good as the most of them."

Ermina finished her toilet in silence and went down stairs, and Helen lingered, unwilling to meet the family in her undecided state of mind. Grace came in search of stray goblets, and Helen, in sheer desperation, stated the case to her, just to hear what she would say. She said nothing for some minutes; she was doubly astonished: first, Horace Munroe was not in the least the sort of man she had thought Helen would fancy; and, secondly, it was such a new experience to have the confidence of her oldest sister that she did not quite know what to do with it.

"Do you like him enough to marry him?" she asked at last, speaking gently, almost timidly.

Helen laughed a little.

"How much is it necessary to like people in order to marry them, according to your code of propriety?" she asked, with a sort of playful sarcasm.

"To single him out from all others as the only man in the world that it seems to you possible to marry, and to marry him seems just the best lot that God could have given you."

"Grace spoke solemnly, and the smile faded from Helen's face; a flush came in its place, and she spoke coldly.

"I am not sentimental like yourself, Grace. I never was; and you must remember I am not eighteen."

"I don't think it is sentiment," Grace said. "It is just plain, common sense. How can people spend happy lives together unless they would rather be with each other than with any one else in the world?"

"How many marriages do you suppose there are in this world constructed on that plan?"

"I don't know. A good many, I think; or there would be more misery than there *is.* Anyway, that would make little difference with me. *I* should never marry unless I had such a feeling."

"Well," Helen said, lightly, "you may demonstrate all your theories when you are married; but, in the meantime, I am not disposed to wait until I make the acquaintance of every man living to see whether I find anybody that I like better than Horace; because, after I found him, he might not like *me*, you know, and that is an item not to be overlooked."

Nevertheless, her heart was heavy, and she went restlessly from room to room, and from one occupation to another, all that day. It was such an apparent trifle that decided the question at last. At the tea-table Tom, knowing nothing about the state of affairs, blundered on Horace Munroe as a subject for conversation.

"He is just about half drunk, father. If he were a poor man he would be called so; but, happening to have some money, people content themselves with saying he is a little wild."

"Did you sell him his liquor?" Mr. Randolph asked, pointedly.

"Why, yes; as to that, I suppose I did. But I can't see that it has much to do with the question. He doesn't drink whisky for the purpose of accommodating me with custom, by a great deal."

"'Woe unto that man by whom they come,'" Mr. Randolph quoted solemnly. "I would rather that it were not *my* son."

Helen played with her knife and napkin restlessly.

"Tom likes to make a great deal out of a little," she said at last. "I don't believe Horace Munroe was ever intoxicated in his life."

Tom laughed sarcastically.

"My dear sister," he said, solemnly, "whatever else you may know, and I am willing to admit that you are very wise indeed, you do not know the habits of young men as well as young men, and I happen to know whereof I speak."

Helen left the table abruptly. But it was not until the rest of the family had scattered, leaving Tom with Maria, between whom and himself peace had been declared, that she enlightened him as to the state of affairs.

"The least you say about Horace Munroe the better, perhaps, until you discover whether or not he is to be your brother-in-law."

"The fates defend me from any such disaster. Why! is there any danger?"

"He has asked Helen to take the oversight of him: though she has not promised. She wanted time to consider. Ermina said: 'If ever a man asks *me* to marry him, I want to be so certain that he is just the individual, that I can safely jump at conclusions.'"

"I am sorry," Tom said gravely. "I wish I had known it. I wouldn't have said what I did for the world, if I had."

"Why not? I should think she ought to know about such things, especially since she is undecided."

Tom shook his head.

"Not with her temperament. If she were undecided before, she is settled now, you may be sure. It doesn't need a dozen words of opposition from me to convince her that there is a conspiracy to ruin Horace Munroe, and she'll stick to him now through anything. I wish I had held my tongue; because, I tell you, Maria, that fellow is going to ruin."

What further assistance Helen needed, in order to come to a decision, Maria unwittingly gave.

"Mrs. Curtiss has sent her bill," she said, coming into the sitting-room where the girls were. "And it is enormous. How three dresses could be made to cover so much evil in the way of charges I can't imagine. I do believe I'll run away and be a nun. I am actually growing a coward over bills. How they are ever to be paid passes my comprehension."

"And there's another awful season coming,"

Ermina said, with a groan. "If the seasons hadn't that foolish habit of changing every three months, we might wear our muslins or merinos, as the case might be, until they wore out. We need pretty nearly everything in the way of hats and ribbons and gloves that girls very well can. I don't know how it's all to end."

Mr. Horace Munroe was a merchant. He kept gloves and ribbons and merinos and muslins in endless variety. Moreover, his taste was very highly cultivated. He disliked anything like shabbiness. Helen stood looking out upon the moonlighted earth, apparently looking at the April mud, but in reality thinking of the rows and rows of well-stocked shelves in the three-story building on Albany street; thinking, also, what a trial it was to wear ties when "they" wore narrow ribbon, just because you could not afford to change. They had ribbons at Munroe's, in the lovely new shades. She had been in the store but a few days before with Mrs. Munroe, Horace's mother. That lady had selected some elegant laces for her new black silk. Both silk and laces were entirely beyond anything that Helen Randolph ever expected to have; but they were not beyond Mrs. Munroe.

"Helen," Grace said, breaking in on the moon-lighted reverie, "Mr. Munroe is in the parlor."

And Helen went to him immediately. He held her hand for a moment as she gave it for good evening, and said, with genuine tremulousness of voice,—

"Helen, is it to be yes, or no?"

In one hand he held his Alexandre kids, of a pale stone color; the faint odor of a rare and costly perfume floated around him. Helen's gloves were out at the fingers. She hated glove mending; besides, they always looked shabby after it. Real, genuine perfumery she could not afford. She looked up into the earnest eyes bent on her, and her voice was low and clear as she said,—

"Yes."

Up stairs, in Helen Randolph's room, the dust still lay on her Bible, and she had been too restless and unsettled for her customary prayer that day. So the question of a lifetime was settled without so much as a glance toward her covenanted guide, whose counsel she had promised to seek at all times. Gloves and ribbons and laces, truly you have weighty responsibilities, and almost omnipotent sway.

CHAPTER XIII.

PRACTICAL ARITHMETIC.

AD you made one of the Randolph household about the time of which I write you would have pitied Maria. There was a wedding in prospect. Now a wedding in a family where the bride with no income at all wants her wedding dress, and her wedding cake, and her wedding presents to outshine those of Mrs. St. Husted, when Mrs. St. Husted's father's income is at least fifty thousand, becomes at once a formidable thing. Maria, as we measure time, is older by a year than when we saw her last. It is four weeks or so since she celebrated her sixteenth birthday in doing up the bride's sixteen-tucked, double-puffed white skirt. Measured by the weight of responsibility and care that it has thrown on her young shoulders that year might count ten to Maria. Helen, by virtue of her new plans and prospects, has thrown off all home anxieties, and Maria is now the acknowledged as well as the nominal head of the household. "Making brick without straw is not my forte," Ermina had said, briefly, with a most expressive shrug of her handsome shoulders when it was faintly suggested that she was the next oldest daughter, and nothing further was said about her assuming the family reins.

A very busy household had they been. "Making brick without straw" had become the constant occupation of each one of them, as the days intervening between the wedding grew less in number. Busy with hands, and brain, and tongue.

"Every spot in this house is historic ground," Ermina declared one morning, after a closely contested argument had been held. "Helen and Maria have a battle in every room and on every chair."

"I know it," said Helen, somewhat plainly. "I am not like most brides. What little I have must be obtained grudgingly."

Then Maria.

"Now, Helen, that is nonsense. You know we *don't* grudge you anything. I only can't see the propriety of a person in your circumstances having three new silk dresses."

"What is the use of constantly twitting me

about my *circumstances?* I'm glad your opportunity for saying that is lessening."

At this point Ermina considered it well to interpose a sentence.

"It is very inconsiderate of you, Maria, when you know that in less than two weeks she will cease to be in *circumstances*—that is a term which can never be applied to her again."

"At least I shall be in circumstances to have a silk dress when I need one, without having the matter discussed and exclaimed over until I am sick of the very name of it." This Helen said coldly.

This is only a specimen conversation. Maria resisted bravely, hoping to save her father at some point from the weary meshes of debt in which he was struggling. But her fighting was in vain, for Helen had a powerful argument on her side, none other than the pale little mother who had been sleeping her quiet sleep for quite a year.

"Helen," Maria would say, "what *is* the need of dressing twice for a morning wedding? It just makes such a confusion, at the last minute changing your dress; and you have such a beautiful traveling dress, too. Why don't you just be married in that, as you are going to start immediately, and then you won't need another light silk?"

" Because I am not going to do it " This was Helen's favorite argument. " *Nobody* is married in a traveling dress; that just shows your ignorance of the ordinary proprieties of such an occasion, or else your indifference to my comfort, I'm sure I don't know which."

Ermina helped a little.

" So far as comfort is concerned, I should vote for the traveling dress in preference to one of those horrid light silks that will spot if you look at it. Nobody will be able to shed a tear for fear it will drop on your dress."

" No danger of any one shedding one. You will all be too glad to get rid of me, I verily believe; but as for making a dowdy of myself on my wedding day, to please any of you, I just shan't do it."

" Susy Perkins was married in her traveling dress," Grace said, in quiet, retrospective voice; and Helen answered her in triumph,—

" Of course she was. It is girls like Susy Perkins who do those outlandish things. I presume they had molasses ginger-bread for refreshments, and Maria would like to have me copy that style, too, no doubt."

" It would be more wholesome, as well as cheaper," Maria answered, promptly, and while she did so Grace finished her sentence,—

" And so did Augusta Horton."

Ermina clapped her hands.

"Now, Helen, Helen! Do you hear that? It is only girls of Susy Perkins' sort who do those outlandish things, you know! and here is Augusta Horton, whose father is worth at least a million, actually having the boorishness to get married in her traveling dress."

"That's of no consequence," would Helen reply, coldly. "If Augusta Horton, on the strength of her father's wealth, presumes to do strange and unfashionable things, I don't court her notoriety."

Then Maria.

"I wish we had some of her father's wealth to pay the bills. *Our* father's life will be utterly worried out of him. I'm sure I'm ashamed to meet him now."

And at this point, with the sound of her father's footsteps in the hall, Helen's eyes would brim with tears, and as her father opened the door her tremulous lips would be framing sentences like the following:

"There is no one for me to appeal to, who will understand and enter into my feelings. If mother were here she would know all about it, and explain things to you that I can not. Now is the time that my loss falls the heaviest."

Then Maria, a torrent of pent-up indignation swelling within her, would leave the room, slamming the door behind her; and Grace, in great grief and dismay, would follow her, leaving Ermina to come in a more leisurely fashion, as became her nature; and then Helen would be mistress of the situation. Such scenes ended generally in Mr. Randolph's detaining the three sisters, after Helen had left the table, to say, in tender, trembling tones,—

"Don't cross Helen any more than you can help during these days, girls. None of you can understand how much she misses her mother now, until you are brought to the same position in life with herself. Her mother would have managed everything. As for the extra bills, we will get along with them in some way. We can scrimp a little, after it is all over."

"Scrimp!" Ermina would exclaim, but never until her father was out of hearing. "Does the dear man imagine that we have done anything else for the last sixty-five years of our lives? Not but that it comes natural to do it; and I wouldn't make any more uproar over silk dresses and things if I were you, Maria. What *is* the use? The snarl will all come out right somehow, and we shan't care a hundred years hence whether it did or not."

Now this talk was none the less sincere perhaps, because these daughters knew in their inmost hearts that the little mother whom they

mourned would have done no planning for them
if she had been there. Had they not planned for
her from their very childhood, and shielded her
in a peculiar manner from the confusion and bewilderments of life? And yet in a sense they
knew that their father's words were true, and
Helen's tears were real. The gentle, sweet-
spoken mother, who never by any chance grew
angry and slammed doors, or talked in a loud
voice, had unusual influence over the harassed
household. She did not know how to pay bills,
but she knew how to sweeten the labors and
soothe the weariness of those who worked to that
end; and it was true enough that she would
have sympathized in all Helen's plans and pro-
jects as not one of them could. So while the
sisters were vexed they were also softened, and
Ermina worked industriously on the light silk.
There were little personal matters of dress to be
worried over. Of course it would not do for the
bride to appear in light silk and the sisters in
mourning robes, and this necessitated what Ermina called " bran " new dresses for each one of
them.

" It is resonable to suppose," said that young
lady, " that if we were not in mourning, between
us all there would be some kind of garment that
might be worn on this occasion; but as it is, we
shall all have to blossom out from the dressmaker's hands."

Aside from the bills that this would make, there was a view of it that jarred on Maria's heart. She had fought bravely against the putting on of mourning; she was equally averse to taking it off.

"I was willing," she said, "to have it understood that I didn't consider black clothes a necessary token of grief; but having yielded to the general notion on that subject, it is dreadful to me to say in effect, 'There! it is a year since we buried our mother. Yesterday we wore crape for her, but to-day we have packed it away and are in blue and scarlet, or anything else that we happen to wear. The time of mourning is over. and we miss her no more.' I hate it," she finished, fiercely.

"How foolishly you talk," Helen said. "Of course we miss her; no one realizes that better than I do. Because we find it necessary to change the color of our dress, is no sign that we have forgotten our mother."

"Then I hope you see the sense of our wearing black dresses in the first place to prove to people that we missed her." And this talk ended like the others, in sewing industriously on silver gray dresses for the sisters. Thus with their endless differences of opinion in regard to every subject under the sun, time had finally brought them up to the marriage morning, to that exasperating moment when the coffee must be left to itself, to boil over if it will, or to get cold if it will, while every one troops to the parlor to hear over again those words which have been repeated in some form ever since creation, and yet which never wear out, nor sound stale and uninteresting, but which people listen to with eager face and beating hearts from the first formula, "Do you promise," down to the important, "I pronounce you." Great had been the trials in the Randolph kitchen since an hour before daybreak. Among the earnest discussions had been those involving guests and no guests. Ermina took up the debate with energy. It was certainly proper enough, and, for the matter of that, aristocratic enough, to have a strictly private wedding; the only difficulty being that Helen did not want it. "She did not believe," she said, "in acting as though one was ashamed of being married. She did not care for a large wedding, in fact no one gave large morning parties; but a few, their most intimate friends, and Mr. Monroe's partners, it was no more than ordinary courtesy to invite those."

Now if you have never tried it, just please sit down and make out a list of the people that you and Mr. Linkenfelter would have to invite to your morning wedding, provided you invited

11

any one. There are, first, your most intimate
and particular friends, yours and his; you will
be astonished at the number who have to be put
in under that heading. Then come Mr. Linkenfelter's business friends; they are not particularly intimate, but they have accommodated him in
a business way several times; he may want
them to do so again; they must be invited.
Then there are the Snyders; you don't care a
straw for them, but then they invited you to
their Kate's wedding when they had very few
other guests; it will not do to pass them by.
There are six of them, counting the married
brother and the two married sisters. They
make quite an addition to your list, but there is
no help for it; down they go. Of course you
must ask the Howlands, for they are living only
next door, and have accommodated you in a
neighborly fashion several times; and across the
way are the Smiths, who will get offended at
something if they possibly can; it won't do to
slight them. And by this time you say, " Well,
the Jones' live right next door on the other side,
and they invited us there to tea last month; I
must ask them. Dear me! what a long list we
are getting." Presently Mr. Linkenfelter says,
" I don't know about this, Fidelia; if we invite
the Carroltons, and we ought to, you know, for
Carrolton sent me that elegant traveling case.

Well, if we ask them, the Burtons live right next door, and are quite intimate, and the Burtons are my heaviest customers. I don't know them much except in a business way, but I think it will be policy to invite them." And the next evening he says, " I've been thinking about the list, Fidelia. Don't you think we ought to ask John and Susy Colvin? John has been in my emyloy before this, and he is a good fellow enough. He is doing quite a growing business, and his store joins mine." Of course you think they ought to be invited, and the next day you receive a note from Mr. Linkenfelter, which reads,—

" MY DEAR FIDELIA :— I find that two of my old chums are in town, stopping at the Clarendon. They will be here on the twenty-seventh. I could do no less than to invite them to our wedding. I am sorry to swell that formidable list, but I know you will see that there was no help for it.

  " Ever yours,   LINKENFELTER.

  " P. S.— One of the boys has a wife with him, and I have just learned that a cousin of the family is traveling in company with them. *Four more!* "

In the evening Mr. Linkenfelter and yourself

count the list. Now weren't you astonished?
Well, this is precisely the manner in which
Helen and Mr. Munroe made out *their* list, and
they were astonished. And Maria had to make
the wedding-cake, with Ermina to beat the eggs
and advise her to put in just a *very* little more
butter, which was just enough to make the cake
as heavy as lead. She didn't make the bride's
loaf.

"I *can* make it," she said, when that question
was up for discussion. "It is just fruit-cake,
and fruit-cake is easier to make than any other.
You put a pound of everything under the sun
into it, and it can't fall if it tries."

"Oh, well, you can't make it look like a
boughten cake," Helen said. "They do something to them that makes them look so different
from home-made cakes. It isn't possible to make
a loaf that looks like theirs."

"Or tastes like theirs," Ermina said, pointedly.

"Well, they don't taste as well as home-made
cake. I'll admit that; but every one has a bride's
loaf from Hackley's. They ornament them
beautifully, and one done at home looks decidedly dowdy after seeing those."

"But, Helen, they cost so much," was Maria's
perpetual rejoinder. "You can't get a loaf from
Hackley's large enough for your purpose for less
than ten dollars, I presume."

"Nonsense! I don't believe they cost so much as that; and if they *do*, how can I help it? If I am to have a wedding at all I want things decent. You are always saying 'they cost so much.' You might as well be a parrot."

The bride's loaf was ordered, and two days before the great occasion Tom brought it home.

"It's intolerably heavy," he said, setting down the mountian of gleaming frost on the dining-table with a thud. "But I've got something in my thumb and finger that is heavier." And Maria left her raisins and Ermina her ruffle to come and look over his shoulder at the weight of the bride's loaf expressed in dollars and cents — $19.62. Those were the amazing figures. Not one word said Maria, she went back to her raisins very quietly; but Ermina, looking at her face, burst into a sharp, keen laugh, in which Tom joined.

"Helen," he said, calling to her as she was passing the door, "Mr. Gordon sent a message to you, that Abby something or other, who is in your class, Kelley her name is, isn't it? has tumbled down stairs and broke her neck, or, no, it's her back. They are poorer than poverty, it seems, since the father was killed, and the young ladies are making up a purse for them. They meet to sew for them this afternoon at Mrs. Granger's, and the little muff wants to see you, it seems."

"Mercy on me! *I* can't go to see her. I haven't time; and as for sewing for her I can't get my own sewing done. That lavender silk is going to fit elegantly, girls. I'm sorry for that poor little thing. I wish I had a cent of money for them. That is one of the delights of being poor; never have a penny to give away. What's that, the cake? Oh, isn't that *beautiful!* I declare, Ermina, it is larger than Fanny Stuart's was, and more nicely ornamented, too. I'm glad of it. They thought hers was something wonderful."

"Helen," called Grace, "Miss Evans wants you to try on your dress," and Helen vanished. Tom's eyes danced with fun.

"I'm glad I've found an appropriate wedding present for Helen," he said, wickedly.

"What is it?" Ermina asked, with eagerness.

"It is a copy of an illuminated text, like one that Hammond got for his sisters the other day. It will be eminently appropriate: "Pure religion, and undefiled before God and the Father, is this, To visit the fatherless and the widow in their affliction, and to keep h'mself unspotted from the world.""

CHAPTER XIV.

SENTIMENT AND DUST.

BUT about Maria's trials during that early morning. In the first place she had secured for "help" Mrs. Charlotte Dickson. Now, if you never had the pleasure of Mrs. Charlotte Dickson's help, she deserves an introduction. She isn't an ordinary hired girl, far from it; she doesn't as a general thing go out to service. Only occasionally, as a matter of special accommodation, can you secure her valuable assistance, during which time you must speak and act and step with caution, for if you chance to remark that the steak is tough or the potatoes not of the best quality, Mrs. Dickson is straightway of the opinion that her services do not suit, and sighs and sheds a few tears, and is sorry that she does not give satisfaction. Also she is an early riser; has the potatoes baked and the eggs boiled at a quarter past six precisely, and the breakfast hour is seven ; of course everything is delicious. Maria had passed through trials unnumbered during the week preceding the eventful morning. During the cake-making, Mrs. Dickson had actually seemed to be an avenging spirit, hovering over open dampers that ought to be shut, and closed slides that ought to be open ; whisking one loaf of cake surreptitiously out of the oven just in time to have it pass through that interesting process known as "falling," and leaving the next one to grow brown and hard while she took an impromptu lunch in the pantry. Oh, the horrors of that horrible week, culminating in the indescribable confusion of that morning. I was mistaken in saying that Mrs. Dickson was always an early riser ; she sometimes overslept. On this particular morning she did so, and Maria, coming in haste to the kitchen stove, found it fireless ; then Mrs. Dickson pronounced the wind in the wrong direction, and the kindlings damp, and the coal soft — the fire wouldn't burn. Did you ever stand waiting for a coal fire, and occasionally give it a despairing poke while you waited? Then you can appreciate Maria's feelings. She decided to set the table while she waited, during which process the following conversation ensued : —

" Mrs. Dickson, where is the other sugar
bowl ? "

" I don't know, I'm sure."

" Why, haven't you seen it ? "

" Not that I remember ; " and Mrs. Dickson
composedly tasted the wing of a chicken.

" Well, won't you please help me find it ? It
is getting late, and we must be at work at something."

" Well, Miss Maria, I'm sure it is not my
fault that the fire won't burn. I've poked at it
for half an hour."

" I didn't say it was. Won't you please look
r that bowl ? "

Thus entreated, Mrs. Dickson wiped her
fingers on the cloth spread over the biscuit, overturned a chair with a couple of plates set on it,
and went to ransacking among the china dishes
for the missing bowl. Ten minutes were spent
in this helpful employment, when the lady's wits
came to her aid.

" Oh, I just remember, that bowl got broke
the very day after I came here. Strange that
I forgot *that*."

" How did it get broken, Mrs. Dickson ? "

" Why, I was settling the china closet, the
dishes were all out of place ; your Grace . set
them up, and she is no hand at work, anybody
knows ; and I just got down that sugar-bowl to

see if it was all right, and Ermina she came
out of the door all of a sudden, and kind of
startled me, and down went the sugar-bowl.
It wasn't my fault, you see."

" I see," said Maria, dryly. " Well, put some
sugar in a common bowl, and hurry, please, for
it is getting very late."

" Oh, there'll be time enough," Mrs. Dickson
said, testily. " I never knew a bride to be
ready in time; it flurries me dreadfully to have
to hurry. 'Don't hurry me and I'll work the
cheaper,' my old man used to say, and there's a
good deal of truth in it."

" I had to leave," said Maria, in detailing
her experience to the girls afterward. " I ran
down cellar to get composed. I was so warm
and so provoked that I was afraid I might flurry
her if I stayed."

Added to the sense of responsibility and care
that rested on her young shoulders, Maria's
heart was sad. The four sisters had never been
very congenial in their tastes and pursuits, but
then they were sisters, and had lived under one
shelter all the days of their lives. The first
break was to be made to-day, and life would
never be again just what it had been. The
sense of change came home to her more forcibly
because of that one grave in their lot at the
cemetery. She had found during the last year

what the word "change" meant. Maria was not sentimental in the common acceptation of that abused word, but she was true-hearted and loyal. Grace came to the kitchen in search of her. Grace had been crying; this sister had those traits about her that the family unhesitatingly pronounced sentimental. "Helen has snubbed you every hour since you were born, and here you are making your nose red and puffy because she is going around the corner to live in a house of her own." This was Tom's indignant remonstrance; yet Grace's tears were not stayed.

"Come," she said to Maria, "almost everything is done. Can't you spare a few minutes to go up and see Helen?"

"What should I go there for?" Maria asked, bluntly, preferring not to understand the tenderness that prompted the petition.

"Oh, I hardly know," Grace said, timidly. "She is dressed, I suppose, by this time, and she will never be in her own room up there again for us to go and visit. Let us go up a few minutes."

"Pooh! she will be in her own room for us to visit a thousand times, I presume. What difference does it make?" Maria answered, rubbing vigorously on the silver spoon she was polishing. Nevertheless, she finished the rest in haste, and, wiping her fingers, said, "Well, come on, then, I can leave for a minute.'

"We have come to take our last peak at Helen Randolph," she announced, as Helen answered their knock.

"Very well; look critically then, for I believe this dress doesn't hang as nicely as I thought it did. I've been provoked about it all the morning."

"So you are dressed and ready? I don't see but it hangs all right. How do you feel?"

"How do I feel! why, just as I always do. How *should* I feel? Only I'm better dressed than I've had the pleasure of being in some time, and I like the feeling of that very well."

Maria turned away abruptly. "It's all clothes," she said. "Helen, you didn't dust your room very well after sweeping." This was an after sentence as she took up the handsomely bound Bible that lay on the upper shelf of the book-rack.

"Mercy on me!" Helen said, shortly. "I wonder if you think I've been sweeping this morning. That is precisely like you. Maria if you ever are married you'll sweep and dust your room and mend your stockings fiftee' minutes before the ceremony is performed. I haven't swept my room since the day before yesterday, and I didn't dust it then."

Maria laughed. "I was wondering when this dust accumulated," she said, as she drew her fingers over the dusty Bible — she herself only read the Bible occasionally, on rainy Sundays — but it jarred upon her that this professing Christian should leave her Bible neglected for three days, especially on days so fraught with life as these. I have often been struck with the promptness of the unconverted part of the world to see the duties that their Christian neighbors ought to perform.

Helen glanced up quickly, and her face flushed a little. "When you marry, I presume you will retire to your room and do nothing but read your Bible for three days beforehand," she said, dryly. "I hope you will have time for it. I am sure it will be much more pleasant than to hurry and drive through the days as I have had to, doing nearly all my own sewing." This last, considering the fact that the three sisters had sewed with and for her, from early morning late into the night, every moment that they could secure from other duties, was somewhat trying to the sort of flesh and blood that is constituted as Maria's was, and she spoke with sharp sarcasm: "Perhaps I will have twenty-one tucks on my third best white skirt, instead of twenty-three, and snatch the intervening time for reading a few verses, that is, if I have by that time discovered, judging from the example of the Christians around me, that the Bible is the 'only infallible rule of faith and practice.'" And then Maria went back to the spoons and Mrs. Dickson. You see what a consistent young woman she was. She was actually provoked at, and disappointed in Helen, for neglecting for three days what she had been neglecting all her life. Something of the absurdity of her own position came dimly across her mind, and that lovely being with whom we so delight to take counsel, furnished her with an immediate solution of her position. "But you make no profession, you know."

Oh, wise and wily Satan! There is a command in the Bible that all *Christians* should study it, and all who do not *profess* to be Christians should let it alone, isn't there? Or, if not, how *do* you contrive to impress such an idea on your votaries?

"Maria is queer," Helen said, as the door closed after her. "Don't you go to being like her, Grace. Strong-minded women are inconvenient and unfortunate beings. I wonder how we came to have one in our family? Grace, *do* you think my dress hangs well?"

"I *think* so," Grace said hesitatingly, her thoughts far away. "Helen, do you dread it?"

"Dread what?"

"Why, the new life, the responsibility, you know; the planning to have everything come out right."

"I've nothing to plan, child, everything is done for me. My house is nearly ready to move into, except curtains and a few ornaments, which I'll risk, but that I can plan when I have a purse to back my plans."

"Oh, I don't mean those things. I know you can plan curtains and vases, but I mean about the — well, the making him happy, the doing your exact duty about the *promises*, you know — they use so many solemn words in the marriage service — it means so much, it makes me shiver all over to think of trying to *live* that service."

Helen laughed. "You are a sentimental little puss, and I am not," she said; "that is the difference between us. I'll risk but that one of the parties will be happy; he will get what he has been planning for several years — so he says. Grace, do you think my gloves are a good match?"

"Very," said Grace, gently. "Can I do anything for you, Helen?" And then she, too, went down stairs.

Helen, on her part, was not so entirely unimpressible as she chose to appear. As faithful and single-hearted a Christian as her sister Maria imagined that *she herself* would be, she

was not, neither was she so tender in her sen-
sibilities as Grace, yet she had both thought and
felt, during these busy days; fill her mind as she
would with thoughts of her elegant lavender
silk and kids to match, and real lace in neck
and sleeves, there was an undertone of unrest,
of wonderment as to whether these things would
last, rather, whether the lasting things would be
as real and as satisfactory as these. She went
over to the book-rack and took up the little
Bible, dusting it first with a common handkerchief which lay near at hand; then handling it in
a very gingerly manner lest it might soil the
lavender kids, she turned the leaves, saying,
with a little sigh,—

"I shall really be glad to get settled, so I can
resume some of my old habits of living. At the
same time she was conscious of a curious mixture
of feelings — a little shiver of regret, and a thrill
of satisfaction — both of these over the one
thought that the *old* habits of living could never
be resumed. Then, as her eyes caught certain
words, the pink flush on her cheek paled a little
— it was so strange to have this thought thrust
into the midst of all her roseate plannings,—

"Whereas ye know not what shall be on
the morrow. For what is your life? It is even
a vapor, that appeareth for a little time, and
then vanisheth away." She closed the book

suddenly, and laid it back in its place. If this were all there were of life — a vapor — of what use were lavender silks and real lace, after all?"

And now we have got back to that important moment when Maria said to the coffee, "Well, if you are determined to boil over, you *must.* Come, Mrs. Dickson." And they went to the parlor. It was all very elegant; the bride looked lovely; everybody said lavender silk and real lace were becoming to her, and she could afford to wear them now. The refreshments were elegant, too, and the bride-cake equal to Mrs. St. Hudson's any day. Mr. Randolph shivered visibly, though the room was uncomfortably warm; but he saw before him, in vision, another bride in white silk and orange blossoms, over whom a May sunshine shimmered twenty-five years ago, and over whom the snow of February was piled only a year ago. Helen thought of it, too - of that white grave — and her face grew paler; over and over in her brain she repeated the sentence, "It is even a vapor, which appeareth for a little, and then vanisheth away."

"Mrs. Munroe, let me present to you my congratulations and earnest wishes for your future — I will not say happiness, because that word is secondary and must have a foundation, let me rather say faithfulness."

It was Mr. Harper's clear, distinct, cultured

voice that addressed the bride. It startled her from her unwelcome thoughts; it startled her into her new life. She was Mrs. Munroe, then, *positively.* She had not realized it before, even when she felt the tremble of her father's lips as they pressed hers. Then there came to the new-made bride a flash of her old dream that she used to dream. "Helen Harper," she said again to herself. Well, it *never* could have been. How silly I am," and then Mrs. Munroe aroused fully to the sense of her position. She was Mrs. Horace Munroe, in point of wealth quite on an equality with any of these, her friends and neighbors, who surrounded her. No danger but she could conduct herself in a manner befitting her position. She had always longed to show some of these dowdy women of wealth what a lady of taste could do if she had their opportunity. The opportunity was hers now. She would show them. Then she wondered what kind of a house Mr. Harper had in New York, and if he really *were* worth two millions, as people said, and what sort of a lady he would marry. "He will never marry any lady in *this* town," she said, emphatically; and this bride of an hour was conscious of a thrill of satisfaction over that thought. She would not have enjoyed the elevation of any of her acquaintances to the height that she had lost. Lost! And she had just avowed that the man whose name she bore was all in all to her; else what did the marriage service mean? How dared she desecrate it by letting it mean less to her than this? Helen Munroe was woman enough to be ashamed of herself.

An hour later she drew back from her brother Tom's parting kiss with a gesture of disgust. Tom saw the movement, and knew the cause, and sneered at both.

"She will have to get used to something stronger than the smell of wine," he said to Maria, still sneering. "It won't do for a lady who has just married a gentleman drunkard to be too fastidious."

"Tom!" said Grace, in utter dismay.

"I tell you, my innocent young sister, he's no more nor less than that; and Helen knows it, for I told her."

"Perhaps your own condition was such that she couldn't depend on your evidence."

This sting of course came from Maria; she felt full of stings.

"Thank you," Tom said, bitterly enough, and dashed out of the room.

CHAPTER XV.

WAYS AND MEANS.

N the multitude of counsel there is safety.'
Is that quoted just right, Ermina? You
ought to be posted on Bible verses. I'm
needed at this council, I presume. Give
us the subject."

"One would think you might know it by
instinct," Ermina answered, looking up at the
handsome, saucy face of her brother. "It is the
everlasting question of ways and means. I'm
sick of it."

"Ways in which money has flown during
the last six weeks, and the means by which it
can be got back again. Is that it?"

"Not by any means. It is ways in which the
bills have accumulated, and where the means
are to come from to pay them with."

"Then I'm off; you don't need me. Here is
Maria, who has studied that question ever since
she sucked her thumb, and looked wise when

she was two days old, and we wondered what
she was thinking about. Her wits will develop the question in some way; if they don't
it isn't worth while developing. 'There's a
time to walk,' Solomon said, and my time for
that has evidently come."

"How does Tom get hold of so many verses
from the Bible, I wonder?" Maria said, looking
after him with a smile and a sigh, both smile
and sigh being called forth by sight and thought
of him.

The year had brought changes upon him. He
looked older by far more than one year, and his
form had developed into manlier proportions;
but — Ah, me! that little word and the blank
after it means a great deal. "I am not afraid
of *myself*," had Tom Randolph said in pride
to the earnest caution of the less self-sufficient
Peter. If he only *had* been! If our young
men of to-day could only learn that important
lesson to be afraid of *themselves*. Among all his
Bible verses had he never discovered *that* one,
"Let him that thinketh he standeth take heed
lest he fall?" Well, he had fallen. The wine-
stained breath was a common thing in the Randolph household now; they had even grown
to be thankful when a month passed with
nothing harder to endure than the odor of wine.
They watched his home coming nightly of late,

either Grace or Maria, or faithful Peter, lest the father might hear the stumbling steps and the thick tongue. Ermina utterly scorned such vigil, and Helen protested that their father ought to know about it, and she should certainly tell him, but she never did; and yet all were equally sure that he knew about it, and that his step was slower and heavier and his hair grayer in consequence. A sad, hard life Mr. Randolph led. What wonder that he sometimes looked with wistful, longing eyes to that vacant spot beside that one grave in his lot at the cemetery. "There remaineth therefore a rest to the people of God." Maria Randolph was not given to going to the Bible for comfort; she had not attained to that degree of common sense; but she knew *that* verse, and whenever she thought of her father she thought of that, and rejoiced over it; for him there remained a *rest*, she was sure of it. I do not know what those who are content to live all their days without any hope of the "rest that remaineth" would do without that blessed rest in which to consign the blessed fathers and mothers who, they know, have met the conditions. Maria had no heaven for herself, did not seek for it, but she craved a heaven for her father, and would not have been content with less.

"Well," she said, turning away from the

window as Tom passed out of sight, " ways and means, as Tom says, here are the ways, piles of them ; thirteen different bills that father knows nothing about, and must not be told about. Now what is to be done ? "

" What is the use of asking that ? " Ermina said, composedly. " What is the sense in going all this over every time an extra expense comes up ? There is nothing to do, and we never do it. We might save our breath."

" Speak for yourself, Ermina. Sometimes we succeed in doing it. We paid three bills last fall without a word to father."

" Yes, by starving the cat and freezing us all. I'm sick of retrenchment and everything else. We can't retrench unless we *die*, so we won't need clothes or bread in the future, and I'm nearly ready for that expedient."

" Oh, come, Ermina, don't be blue ; that isn't your forte, as Helen would say. Doesn't it seem queer not to have Helen present at our family snarl ? "

" I wish her bills were not present for us to snarl over."

" So do I with all my heart. Girls, suppose we send them around to the store directed to Horace ? Imagine Munroe senior putting on his glasses and examining them : ' To cutting, fitting and trimming three dresses, thirty-five dollars and eighty-seven cents; to three pairs kids, six dollars and seventy-five cents; to one pair extra Alexandre's, three dollars and seventy-five cents, and so on indefinitely. Now, what would he think of his new daughter, do you imagine? Wouldn't it be rich?"

In arranging and laughing over this plan, that neither of the sisters would have carried out if their very bread had been the alternative at stake, Ermina's non-committal good humor returned. Many and varied were the schemes proposed for raising money, some of which were unhesitatingly laughed down, and some disposed of with sighs, as nice but impracticable.

"There is nothing *to* do for three respectable young ladies, who can't drum on pianos with sufficient force to be justified in teaching drumming, and who have no one talent in particular to emphasize, as people in books are always doing." This Ermina said.

"I have read somewhere," said Grace, thoughtfully, "that every human being had one special talent, sometimes undeveloped, but always there, ready to be called forth in emergency. I have often wondered if that were true, and what mine could be."

"The emergency has certainly arisen," Maria said. "The question is, where are the talents? I wish they would start into action soon, for I am tired of plodding on without them."

An interruption occurred. Their neighbor, Susie Truesdell, tapped on the door, then opened it and put her head in.

"Good morning," she said, brightly. "Excuse me, I'm in a hurry. I've been to the post-office, and I saw a letter in your box; it is right next to ours, you know, so I took the liberty of bringing it to you. No, I can't come in, thank you. I must run along; mother is waiting for these hops."

So the three girls put their heads over the letter.

"Who can it be from?" Grace said, curiously. "It is addressed to Miss Randolph. That must mean you, Ermina, nowadays. I wonder if it is from some one that knows Helen is married?"

"I should think much the easier way of finding out would be to open the letter," said matter-of-fact Maria.

Thus reminded, Ermina clipped the end of the dainty white missive, and disclosed a closely-written sheet in a dainty feminine hand.

"That miserable running Italian!" she said, in disgust. "I wish she had taken lessons in respectable penmanship before she wrote to me, whoever she is."

"It isn't to you especially," Maria said, looking over her shoulder. "It says 'Dear Cousins.' Who on *earth* can it be from? Let's look at the signature."

"No," said Ermina, positively; "we'll look at the signature when we get to it. Sit down, Maria; it makes me nervous to have you looking over my shoulder. I'll read it aloud."

"DEAR COUSINS:—I hope you will let me call you such, though I am only your mother's cousin; but I remember you all very well, only I can't think which of you is the oldest, so I have to direct my letter awkwardly enough to 'Miss Randolph.' I've written it on the envelope, and it looks ridiculous. I hope you won't laugh at it, because there is really nc other way to do. I can't remember your names, only Maria, and it seems as if she were a baby; she was, when I saw her, a very quick-motioned, mischievous baby; she had beautiful eyes ('who in creation is it?' here interpolated Maria); but I suppose she is a young lady now, for that was nearly sixteen years ago. I am twenty myself. Auntie Faye says it is utter nonsense to suppose that I remember Maria, but I do distinctly.

"But you don't know who I am, *do* you? And you don't know what I want. That last is a difficult thing to ask, so I will hurry and ask it just as quick as I can. I want to come and board with you all summer. Now isn't that a breathless idea? Then there is another thing you must know right away, and that is, there are two of us, baby and me! ('My patience!' ejaculated Maria. 'Ermina, I *do* wish you would look and see who it is.' Ermina read on.) Baby is *all* mine, and he is all I have now in the world; my little brother, Percy Halsted, he is a perfect little darling. I know you would love him — everybody does. Mamma died when he was three weeks old, and papa died just before he was born, so little Percy is all I have. I have taken care of him always, and every beat of his precious little heart is more precious than a diamond to me. He is a year and five weeks old, just the age that Maria was when I saw her; at least Auntie Faye says she could not have been more than that. I want to get out of the city with my baby this summer. Auntie Faye, with whom I live, is going to close her house and go to Newport with her son. I don't want to go to Newport; it doesn't seem as though baby could breathe there. I want to find some friends — some relations, you know, who are really and truly our own. I *do* belong to you, if it *is* ever so distant, and I want to know you. Won't you take us to board, baby and me? We would be as little trouble as we could, and we would pay you well in love and in money. I have enough of the latter stuff for all that baby and I will need in this world. I am William Halsted's daughter, you know. and he left me a fortune; and a fortune is a cold, hard thing to have. I don't think much of it; if I only could have kept my dear ones! I can't talk about that just yet. Well, may I come? I wish I could think of your names and how you look. I remember that one was tall and fair, and seemed to me like a queen. I know your dear mamma is dead, like mine. Your papa wrote to Auntie Faye when she died. I feel very sorry for you. At first I thought I would write and tell you so at the time, but I didn't, because written words look so empty and soulless. I know just how lonely you are, because I have experienced it for myself; but then there are four of you, and only one of me, and, besides, you have your father; but then I know that a mother's grave is something that can never be closed over. Say I may come, please. I want to very much. I would like to come in about three weeks, if you will let me.

"Your loving cousin,
"FAITH HALSTED."

"Well!" Maria exclaimed, when the last word was read. "Who ever heard a letter like that before?"

"I think she is rightly named," said Ermina. "She seems to have unlimited faith in everybody."

"I think it is a beautiful letter." Grace said, warmly. "It sounds as though she sat here talking with us."

"Who is she, anyway?" said Maria. "Ermina, do you remember her?"

"Of course I remember her — a little white creature, in white muslin dresses and blue ribbons. She came here with 'Auntie Faye' as she calls her that is mother's aunt on the germain side. Helen and she and I used to play keep house, and she was our little girl. She was a year or two younger than I, perhaps more, and ever so much smaller; but she used to manage to have exactly her own way. We never could quite tell how."

"Well, she evidently has some of the 'stuff' that is very scarce in this house. If she will pay a good price for her board, I move that we write to her to come." This was practical Maria's conclusion.

"It will be soothing to Mrs. Horace Munroe's nerves to think that she is really a cousin, provided we *do* have to descend to taking boarders. Peter Armstrong has been almost too much for *her* constitution." This was Ermina's expression of opinion.

"It would be nice to have a darling little baby in the house," said Grace; hereby indicating *her* character as plainly as her elder sisters had theirs.

There was a general discussion of the impor
tant subject at the dinner table. Tom's opinion
was that there were girls enough in the family;
that it would be poky to have another one,
and that babies always squeaked in the night,
and pulled hair and whiskers in the daytime.
But during these days Tom Randolph's opinion
had as little weight as it was possible for an
opinion to have, and it was passed over in
silence. There was a show of appealing to Mr.
Randolph, who declared nervously that the matter was in safe hands. He should asquiesce
in any decision that they chose to make, and
added,—

"We must invite her to make us a visit
anyway. Her Aunt Faye was your mother's
favorite aunt."

Maria's comment on this sentence of her
father's, was,—

"It seems to be impossible for a Randolph to
give up the idea that we are well-to-do, hospita-
bly-inclined people. I wonder if it wouldn't
utterly surprise father to know that we really
haven't a cent of money in the house, and
haven't had for three weeks. When Faith
Halstead gets invited here, I'm inclined to think
that it will be on condition that she pays a good
round sum for her board every Saturday night."

"Where *are* you going?" questioned that

rame sister an hour later, as Ermina came through the kitchen dressed for the street.

"Going to walk out for my health," said Ermina, gathering up the silver-gray dress lest it should come in contact with the coal scuttle. Perhaps it was not in human nature not to feel aggrieved, for the afternoon was bright and sunny, and the kitchen was as hot as a furnace. There were piles of dishes on the table, waiting to be washed, and the kitchen was to undergo that horrid process known as mopping.

"It wouldn't particularly offend me if she should take hold and help with this work," Maria said, energetically, as the silver-gray dress rustled by and vanished.

"Perhaps she has the headache," said gentle Grace, who was ironing Helen's black and white striped calico, with three ruffles on the skirt.

"Headache!" said the lady at the dish-pan, rattling cups and saucers fiercely. "So have I the headache, and the heartache too, maybe — if I *have* any heart. What if *I* should put on my gray dress and walk out this nice day. I've a great mind to do it sometime, and see how my lady would enjoy it."

Two hours afterward both mopping and ironing were done, and Maria was resting from her labors in the old-fashioned rocking chair, reading the local column of the daily paper, when Ermina walked gravely in.

"I have been in search of my mission," she said, dropping on the lounge, and using yesterday's *Standard* for a fan. "You will doubtless be charmed to hear that I found it."

"On the street?" said Maria, coldly.

"No, in a back room whose windows look out on a coal-yard. I concluded that if I had any undeveloped talents, they lay in managing a Grover & Baker sewing machine. So I have engaged myself to Madame Roller, as a machine hand. Her advertisement, perhaps you observed, has been in the paper for several days."

Maria dropped the paper and sat erect.

"Ermina Randolph!" she said, her voice full of exclamation points.

"Yes, just so," answered Ermina, gravely. "How do you imagine Mrs. Horace Munroe will enjoy me for a sister now?"

"How came you to do it?"

"I wanted to develop my talents, as I observed, and I never discovered a hint of said articles in any other direction. I went on this particular afternoon because — I don't mind telling you that — I preferred to be in the full exercise of my gifts before the arrival of Faith Halsted, if she is to come."

Be it known that this was a triumph over Ermina Randolph's proud and indolent self, which was understood and appreciated by her youngest sister.

"It is twenty times harder for her than for me," she soliloquized; "because she cares for what 'they' say. It is her nature to care, and I really think I rather enjoy shocking 'them.' It was real noble in her. And to think that I grumbled about her not staying to help with the dishes!" Then, aloud, she said,—

"Well, you walked out for the health of other people as well as yourself, I think, this time. As for Helen, she can't expect us to live on the strength of her grandeur. It will be easier for father, Ermina."

That evening Ermina wrote to Faith Halsted that they would be glad to welcome her when ever she should choose to come.

13

CHAPTER XVI.

PUZZLING PEOPLE.

HERE was an air of expectancy about the Randolph household; they were in what Maria called "a state of cleared-upness," and gathered in the back parlor at an unusually early hour in the afternoon.

Tom had gone to the station to meet the new-comers — Faith and Baby Halsted. He had gone rather against his will; in fact, this innovation was not of his appointing.

"I don't want to go prowling through the depot in search of a strange girl with red hair and a baby," he growled, when the arrangement was being made. "She will be dowdy-looking; women with babies always are. And I shall be expected to carry the baby, and it will have a stick of candy in one hand and a hunk of gingerbread in the other."

194

" All of which will be much more respectable than a great many positions in which you must have found yourself of late," Ermina observed, serenely. "At any rate, you will have to go; we can't expect father to do it, and as we *have* a brother, it is supposed to be his place to be courteous to company."

"Especially the boarders," chimed in Maria. "Don't let us lose sight of the fact that this 'company,' is going to pay a wholesome price for her board, every week of her life."

" You would have been considerably wiser if you had allowed her to set her own price for board. She is worth five hundred thousand, to speak within bounds. Horace is acquainted with their business lawyer, and we met him in New York; he says this girl has as much as that in her own right, and that she is Auntie Faye's heir; besides, she would have paid you a splendid price for her board, for they have the name of being liberal people."

This bit of advice and information came from Mrs. Horace Munroe, who was at home spending the day, overlooking the arrangements for receiving the new comers, and giving advice freely on all subjects. Ermina's lip curled visibly, and Maria, as usual, spoke her thoughts.

" We haven't reached as low a notch as that, Helen, if we *are* poor. She asked us to name our price, just as any lady of delicacy of feeling would have done, and we did it; a good fair price it is, too, more than she would have to pay in hundreds of places where she could have gone; but it no more than pays us for the extra expense and trouble it will be to us, and I for one wouldn't have taken a cent more than that. When I take to begging for a living it shall be out-and-out begging; I won't whine around any one and say, 'you are rich and we are poor, and you are our twenty-third cousin, you know, so please give us five times the worth of your living, for sweet charity's sake, and call it *board*, you know.'"

Mrs. Munroe laughed.

"You are ridiculously fastidious in your no-tions, child," she said, with infinite patronage in her voice; "but you will recover from some of your follies by the time you have rubbed through with as much life as I have. Take what you can get, and have as nice a time as you can in this world, is my motto."

She spoke serenely — much more serenely than Helen Randolph was given to doing. She looked well, too; black silk dresses and real lace ruffles were undoubtedly becoming to Helen Munroe. She seemed made to adorn them.

"One would never imagine that she had

turned her dresses upside down and wrong side out, and darned forty holes under the ruffles."

This was Ermina's comment on the serene, faultlessly-dressed lady; and this just expressed it. She looked like one born to the position which she was now filling, so easily and gracefully had she slipped into the " real " things, at least so far as lace and silk and velvet were concerned.

Many were the surmises concerning the appearance of the coming lady.

" I think she is tall and thin and pale," Grace said. " Don't you believe she is, Ermina? "

" I don't believe anything about it. She was perhaps three years old when I saw her; or four, didn't she say? and I must have been very little more than that. It is a poor age for determining whether one is, ' tall and thin and pale.' She was a pretty little thing; wasn't she, Helen? "

" Not particularly pretty; but she contrived to make every one imagine that she was. I never quite liked her. Everybody humored her so continually that it gave me a sense of never having my own way."

" That must certainly have been trying to your disposition," Maria said, merrily. " I can't conceive of there having been a time when you didn't try pretty hard for *your* way."

" Maria," said Mrs. Munroe, as she finished one of the little crimson wheels that she was crocheting, and laid it against the black ground of her dress, to try the effect; "I hope, for your sake, that she won't be '*sharp*.' Two sharp people in one family would be very .asping to the nerves, and, as I remember her, I should say that it was the most likely thing in the world that she is sharp. I'm glad I don't live here."

This last with a complacent glance at the house nearly across the street, with its lace curtains at the windows, and its body Brussels carpeting that her mind's eye beheld. Mrs. Munroe had always looked with longing eyes upon body Brussels carpets, now she trod on them with satisfied feet, every day of her life.

Futher comment was interrupted by the roll of carriage wheels, and the exclamation from Grace,—

" There they come ! "

" In one of Smith's hacks," said Mrs. Horace Munroe. " That's just like Tom, when he *knows* Stuart's are ever so much nicer."

" Why, she isn't larger than a minute," Ermina said, peering from the window at the small creature who sprang briskly from the carriage, after giving a parcel carefully into Tom's hands.

" Tom has the baby ! " exclaimed Grace, in a

tone of intense satisfaction. "He declared he
would not touch him."

"What *else* could he do with him?" Maria
said, composedly. "Why don't they bring him
in, and not stand bothering over the baggage?"

"Stand back from the window, Maria," Mrs.
Munroe said, authoritatively. "It is in wretched taste to stare at people. Grace, *do* sit down.
Ermina, aren't you going to the door to meet
her? You forget that you are Miss Randolph,
now."

"On the contrary," said Ermina, coolly, "I
have a realizing sense of it; you are the only
one who seems disposed to ignore that important
fact. Please to remember that we do not live
in a stone house, with lace curtains and lambre-
quins, so we have a right to *stare* just as much
as we please. No; I'm not going to the door,
as if we were slaves and she our queen. Tom
knows the way in."

Apparently he did, for at this point the door
swung open and Tom set a bundle down in the
middle of the room. Said bundle shook itself
and revealed inside of its white cloak, a small,
fair, blue-eyed baby, who looked around the
room with a delighted smile, clapped a pair of
small, fat hands, and said, emphatically,—

"Ta, Tare!"

"Oh, the little darling!" said Grace, rushing

toward him, and the rest were welcoming his sister Faith.

"Which is which?" she said, looking earnestly from one to the other. "Oh, you are Maria — now *aren't* you? There, what a triumph! I told Auntie Faye I remembered your eyes; now I have proved it. And this is Helen — or, no; Mrs. Munroe. You live nearly across the way, Tom says. Isn't that splendid? baby and I can call on you every morning. Oh, isn't my baby a darling?"

Altogether, Mrs. Munroe's dignified reception, in which she was to prove to this young heiress that *she*, at least, was equal in position and culture to herself, seemed not to fit the present occasion. One might as well have to be ceremonious with a robin. Some way they all forgot dignity and propriety, and were in full tide of eager talk when Tom came from the trunks and the hack-driver.

"Isn't she a case?" he said to Maria, following her to the kitchen for a confidential chat. "I don't know whether she is as 'harmless as a dove' or as 'wise as a serpent,' or both, or neither; I know I never met such a creature since I was born. Why, Maria, she knows more about our neighbors than you do; she asked all manner of questions concerning them, and was as interested in the number of children each of them owned as if she meant to start a select-school in this neighborhood to-morrow, and live on it the rest of her days."

"Indigestible living," said Maria. "Tom, won't you get me a pail of water? she might not think it aristocratic in me to go myself, and she stands looking out of the window — I see her."

They had a very merry tea.

Mr. Randolph came home early, dreading the presence of a stranger — eager to have the meeting over and to get back to his office.

The new-comer stood at the window as the gate clicked.

"Is that he?" she asked, eagerly. "Is that Uncle Randolph? Who is that other gentleman — a young one?"

"That is my husband," Helen answered, with conscious pride.

Mr. Munroe was a handsome young man — she expected him to make an impression.

"Oh," Faith said, "then it's all in the family. We'll go and meet them. Where's my baby?"

And catching him from Grace's arms, she perched him on her shoulder, and ran gayly out to the hall. They heard her clear, ringing voice,—

"We're coming to meet you, Uncle Randolph; baby and I. We are going to call you 'Uncle

Randolph,' both of us, because we have no uncle of our own, and we've always wanted one -- kiss the new uncle, Pearly. You don't mind being our uncle, do you, sir?"

Baby touched his cool, pink tongue to Mr. Randolph's sallow cheek, and immediately thereafter seized upon his gold-bowed glasses by way of recompense.

"Yes, I mind it," said Mr. Randolph, heartily; "I shall be most thankful to have a niece and nephew. You don't remember my wife, I suppose," and his voice faltered. "You are just her size."

"I remember her *distinctly*," Faith said earnestly. "Not her face, you know, but her kisses. I was homesick, and she kissed me like mamma. I never forgot them."

Mr. Randolph bent over and kissed her on cheek and lip, leaving the touch of a tear on her face. He was not given to caresses, was not a demonstrative man; but he, too, remembered tender-clinging kisses that he used to have and received no more. Faith Halsted's place in his heart was secured. Mr. Munroe had meantime been divesting himself of his duster and making silent advances toward friendship with the bright-eyed baby. He turned to Faith now.

"I am not to be left out in the cold I trust," he said, with a winning smile. "I think, according to the compact which has just been formed, I must be a cousin."

"Oh, yes," said Faith, heartily. "You are Helen's husband; she told me so; she said it as if she thought you were very nice; and as for baby and me, we are glad of all the relations we can get; we have been alone a long time. Do you like baby kisses? Pearly, have you a kiss for Cousin Horace?"

But Pearly was seized with one of those obstinate fits peculiar to babydom, and would neither kiss nor shake hands nor make a bow; in fact he ignored the gentleman completely and tugged mercilessly at Mr. Randolph's whiskers. But the introductions, which Mrs. Munroe had planned to conduct with due ceremony, were over, and the whole company went gayly out at Maria's call to the table. In the little sitting-room that same evening Faith made the acquaintance of Peter Armstrong. The early spring evenings were cool for baby natures, and at sunset a fire was built in the cosy back sitting-room, which, with the large room adjoining, had been given up to Faith. Tom's business calling him elsewhere, Peter volunteered to be fire-builder, and was bent down in front of the stove when Faith's clear voice addressed him.

"You are Peter Armstrong, I think, and I am Faith Halsted. Shall we shake hands on it?"

Peter stood up suddenly in great surprise a small white hand, on which a single diamond gleamed, was held out to meet his red, rough one; this was an utterly new experience to him, nevertheless he held his red hand out for her to do with it what she would, and she clasped it cordially.

Pearly sat in the middle of the floor, gravely watching the operation, and at this point he laughed, showing half-a-dozen dainty pearls, and clapped his small fat hands.

"Baby approves of our acquaintance," said Faith. "You must consider that a compliment; he doesn't like everybody."

Peter smiled broadly and snapped a clumsy thumb and forefinger at baby, whereupon that small being went into a perfect ecstasy of laughs, and crows, and spatting of hands. Baby believed in Peter. Faith's next sentence was as unexpected and quite as bewildering to her new acquaintance as the hand-shaking had been.

"I'm much interested in your method of reading the Bible," she said, simply. Peter stared.

"*My* method!" he repeated, in a dazed sort of a way; he hadn't the least idea that there was such a thing as method about his reading.

"Yes, Tom told me. I like it ever so much; if my name had been Mary or Sarah I should have done the same. How did you happen to think of it?"

Now, Tom's information had been given on this wise: Finding his companion interested in every man, woman, child, and even animal, that they saw during their ride from the depot, he had said, among other things, as he chanced to see Peter crossing the street, "There's Peter Bible."

And she responded, "Peter Bible! what a very queer name."

"He's a queer fellow," Tom had said; "that name is one of my coining; part of it at least; his name is Peter, but the Bible part grew out of the fact that he has lately taken to hunting up the old fellow who figured in those days, and comparing notes with him." Then Faith had asked numberless questions concerning Peter Armstrong, and secured his history, so far as Tom could give it. So now she said, "how did you happen to think of it?"

"Tom told me about him," Peter said, simply. "I don't know much about the Bible, ma'am. I'm reading it over for the first time; but he mentioned to me that there was a Peter in the Bible, and I naturally wanted to know about him."

"Well, how do you like him?" Faith asked, as she rescued a match and a pair of scissors from Pearly's grasp.

"I'm disappointed in him," Peter said, grave

ly, the sad, perplexed look which she had first noticed sweeping over his face as he bent down again to the fire. Faith tried to suppress a laugh; one of her propensities was to laugh at inconvenient times, but it certainly did seem funny to hear this rough-faced, roughly clothed boy express his disappointment in St. Peter with his eighteen hundred years of glory about him.

"What has he been doing?" she asked, when she could command her voice.

Peter sighed heavily. "He's so queer," he said, gravely. "He does things when you least expect him to. Now, night before last I was reading about the wonderful things that Jesus said to him, how he called him blessed and said, 'Thou art Peter, and upon this rock I will build my Church,' and I thought how happy Peter must have been, and it seemed to me he could never do anything wrong again, and last night, only a few verses after that, I came upon this one: 'Then Peter took him, and began to rebuke him, saying, Be it far from thee, Lord; this shall not be unto thee.' And he was speaking to Jesus *himself!* Only think of that now. 'Began to rebuke him!' That does beat all I ever heard of. I don't know who could help being disappointed in him."

The laugh was gone from Faith's face; in its place was sadness. "I know," she said, musingly, "how like ourselves it is."

"Ma'am!" said Peter, in wondering amazement. "*Do* you think it is the way folks would
do now? I can't think it. I *know* I wouldn't
speak that way to the Lord himself."

Faith smiled. "I am thinking of one part
of the words and you of another," she said. "I
was thinking of 'This shall not be unto thee.'
How often we say it in spirit; I have done it
myself, and gone away and forgotten it."

"I don't understand," said Peter, humbly.

"Why, have you never promised the Lord
'this shall not be; thou shalt not have it to
bear; I will not bring this reproach upon thy
name again; I will not grieve thy spirit any
more;' and before the day and perhaps the hour,
was past, have done 'that thing,' or worse than
that, again and again?"

Peter laid down the armful of kindlings he
had been gathering up preparatory to departing,
and, rising to his feet, stood looking at Faith
with earnest, searching eyes. "I see," he said.
at last. "Why, yes, I understand you, but I
never thought of it, never; but Peter didn't
mean that way though; it wasn't respectful
in him."

"I know it; I am not excusing Peter; I
think he repented bitterly, but I was thinking
of myself as being led through different steps
into a like boastfulness of faith and devotion."

"I see," Peter said again. "There's two ways of reading that story; one way is to find fault with Peter who is in heaven and out of all the fuss and trouble forever, and another way is to measure my own heart by it and see whether it will stand looking into. I understood about the faults of Peter, ma'am, but I never thought anything about the other part until this minute, and I am truly obliged to you."

CHAPTER XVII.

OPPOSING ELEMENTS.

T is the merest act of commonplace courtesy," Mrs. Munroe said; and she spoke
authoritatively. She stood in the kitchen
doorway; time—a warm spring day among
the closing ones of May. It was eleven
o'clock, and Maria was in full tide of preparation
for the noon-day dinner, her sleeves tucked
above her elbows, a large calico apron covering
her neat calico dress, and she pared potatoes
with an energy that betokened a perturbed state
of mind. Her cheeks were red, too, but that
might have been from the fire, for the kitchen
was insufferably hot. Mrs. Munroe lifted her
straw hat from her shapely head and fanned
herself leisurely while she talked. Her dinner
hour was one, and the dinner itself was in the
hands of Becky — a pattern cook, who had lived

in some of the Munroe families since babyhood
So Mrs. Munroe, in her blue and white plaid
wrapper, with linen cuffs and small standing
collar, fastened with the spray of lava which
was one of her husband's gifts, looked the picture of refinement and leisure. She continued
her sentence, unmindful of the glow on Maria's
cheeks: "I don't see how you can avoid it.
Everybody does such things."

"But I tell you, Helen, we have *got* to avoid
it. We haven't the money to waste in any such
senseless way."

"Senseless! You are very sweeping in your
condemnations. If you live in the world you
must act like other people a little, even if you
do feel yourself superior to them; and that has
always been your trouble — having too high an
estimate of yourself. As to money, that is nonsense! How much will it cost, I wonder, to have
half a dozen friends to take tea with you? You
needn't make a great flourish. In fact, it would
be in bad taste for persons in your circumstances
to do so; but a few intimate friends. I'm sure
I don't see how you are to avoid it, unless you
girls mean to decline all invitations for yourselves. While poor mother was living she was
so much of an invalid, that people didn't expect
to be invited here, and of course they didn't
expect it while we were in mourning; but now
it is different."

Maria splashed the potatoes about in the rinsing water with such energy as to give her apron a shower bath, and spoke with unusual sharpness.

"I wonder, Helen, if getting married has destroyed all the common sense you ever possessed. You know that mother was never so much of an invalid but that she would have enjoyed company if we had been able to afford it, but we weren't, and we aren't now."

"Well, don't talk so loud. How you do fly into a passion over every trifle. That is a very unlady-like trait. You ought to break yourself of it before you are older. I wonder how you came to be so mercenary, Maria? I'm sure there are other things of importance as well as money. You talk as if that was the only thing worth any consideration."

"I have to consider how to get along without it so constantly, that it is no wonder it is often in my thoughts." Something had calmed Maria. She spoke more in her usual tone of cool indifference.

"I know," said Mrs. Munroe, thoughtfully. "You have had a hard time of it, and I think you have managed very well, considering your age; but I should think things must be very much better with you now. Tom receiving a salary, and Ermina working in that horrid shop

—but they give her very fair wages—and Faith pays a good price for her board. There's considerable coming in."

"And considerable going out," said Maria as she landed the wire full of potatoes into the bubbling kettle. "There are old bills to pay, and Ermina has undertaken to help pay them. Father's quarter's salary won't begin to do it; and we were out of everything under the sun, from flour to brooms, to say nothing of clothes. There are ways enough for the money, I can assure you."

"But for all that," said Mrs. Munroe, going back persistently to her first idea, as such natures do, "*I* think you ought to give a little company Of course I don't speak for myself, although it is common for brides to be invited to their former homes for entertainment, and I presume Horace's folks think it strange that we are not; but *I* could get along without it—only there is Faith, coming here a stranger, our cousin, and it is so singular not to pay her any attention; besides, you girls owe it to yourselves. What society will you have if you ignore its claims upon you as we have been doing?"

"The claims of society are a humbug," said Maria, basting her roast beef until its savory odor filled the kitchen. "I always thought so. Here we, as poor as mice—poorer for that matter

—must twist and turn, and scrimp, and make pound-cake and other stuff, and invite a company to jam into our dining-room, and make fun of our nicked dishes and our tin coffee-pot, so that they will invite us to similar shams if they are poor, or show us how unutterably shoddy our efforts were if they are rich. That's society."

"Oh, well," said Mrs. Munroe, fanning herself with more energy, "you can't have the millen· nium come right away, even if you want it; and I get along very well with the world as it is. It is nonsense in you to talk about a *jam*. Your dining-room is large, I'm sure, and its very respectably furnished, and a few friends to tea would be very pleasant. You could have spoons and napkins and such things from my house, and Becky to help you. She would show you just how to do everything; and as to the silver, why, you could have my coffee-urn and cake-baskets."

"I should never do it in the world," sputtered Maria. "If we were foolish enough, in our circumstances, to give a tea party, I would insist upon its being according to *our* circumstances, and not yours. I'll serve no coffee from borrowed urns, you may be sure of that. Spoons and napkins are bad enough, but they are common necessities."

"That's pride," said Mrs. Munroe, complacently.

It was not this conversation, nor a dozen others like, held when the combined forces were gathered, for both Ermina and Grace took earnest sides with Maria, that finally settled the question of company. It was Mr. Randolph returning, after he had started for the office, to say, in hesitating tones, to Maria, who occupied the dining-room alone,—

"Could you manage a little company to tea, Maria? Helen and Horace, and a few of their friends. Helen feels as if her new family relations ought to be recognized, I presume. Could you bring it about, daughter?"

"Why, yes, sir," Maria said, speaking slowly and hesitatingly, with a glow on each cheek. Helen married was worse than Helen at home among them. "We can, if you think best, but we don't consider it at all necessary; and, father, having company is rather expensive business."

Mr. Randolph winced, as he always did when finance was the subject of conversation. Poor man, there was nothing he would have liked better than a fortune — unless, indeed, it were to be at rest somewhere, where money was never mentioned. Mr. Randolph's tastes, like his daughter Helen's, were royal."

"Never mind," he said, hurriedly. "A few shillings more or less can not make much dif-ference in the end. I would not try to do much.

Something very simple, and within our means.
People know we are poor. They must take the
will for the deed. I do not like to hurt Helen's
feelings by passing her new connection over entirely. You will manage it right, daughter; you
always do," and then Mr. Randolph went away,
leaving Maria the picture of dismay. She had
not meant to yield this point. She knew "they"
were in the habit of making company for a
married daughter, but she was personally very
indifferent to "them," and she had reckoned
on battling the matter out with Helen. She
had not counted on the half dozen words that
Mrs. Monroe let drop sadly in her father's hearing, "If mother were here, Horace, your mother
and father would be cordially welcomed to this
house. We miss mother in everything."

So the cake making and the discussions commenced again. Maria having yielded against her
will, did it with a very ill grace, and made herself extra trouble, as angry people are apt to do.
Three several afternoons did Becky present herself, her hair done in the neatest little knot
imaginable, her apron large and clean, and
announced herself ready to make cake, or do
"anything that Miss Maria wanted of her."
Miss Maria wanted nothing. Not an egg would
she let Becky beat, not a raisin was she allowed
to touch. Mrs. Munroe came over and stood in

the kitchen door, in cool, summery toilet, and fanned herself, while she told Maria that she was certainly very silly; Becky knew how to do everything much better than *she* did; and that she (Mrs. Munroe) had put herself out, in order to let Becky help over here.

"Put yourself in again," said ungrateful Maria, "as soon as you choose. We have lived thus far without any of Becky's assistance, and we shall continue, for a little while."

"But you are not accustomed to entertaining company," persisted the eldest sister; "and you are nothing but a young girl. Now, she knows how 'they' arrange everything. She has assisted some of the very first families in town."

"Did you ever hear of the man who told his transient boarder that if she couldn't stand, in the eating line, for one week, what he had to endure all his life, it was a pity? I might say the same to my guests. I am sure I have done the cooking for you ever since I could talk, nearly, and you are still alive. We'll venture it one night longer." This was all the reply that the inexorable Maria had to make, and she burned her cheeks and her finger, and made all the cake herself. Delicious cake it was, too. She had that accomplishment, I think no one who has ever attempted to compound the depraved stuff will deny. There were other things about which she obstinately insisted on her own way.

"How on earth came you to think of inviting Nettie Thatcher?" was Mrs. Munroe's exclamation on one of the aforesaid afternoons.

"It wasn't a very hard thing to think of,' Maria said, composedly. "I've performed more severe mental labor than that many a time."

"Don't for pity's sake try to be funny, Maria; it is too warm for that. But what possesses you to think you must mix people up so?"

"I'm not mixing them up. It is entirely your work. If I could have had my own way I should have left them all in peace and quietness, to get their suppers at their usual hours, instead of coming here and waiting for it until bedtime. But since it had to be done, I thought Nettie might as well wait as the rest of you."

"Well, I thought you had more sense than *that*. She never expects to be invited in our set. You certainly couldn't have thought that you would hurt her feelings by leaving her out, for no one invites her?"

"Why don't they?"

"Well, for several reasons. In the first place, she doesn't belong, as I said, to our set in society."

"Why doesn't she?"

"How do *I* know? I don't suppose she has a suitable thing to wear."

"That's *her* concern, not mine. I don't have to clothe the people, only to feed them, for that matter. I've heard you make the same remark about yourself many a time, yet you didn't consider it a reason why people should ignore your acquaintance."

Mrs. Munroe laughed complacently. It was a source of unceasing comfort to her that she would never be obliged to make that remark again. Then she turned to the charge.

"What is the use of talking this nonsense. I insist that there is no sense in your thinking of inviting Nettie Thatcher. She is not in our circle of society, and we can't put her in."

"She is a member of the same church with yourself, Helen."

"Oh, well, now, that has nothing to do with the subject. People may talk about equality and all that sort of thing to the end of time, and there will still be classes, or grades, or sets, or whatever you please to call them."

"But what shall make them, Helen — education, or worth, or money? For instance, Nettie Thatcher is a good-principled, noble-hearted girl, with a very fair education, as good as yours or mine certainly, and she is refined and gentle in her manners. The entire difficulty lies in the fact that she works in a mill. Now, what common sense is there in that?"

Mrs. Munroe sniffed energetically, and her reply was very much to the point.

"You are burning that cake, Maria; I smell it. Scorched cake is horrid stuff. Becky never has the least bit of burn on hers. What a simpleton you are not to let her help you! Something horrid will happen, just because of your obstinacy. I expect to fairly die of mortification."

"In that case, your troubles, so far as my cake is concerned, will certainly be over," Maria said, composedly.

"Well, at least I hope you won't insist on mortifying Nettie Thatcher with an invitation which she won't know what to do with. *You* can't make the world over, and it isn't worth while to try. Nettie seems well enough satisfied with her own sphere. Don't mix things."

Maria closed the oven door with a bang.

"It's of no sort of use to hold an argument with you," she said, hotly. "You would dance around in a bandbox all day, and never discover that the bottom was out; but you can compose your mind on one point. Nettie Thatcher has been invited, and has accepted the invitation."

Mrs. Munroe's cheeks reddened angrily.

"Then all I have to say is," and she said it in a somewhat high key, "I think you are a very headstrong, obstinate girl, and you take a great deal on yourself for one of your age. I am sure I don't see why Ermina don't control you better. I would rather not have *any* company than to have people who never saw each other before, and never will again, sit stiffly around trying to make talk, when they have *nothing* in common. I wonder what Mr. Harper will think of such a company. I guess he will wonder where you picked up Nettie Thatcher."

"I will clear out a clothes-press for the gentleman, if you think he can not breathe the same air that Nettie does for one evening," Maria said, now thoroughly exasperated; and her sister gathered herself up in wrath and went home, leaving the kitchen in outward peace for the rest of the day.

There was one redeeming feature of Mrs. Munroe's character. She never *stayed* angry. The next morning's sun found her as peaceably disposed toward the family across the way, and as ready to aid them as ever. She came over just before the dinner hour. She had a new scheme, which she brought before Ermina, who was slicing cold meat for the hurried dinner; for it was the day of the coming entertainment.

"Dinners are of no account in this house to-day," as she shaved the great pinky slices. "It is the supper toward which our stomachs are eagerly looking. This is simply to stay them until seven o'clock."

Mrs. Munroe, thus reminded of the tardiness of her plans, came to the point at once.

" I wish we could have a little currant wine to serve with the cake this evening."

Ermina, in her astonishment, forgot the matronly name, and exclaimed,—

" Why, Helen Randolph!"

" Well, I do," said Mrs. Munroe, firmly. "It is simple, and at the same time elegant. They have it at a great many little parties where other liquors are considered objectionable; and your cake is so ridiculously plain you need something to set it off. You humor Maria so, in all of her whims, I wonder at you."

Ermina laughed. "It is she who humors me in mine, when she occasionally allows me to have my own way," she said, good-humoredly. "But I consider it no more than fair that the one who does all the work should do some of the managing. As to currant wine, you might as well propose a glass of prussic acid all around. You seem to have forgotten father's opinions?"

" Oh, father! I could coax him over to my side in less than five minutes. I really think you ought to have something of the kind, and that is so simple that the most morbid temperance people use it. City people don't look at these things as we do, anyway — in large cities, I mean. Mr. Harper now is a temperance man, quite an earnest one, I've heard, and I've no doubt that he would think father's ideas ridiculously narrow and strait laced. We have some splendid currant wine that Horace's mother made two years ago. It was Horace's idea to offer it here this evening. He thinks it will make things more free and easy. If it were not for Maria we might bring it over quietly, and serve it without saying anything to father; but I suppose she would make an outrageous fuss."

"If it were not for Maria, and Ermina, and all the rest of us, you would better say. That will never be done in this house, I assure you. You are welcome to get father's consent if you can, though I think he has trouble enough without bothering his brains about such things; but everything that has to do with him shall be fair and square — no slipping in and doing things quietly. I won't consent to it."

"No one thought of asking you to. You are as bad as Maria. I'm not afraid but that I could get father's consent to it in two minutes."

"Very well," said Ermina, composedly. "Try it, and I wish you joy in the undertaking. He is coming. You will have an opportunity to vanquish him before dinner if it is only to take two minutes."

CHAPTER XVIII.

THE FORCE OF ARGUMENT.

"FATHER," said Mrs. Munroe, turning to meet the weary, sallow-faced man, "you don't look as well as usual to-day. Are you feeling badly?"

"No worse than usual, Helen," he said, trying to smile cheerily. "I haven't much to boast of in the way of strength."

"*I* think you need a tonic of some kind. Horace's father has been real miserable for several days, and Dr. Marvin ordered wine bitters for him. He thinks they are helping him. I wish you would try currant wine, father; that is harmless enough, and it is real strengthening. I'm going to bring some over to-night for the company, and I want you to try it. Will you?"

From the time of her earliest recollection her father had worn to Helen Munroe the same kind, patient, tender face; easily moved, easily coaxed, apparently; one of those men whom natures like Ermina's and Maria's shrank from wounding or jarring in anyway: hence his wish had grown into being their law; one of those men whom natures like Helen's wheedled into doing dozens of things which he did not want to do — to which his higher nature objected — simply because he shrank morbidly from argument, from strife, from *scenes* of any sort. Very rarely had Mrs. Munroe seen him either excited or determined. She did not understand her father. He turned toward her now, a bright red spot burning on the sallow cheek, and his voice was slow and low:

"Helen, it is very seldom that I assert my decided views in regard to things. It is very seldom, *indeed*, that I issue any commands: but I thought my children understood my position in this matter. There can no currant wine ever be served in my house to guests of mine. Don't forget it." Then he turned and went with quick, trembling steps out of the room.

"There!" said Ermina, angrily. "I hope you will enjoy your dinner; you have spoiled father's. *Do* go home."

And Mrs. Munroe immediately went.

"You will have to give up your currant wine plans," she said to her husband when they met at their late dinner. "Father is really fierce about it. He actually frightened me." Then she told him her attempt and its result.

Mr. Horace Munroe laughed. That thin, pale old man, old before his time, with not business capacity enough to have risen even yet above clerkship, with not mental power enough to care to converse for half an hour with anybody — the idea of being cowed by him, or of not doing as one liked in spite of him! He did not say all this to his wife; he did not say a word of it. He was learning Mrs. Munroe's nature. There were things that it would not bear. She could get thoroughly exasperated with her sisters. She could feel at times utter contempt for her brother Tom. She could even lose patience with her father; but woe to the foolish being who dared to sympathize with these feelings! To be out of sorts with her *own* flesh and blood was one thing, to allow any one else to do so was utterly another. Mr. Munroe was wiser, therefore he kept all his thoughts to himself, and laughed, and said,—

" Well, their loss is our gain. Never mind," and then dismissed the subject.

Very early in the evening Mrs. Munroe crossed again to her father's house, ready dressed for the reception which she had gotten up for herself. She was dressed in the much-talked-

15

over lavender silk, with its elaborate trimmings and elegant laces. She felt called upon to apologize to Ermina's stare of astonishment.

" You know I am a bride, Ermina, and they always expect brides to dress a good deal the first few times they go out in company."

" I'm glad there's no prospect of my being a bride," Ermina said, coldly. " ' They ' seem to expect them to be guilty of all sorts of absurd and preposterous things. What are you going to wear to parties, Helen ? "

" I really don't believe you ever *will* be one, Ermina. You are altogether too blunt and sharp." The *question* she ignored.

Ermina laughed.

" Both blunt and sharp. I should think I might be about right then, as they are both extremes. But I don't know that you are any sillier than I am. I expect to swelter in this gray dress; but I *must* wear it, because it cost a dollar a yard, and my comfortable one was only twenty cents. We are all fools together. That's the conclusion that Peter Armstrong has arrived at, and I agree with him."

This suggested a new trouble to Mrs. Munroe.

" What have you done with Peter ? " she asked, anxiously.

" Done with him ? Ironed his best shirt to the last degree of smoothness, and cut the fringes off his cuffs, and made a new bow to his necktie. He is in very good order for the occasion, I assure you."

Mrs. Munroe stood aghast.

"He *isn't* going to be here with the company? Now, *is he?*"

"Why, of course he is. Isn't he one of the boarders, and hasn't he as good a right to his supper as any of us?"

Mrs. Munroe sat down in the nearest chair, in speechless indignation.

"I never *saw* such works!" she managed to say at last. "You are quite as wild as Maria. Why, I *used* to think that *you* had common sense. The idea of Peter Armstrong being at a tea party! He never knows what to do with his feet nor his hands."

"His feet are all right this time. He has made them shine beautifully; and as for his hands, no doubt he will make them useful — he generally does. *Don't* fret about things, Helen. *I'm* Miss Randolph, you know; your responsibility in this family has ceased."

"That is very evident," Mrs. Munroe said, tartly.

Then both ladies went in search of Maria. They found her in the dining-room, busy over the table, which was fragrant with flowers and leaves.

" This table really looks *very* pretty," Mrs.
Munroe said. " Who arranged it? It must be
Grace's work. She has the most tasteful hands
of any of you. Why, Maria Randolph ! "

" At your service, ma'am. What can I do for
you ? "

" I should think it was quite time you were
dressed for the evening."

" Dressed ! Hear the woman ! and I've been
prinking for the last hour."

" And arrayed yourself in a calico dress at
last ! "

" English cambric, ma'am ; cost twenty-five
cents a yard, and cheap as dirt at that. I have
the clerk's word for it."

" Maria, what is the use of being so disagreeable ? I'm sure I don't like to do things to
mortify you. Why should you care to treat *me*
so ? "

Maria turned toward her in genuine astonishment.

" I hadn't such an idea, Helen," she said, earnestly. " I didn't think it would make any
difference to you what I wore. In fact I didn't
think about you at all ; and I had several reasons
for choosing this dress. In the first place my
poplin is insufferably hot — *warm* doesn't express
it — and, besides, it's too long for table serving.
Then I remembered what you said about morti-

fying Nettie Thatcher, and I determined that I wouldn't mortify her by appearing better dressed than she might be."

"You are very considerate," Mrs. Munroe said, coldly, turning away as she spoke. But she said no more against the pretty cambric dress.

The guests began to assemble, few in number, and, for the most part a choice selection. Mrs. Horace Munroe was conspicuous in her lavender silk, even her mother-in-law wearing a plain black one; but she drew consolation from the thought that she was a bride, and was expected to be conspicuous. Not the least interesting among the young faces was that of Nettie Thatcher. Her dress, too, was certainly unobjectionable. It was one of those soft, still grays, of a material so vague that even Mrs. Munroe's practiced eye failed to determine to what class it belonged, nor how much it might possibly have cost a yard. Her ornaments were rare and exquisite enough; they were small, blue wildwood flowers. Mrs. Munroe, standing near her, moved dexterously forward as Mr. Harper entered, and her voluminous skirts and ruffles and puffs served to hide the quiet little wildwood flower behind her. "There is no necessity for performing conspicuous and disagreeable introductions," she said, in undertone, to Grace who sought her shelter. "He will not know there is any one behind me. He is fastidious in his tastes, and extremely inconvenient in his questionings." He came very soon to her corner and greeted her with a cordial shake of the hand, and almost his second sentence was,—

"Whom are you hiding behind you, Mrs. Munroe?" Then, as his eye caught a view of her, "Ah, Miss Nettie!" he said, and there was unmistakable pleasure in his voice. Immediately he held out his hand to her, and Mrs. Munroe had the pleasure of hearing their conversation: "I haven't seen you in an age, Nettie."

"Not since Saturday evening."

Mr. Harper laughed.

"Was it so recent as that? Well, it seems longer. How are matters progressing?"

"Very smoothly, so far as I can learn."

"How does it happen that you have been beguiled out of your retirement?"

"It doesn't take much to beguile me, when people give me a chance to come." Her laugh was low and sweet.

"Who gave you the chance? Was it Miss Randolph's invitation?"

"No; Maria's."

"Oh, I don't think I know her."

"Don't you? Come with me, then, and we'll find her."

And immediately the soft gray dress was shaken out, and Nettie Thatcher crossed the room with the only *very* distinguished guest they had.

This Mr. Harper, about whom so much has been hinted, deserves a more extended mention. He was not a resident of the little city where the Randolphs lived. In fact, he was the junior partner of one of those mammoth firms in New York. He had charge of the foreign branch establishment, and lived abroad. He was spending a year at home — that is, in this country — sending out one of the confidential clerks of the firm to take his place, while he attended to various outside business matters. And ever and anon he came back to the old homestead, situated in this little city, spending days, and sometimes weeks, with an old aunt, the sole remaining branch of the old family tree, and the only mother he had ever known. Great was the estimation in which he was held in the city. Thus much about him. What sort of a man was hidden behind all this external of wealth and importance you may discover for yourselves as chance makes you acquainted with him. Later in the evening he stood beside Ermina.

"You are looking weary," he said, bending a little and speaking in a low tone.

"Am I?" she said, gravely. "That is an unpardonable offense. As hostess I ought to look as fresh as a June morning, no matter if I *have* been on my feet since daylight; but I *can't*. Even my looks refuse to be hypocritical."

"Have you schooled them *not* to be?" he asked, earnestly.

"Not I. They schooled themselves. Hypocrisy was left out of my nature. I can plead guilty to every other sin in the calendar, but I haven't enough of *that* to get on comfortably with this flattery-loving world."

"What a pity." He said it quietly, and apparently in perfect sincerity.

Something prompted her to answer him with equal gravity.

"What do you mean? What is a pity?"

"Do you know Burns? and are you acquainted with that honest bit of life he wrote, commencing, 'Oh, wad some power the giftie gie us?' I was thinking what a pity it is that he was right, that people know so little about themselves."

"Do you mean me to make a personal application of that remark?"

"I hoped you would," he said, with a bright smile.

"Then I should think you meant that *I* was hypocritical without knowing it."

"If I mean just that, what then?"

"Well," said Ermina, in undisguised astonish-

ment, " I *certainly* don't think *you* are one. I am
sufficiently interested in myself, however, to make
my acquaintance; so if you really mean just that,
will you tell me how?"

"I beg your pardon," he said gently. "I think
I am presuming a great deal on a first acquaintance; but I have imagined you to belong in a
measure to that class of persons who vail their
better selves, who hide their tender and gentle
and sympathetic feelings under a mask of cold-
ness or brusqeness."

" People are educated into doing that," she answered quickly, " because there is so much sham
tenderness and mock sympathy."

" Because there is counterfeit money in circu-
lation, Miss Randolph, you and I must counterfeit some for ourselves. Is that it?"

Ermina laughed a little.

" I believe I am a poor logician," she said.
" But, Mr. Harper, don't you think hypocrisy is
the besetting sin of polite society?"

" One of them; and the *want* of it is the besetting sin of *some* people?"

" What can you mean? It is certainly not one
of the Christian virtues in any case."

" I am not so sure of that. There is a kind-
ness of spirit, a gentleness of manner, a willingness to yield to the feelings of others, that by
many would be termed hypocrisy, that to me is

one of the Christian graces. I have seen just such lovely characters, and have heard their owners denounced as hypocrites, simply because they did not speak *all* that they might think. What do you imagine Paul meant by becoming all things to all men ?"

"I don't remember ever having given it a thought."

"Haven't you? It seems to me that he desired to cultivate that grace of sympathizing with other people's views and feelings, and even whims, so far as it was possible."

"But don't you think there is danger of carrying the theory too far ?"

"Not if we adopt the other part of Paul's doctrine, 'That I might by *all* means save *some.* The Christian who takes that as his motto, works for that, prays for it, will not be likely to get far astray in regard to it."

"How many people live according to that standard do you imagine ?"

"Let us hope that *many* do; let us be *sure* that *you* and *I* do."

"I am sure that I do *not*," she said, emphatically.

"But you wish to ?"

"No, I cannot even be said to *wish* to, since I have never thought of the subject in that light before."

" You are a Christian, I think ? "

" Why, I am not even sure of that.   At least not in this hypocritical sense.   I am a member of the church, if that is what you mean."

"I do *not* mean that," he said, quickly.   "In one sense it matters very little what I profess if I do not *possess*."

" Your talk about St. Paul reminds me of St. Peter," she said, with a sudden change of tone. " We have him here to-night; that is he leaning against the side window.   He don't know what to do with his hands nor his feet, nor the rest of his body, for that matter.   I think I ought to go over and talk to him — not to carry out your theory, however, for I would rather have a talk with him than with two-thirds of our guests."

" Who is he ? " asked Mr. Harper, very much amused.

" He is our boarder," she answered him, with sparkling eyes.   " Hypocritically, we take him because it is convenient to have some one to do errands for us, and because we were sorry for the poor boy, and wanted to give him a pleasant home ; but *honestly*, because Mr. Evans, for whom he works, pays a fair price for his board, and we needed the money."

" Will you take me to see him ?   I have noticed his face, and there are reasons why I am interested in him."

So the *next* thing Mr. Harper did was to cross the room to Peter Armstrong and shake hands with him.

Maria's cake was certainly appreciated, the dainty little supper was thoroughly neat in all of its appointments, and Maria herself was feel-ng that if it were not for to-morrow, and the bills, and the folly of trying to be like well-to-do people when·you were poor people, she would quite enjoy herself; as it was, she tried to lay aside all thoughts of the morrow for a little space, and was doing the honors of her end of the room, when a diversion occurred at the other end. Her brother-in-law. Mr. Munroe, came from the pantry with a tray and glasses, and the glasses were glowing with wine! Maria set the spoon-holder down with a jingle, and paused in the midst of her sentence to Mr. Harper. Mr. Mun-roe came gayly forward, and spoke to those nearest him in his clear, cultured voice.

"Now, good people, I will give you the privi-lege of drinking to my wife's health in some very delicious currant wine. We do not believe in stronger beverages, some of us, at least not this evening; but this is a very rare quality, and I know will be enjoyable."

There was a laughing gleam in his handsome eyes as he began to pass the glasses, but he had **certainly reckoned without regard to his host.**

A sudden hush fell on the guests, for Mr. Randolph had risen from his chair at the other end of the room, and those who were nearest him saw that his sallow face was very pale.

"There is some mistake," he said, speaking steadily and in a voice sufficiently clear to be heard by every one in the room. "My son-in-law is a new member of my family, and may possibly be excused for not knowing my views. But it were discourtesy to my guests not to make them acquainted with them. I am known in this place as an advocate of temperance, of total abstinence. I do not believe in wine made of *any* kind of fruit, whether it be of currants or grapes. I never offer wine to guests of *mine*, and never mean to."

"Randolph," said Mr. Harper, touching Tom on the shoulder, as the elder Mr. Randolph sat down, "be proud of your father."

"I am," said Tom, his eyes glowing. "I'll be hanged if I don't like square out and out independence, even when it fires a shot right at me."

CHAPTER XIX.

REAL OR IMITATION?

THE next thing they did was to go shopping — Ermina and Faith and Mrs. Munroe. The last-named lady was fond of shopping. Once it had been a trial to her, because of the windows and shelves and cases full of beauty that she must needs pass by; but nowadays her purse was well filled. At least it always seemed so to her, unless she came in contact with Faith Halsted. Mrs. Munroe's wealth would always be that of degree. When in the presence of her sisters, with their carefully counted pennies, she felt rich; when she was with Faith, in view of that young lady's half million, she was poor, and somewhat discontented. It was this feeling that served to put her in a petulant, argumentative mood whenever she came in contact with Faith. Ermina went shopping because she had a half holiday, with nothing in particular to do; and she said it was refreshing to look on occasionally and see other people spend money, even though she had none to spend herself. Faith went of necessity, because things would wear out and must necessarily be replaced. In her haste to get settled for the summer she had left much of her summer sewing to do after she reached her new home. Mrs. Munroe went because, as I told you, she enjoyed it. They were a pretty trio in their cheerful summer toilets. A trifle overdressed Mrs Munroe was for the street. It was her besetting temptation. But Faith was as simple in her toilet as Ermina herself; and that young lady was wont to remark that " severe simplicity " became her complexion and her purse. I don't remember whether I have ever told you how Ermina looked. I am anxious that you should know. She had large gray eyes, and hair so brown that sometimes people imagined it to be black. She had a somewhat large mouth, in which one caught glimpses of rows of white teeth. And now you know almost nothing about how she looked. As if eyes and hair and teeth told anything about *the look*. I wonder what it is. Everybody has eyes, and quite a

good many people have hair and teeth of their
own, even in these days; and yet we never get
mixed up, mistaking other people for our sisters,
or our husbands or fathers — *the look* is there,
the distinguishing something that makes each
person distinct from every other person. Ermina had the look, in a marked degree. No one
ever said of her, " There goes one of the Randolph girls." She was Ermina Randolph to
everybody that knew her. On this sunny afternoon, as the three ladies took their seats in a
street car, Ermina in her plainly made silver-
gray dress looked every inch a lady. Mrs. Munroe
was, as I said, just a *little* too much dressed, and
Faith was so small and slight that every one
thought her a fair young girl not out of her teens
by some years. The cars filled rapidly and
there presently occurred that interesting condition peculiar to street cars — more people than
seats. Among the standers was a woman belonging to that class to whom belongs the term
" common people " — whatever that may mean
in this country of free schools and republican
principles. I think it generally means that the
women wear calico dresses, where the other class
wear some other material. A refined distinction
you will observe. This particular woman was
in clean, neat, recently starched calico, of a
quiet, neutral tint. In her arms she carried a

plump, well-to-do baby, whose head bobbed from side to side incessantly, partly because of the jar of the car, and partly from his intense desire to see all that was to be seen. She stood opposite Ermina, who indulged in a mental calculation on the probable weight of the child, and then glanced down the car at the row of fashionably dressed young men, who were making merry over the personal appearance of some of the passengers. Suddenly Ermina arose, and as the car had stopped to receive a package and a message, her voice could be heard distinctly.

"Take my seat, madam. It is difficult to stand and carry a child," and, as the woman objected, "I *insist*, madam. I am abundantly able to stand." Instantly the three young men were on their feet, and the nearest one tendered his seat in unmistakably pressing terms.

"No," said our gray-eyed lady, coldly and proudly. "No, thank you. I am quite able to stand, and the lady to whom I gave my seat was *not*."

Mrs. Munroe took her to task for it afterward.

"What *is* the use in being so different from everybody else, Ermina. It certainly isn't your business to provide women and babies with seats. You spoke out so rudely, too, to those gentlemen. The one who spoke to you was General Thornton's son. Did you know him?"

16

"No," said Ermina, decidedly; "and I don't want to. A *gentleman* would offer his seat to a woman and a baby, provided he felt able to stand at all. I am not quenched, Helen, ever by *your* disapproval. I am glad I spoke out."

"Well, *I* say you were bold, and unnecessarily rude. Don't you think so, Faith? I was mortified. It does seem as if we were fated to have something ridiculous or mortifying happen whenever Mr. Harper is present to look on."

"Mr. Harper!" Ermina repeated, with a little start. "Where was he? I am sure he was invisible to me."

"He was standing on the platform, and saw and heard the whole proceeding, I know by the appearance of his face."

"Oh," very composedly, "you studied his face, did you? I am glad he had no seat."

"Why in the world are you glad of that?"

"Oh, simply because I consider that posture beneficial to health and strength, and I have a benevolent interest in his welfare."

Faith laughed.

"*I* am glad, too," she said, in an aside to Ermina. "I like him."

"Well, I'm sure I hope you are rested for our shopping, after standing for half an hour in a street car. Utterly unnecessary it was, too. I presume that woman is used to standing at the wash-tub all day. Faith, *did* you notice the cotton lace on that child's cloak and hat? I declare, it perfectly disgusts me to see how such people try to imitate us."

" Me, for instance," said Ermina, utter unconcern in her voice. " I have an imitation lace ruffle in my dress this minute.'

Faith laughed again.

" So have I," she said, brightly; " and *I* think I look very nice in it."

" I wonder if *you* wear imitation lace!" Mrs. Munroe said, utter surprise in her voice. " I am sure it's very pretty. I thought it was real."

" That's the beauty of the imitation. I am obliged to judge by the price of it half the time, which proves that the imitation is almost as pretty as the real."

" Oh, *I* can tell it as a general thing," said Mrs. Munroe with marked emphasis on the " *I*." (N. B. — If you know any fashionable lady, who never bought half a dozen yards of " *real* " lace in her life, you may be sure she will be the one to declare her ability to distinguish the real from the counterfeit, even in the dark.) " But yours is a remarkable good imitation. Ermina's, now, is almost as bad as that ridiculous woman's. Don't you dislike to see such attempts to deck out a baby? The child would have looked better in calico."

"I don't think so,", Faith said, stoutly. "I liked the poor woman just because she had taken such evident pains to make her baby look pretty. If she can not have the real things for her darling, she gives him the best that her purse will afford."

"That is mere sentiment," Mrs. Munroe said, in an oracular tone.

Then they both went into Caswell & Hollister's store. Those gentlemen kept a line of goods not to be found at Munroe's. Ermina was staid at the very entrance.

"What lovely calicoes! I think I never saw any prettier. Helen, they have none like these at your store?"

Mrs. Munroe surveyed them coldly.

"I'm sure I don't know whether they have or not," she said, in an indifferent tone. "They are common, ten-cent prints. I don't patronize that class of goods, and never notice whether we have them or not."

Ermina's interest increased.

"Are they only ten cents?" she questioned, eagerly. "That sounds as if it might come within the bounds of my purse, and I really need a couple to sew in. I believe I'll buy some."

"Ermina, what nonsense! Cambrics are only twenty cents, and English calicoes you can get for fifteen."

"But if I can get what will answer the same purpose for ten cents, why shouldn't I?"

"They won't answer the same purpose. No one wears those common things."

"I do," said Faith, emphatically. "I have two. Paid ten cents a yard for them in New York. No, I declare,—one was nine cents; and I have them made up beautifully. They are the prettiest dresses I have—in their sphere, you know."

Mrs. Munroe gave her rich cousin a stare of genuine astonishment, and questioned her energetically, while Ermina reveled in buff and gray tints, among the ten-cent calicoes.

"Why in the world do you buy such cheap things, Faith? I'm sure you can't plead economy."

"Why not?" Faith asked, good-humoredly. "Why should I waste money because I happen to have more than some people?"

"But do you consider buying cambrics a waste of money?"

Faith laughed merrily. "What a logician you would make this afternoon!" she said. "We were not talking about cambrics—you were denying me the duty of economizing."

"Well," Mrs. Munroe said, drawing her Paisley shawl about her shoulders with an impatient jerk, "I suppose you are not so obtuse but that you take my meaning. Do you pretend to say you think common, coarse calicoes are as good as cambrics?"

"I don't remember having said anything of the kind, Cousin Helen. There are places to go to where I should rather prefer a cambric dress to a calico; but there are also places where the ten-cent dresses fit in beautifully, and I won't be so silly as to keep myself from buying them merely because they only cost half as much as some other goods. I detest that sort of shoddyism."

Ermina laughed. "That is good," she said, heartily. "I think you have touched the root of the question. I am just waking up to see it. The price per yard marks the importance of American costumes, and not the 'pretty,' at all. Now, for instance, I'm sure anybody with eyes must see that this pale sea-green ground, with dots of deeper green all over it, would be very pretty, if it were not for that fatal ten-cent ticket on it. Helen, I'm sorry to shock your taste so deeply; but I must have a dress of this; it suits me — and my pocket-book — two important matters."

"There might be another reason given for economical dresses," Faith said, with the far-away look in her eyes. "This whole question of dress is a misterious, and sometimes a painful puzzle to me. Where to draw the line — how far, as responsible stewards, to spend money that is intrusted to our keeping, for the simple purpose of adorning our own bodies — I'm sure I don't know. Whether to buy *any real* lace at all, when there is actual starvation in the world, both of the body and the soul, is a strange query. What do you think, Ermina ?"

"I never thought about it at all," Ermina answered, bluntly. "I never had any money to buy *real* lace with, nor *real* things of any sort, and never expect to have."

"But do you never try to make other people's duties plain to them?" Faith asked, with a merry twinkle in her eye.

"Plenty of times, so far as their duties toward me were concerned; but I never troubled myself about their relations to the heathen. I should think, though, it would be rather an easy question to settle, if one wanted to settle it conscientiously — it would simply involve a little close looking into things, to discover which was really of the most importance, lace or soul."

"What a startling way of putting it!" Faith said, thoughtfully.

"What an *absurd* way of putting it!" Mrs. Munroe said. "Ermina, you are tumbling those prints about in a shocking way. Do come on!"

"I can't," said Ermina. "I want to buy a dress, I'm sure. I am waiting to be served. The clerks are all busy — lace is uppermost, you perceive, this afternoon."

"But, Ermina, if one really takes that view of the question, where will it end?" This Faith said, speaking earnestly. "Since there really *is* starvation in the world, why should we have *any* of the things that we do? It is not a question of real lace and silk and velvet simply, but of merino and poplin, and carpets and pictures, and music and flowers, even. Where is the dividing line?"

Ermina laughed. "I don't know, I'm sure," she said, lightly. "It is a puzzle. I think about it as little as possible, and buy my ten-cent calicoes because I can not afford any better, and for no other earthly reason."

"You are a ridiculous couple!" Mrs. Munroe said, shortly. "If you really are going to stay here and tumble over horrid prints, and moralize all the afternoon, why, I'll go on. I came to match blue silk."

Mr. Harper had a way of appearing to people at unexpected moments. It was when the green calico had been purchased, and the ladies, returned from a vain search after the right shade of blue silk, halted again before the calico counter, while Faith picked out a dainty morning slip for Pearly, that he came over to them.

"Didn't I hear you puzzling your brains over abstruse questions of starvation and plenty?" he said to Faith, in a familiar tone. He and Faith had been friends since the latter's early childhood.

"We didn't know that you heard us," she said, brightly. "But since you did, perhaps you can help us."

"Not very materially, I fear. You must ask my sister about that. She is in town. Did you know it? When will you ladies call on her? There is one sentence, Faith, that might help, I should think: 'Whether, therefore, ye eat or drink, or whatsoever ye do, do all to the glory of God.' Have you thought of that?"

"Yes, and it increases the puzzle. We just don't *live* it. How can we?"

"Ask my sister."

"Who is his sister?" Mrs. Munroe asked as they went down Chester Street.

"She is Mrs. Laport, of Boston, daughter of Kenneth J. Carlton, of Washington. I don't know her; they have been abroad since her marriage."

"They are immensely rich, are they not?"

Mrs. Munroe's tones were respectful; they always were when she spoke of riches.

"Very," Faith said, simply.

"Humph!" said Ermina. "What can *she* know about the subject of silks and souls?"

CHAPTER XX.

A PROTECTOR.

T was a beautiful room, not small,— Mrs.
Munroe disliked small rooms, and had as
little to do with them as possible,— but
it was so daintily furnished with household conveniences and comforts as to give
an idea of cosiness and diminutiveness. The
walls were hung with a delicate tint of buff, bordered with a deep maroon, rich maroon carpet
on the floor, chairs and sofas and little cunning
ottomans all in rich maroon rep,— even the
spread for the tiny round table was of the same
glowing color. It was Mrs. Munroe's sitting-
room. There were little corner stands, with
books and papers, and sewing materials; and
brackets, with vases and flowers; there was
everywhere that beautiful, systematic, unstiff

251

ness of arrangement which a tasteful lady knows how to bestow upon the family room. In the center of this fair room sat the lady of the house, her toilet quite in keeping with her surroundings, the colors of her dress blending harmoniously with the prominent colors of the room. Mrs Munroe had an eye for details. Sometimes, how ever, the most fastidious lady is obliged to endure contrasts. Mrs. Munroe's companion was a contrast. He sat in one of the luxurious maroon chairs; his hat, tipped on one side, showed plainly that a blow or wound of some sort had blackened his left eye; his coat was torn away in front, as if he had rescued it from a rude grasp; his boots were thick with black, filthy looking mud; his face was flushed, an unnatural red; and his breathing, or rather snoring, had a strange, unnatural sound. Mrs. Munroe had let her java canvas slip from her silken dress to the floor, and sat with clasped hands, looking steadily at the sleeping object before her. It was perfectly plain to any looker on that his sleep was that which is caused by taking a glass too much. A drunken man! Well, if he were only Jim Smith, living over the wretched little corner rum-hole, that would be the proper name to use; but inasmuch as he was Mr. Horace Munroe, of the firm of Evans, Munroe & Co., people hesitated, and generally said that he was a little overcome with liquor. There were no tears in his wife's eyes. Helen Munroe was not one who had tears to spare for many occasions — this one did not call them forth; but if you have never pitied her in your life, I hope you do now — she needs pity.

It is an old story, it has been repeated until it is familiar to every one, and I think we American people must enjoy its recital, we take such pains to manufacture just such homes as these. I suppose it never grows commonplace to the suffering wife. There were features about this family life that made it peculiarly terrible. Mrs. Munroe had in the place of an absorbing love, such as the marriage relation should be built upon, only a composed, quiet friendship for her husband. Perhaps you think that would make the trial less hard. I tell you I *don't* think so. I have known drunkards' wives clinging to their husbands with almost Godlike pity and patience as they sank from one depth to another, and those wives were sustained by that blessed love that God had given them for their husbands; it enabled them to bear up under trials that would otherwise have crushed them, to cling where they would otherwise have spurned, to hope when others despaired. I say it was harder for Mrs. Munroe because she did not love her husband. She liked the position that he had given her; she liked her beautiful home, and all its tasteful appointments, but sit-

ting there that evening, looking at the red-faced,
swollen-eyed, filthy creature whose name she bore,
whose wife she was, she hated the very sight of
him; and if there is anything more terrible in all
this pitiful earth than that, I don't know what it
can be. I have heard people tell of what strange
and queer, and sometimes trivial, thoughts came
to them when they believed themselves to be
drowning. Some of the thoughts of this young
wife were equally strange. She sat, with dry,
wide-open eyes, and stared at her husband. How
strange that such a pitiable wretch should bear
that name! "Love, honor and *protect*," she said,
repeating a scrap of the marriage service which
came to her just then, repeating it with curling
lips of scorn. The city clock struck nine. She
counted the strokes from the force of newly-ac-
quired habit; she compared the time with her
little gold watch, that was a present from her
husband. Always, in the house nearly across the
street, as the clock struck nine the head of the
house took down the family Bible and the household gathered for prayers. Suppose it was their
custom in this family,— how would they manage
it this evening? "He is much too drunk to
kneel," she said, aloud, and then she laughed —
a terrible laugh. Such natures as Helen Munroe's are sometimes brought, through heavy trial
and pain, to kneel in utter self-abnegation, and

find peace. Sometimes such natures as hers are brought to mad-houses through like trials. Her laugh was like that. She went on with her half-insane thoughts. " What if he were not my husband ? What if he were some miserable street loafer who had blundered in here, I wonder what I should do with him ? I should probably scream to *my* husband to protect me from him ; but who is there to protect me from my *husband?*" Then she laughed again. " Perhaps I should kill him; perhaps I shall anyway, then I should be a widow. I don't think murder would be a very hard thing to do. I can think of worse things." The front door-bell rang, there was a slipping of bolts, and voices in the hall, the girl's (a foolish young second girl, it was Rebecca's evening out) and a gentleman's. Mrs. Munroe heard neither bell nor voices; she heard her husband's breathing. The girl knew that her mistress was in the sitting-room, and that Mr. Munroe had recently come in — that was all she knew. Nothing was more natural than that she should throw open the door of the sitting-room to Mr. Harper. He came forward with quick step and cheerful voice.

" Good evening, Mrs. Munroe. I fear I am intruding on the quiet of family life ; but I have a little item of business of some importance. Can I see your husband ? "

Mrs. Munroe was a woman of two natures —

one was made up of fierce, strong pride. She sprang to her feet, her first impulse, to take Mr. Harper by the shoulders and thrust him from the room. Anyone but him! Oh, for *that* man to know the depths to which she had fallen, was the bitterness of horror. Her second thought was the utter impossibility of keeping secret their dreadful condition and the utter incongruity of his errand. She laughed in his face that fearful laugh.

"It is an infinite pity to have disturbed such delightful family communion as ours. I hardly know how to forgive you. Oh, yes, you can see my husband. I presume he will be very happy to discuss *important* business with you. There he is."

All this in almost a moment of time, and she pointed her scornful finger at the sleeping man. Mr. Harper wheeled in bewilderment, following the pointing finger. One glance at Mr. Munroe's face and dress and position, and he comprehended the situation. Then an almost infinite pity took possession of him, and an almost equal embarrassment — what to do, what to say, rather, what *not* to say. He stood in utter silence and dismay until a glance at an opposite mirror, in which was reflected Mrs. Munroe's stony face, recalled to him the necessity for doing something. He turned to her.

"Mrs. Munroe, nothing can justify my intru·
sion upon you, but the hope that I can do something for you. In what way can I best help
you?"

"I want no help," she said, with hardness in
her voice. "What help is there for me?"

"May I bring some one to you,—your brother
or sisters?"

Again Mrs. Munroe laughed.

"My brother!" she said, in an utterly scornful tone; "he is probably in the same delightful
condition. They have been on a *pleasure* excur-
sion, you understand. As for my sisters, they
are the last persons on the face of the earth that
I want to see. No, thank you, my husband is my
legal protector. I must look to him for help."

Mr. Harper actually shivered.

"Don't," he said, in a pleading tone. "It is a
bitter trial, but don't receive it in this way; you
are only making the burden heavier. May I help
him to his room, and make him comfortable?"

"No," she said, fiercely, "you may not. Comfortable! What does it matter?"

"But what are you going to do?"

"Nothing; let him finish his nap. I hope he
will waken in a refreshed state of mind."

"But, dear madam, he is your *husband*."

"I know it," she said, in a husky voice. "God
pity me."

17

Still Mr. Harper stood irresolute. To leave her in loneliness, and in such a state of heart, seemed impossible; to remain longer with the insulted wife and the drunken husband, seemed equally impossible.

"May 1 not go for your father?" he asked, with a sudden hope in his heart.

Mrs. Munroe's lip quivered, but she resolutely shook her head.

"Not for the world. This would *kill* my father; besides — he warned me. No, Mr. Harper, I am utterly alone."

"Never that," he said, earnestly. "You have the unfailing, ever-present Friend, the One who knows your sorrow. May I not beseech you to carry this burden to him?"

"I never understood such talk," she said, bitterly. "It never comforted me in the least — it doesn't now. God has everything in his hands; he can control the world. Why does he permit such burdens to come upon people? Why does he allow my husband to make a beast of himself? Would *you* allow it, if you could help it? and are *you* more humane than God?"

Mr. Harper hesitated — it was such a strange time for the discussion of theological questions.

"Dear madam," he said, speaking very gently, "when you accepted Christ as your Friend, did you not engage to take *some* things on trust, — to believe that what *you* could not *see*, was yet clear to the eye and the heart of your Saviour, and that he ruled?"

"No," she said, passionately, "I don't see it at all; it seems to me exactly as though Satan ruled. Who but he could make such an object of my husband as that? And if his plans succeed, instead of God's, which is the greater?"

"They will not succeed," he said, quietly, "unless you let them. God is on your side, he will surely deliver you if you trust in him; if you turn from him how *can* he help you?"

She had quieted again, but answered him sullenly,—

"I know very well he needn't have made a brute of himself unless he had chosen; but having chosen to do so, I don't see how I can help it."

"Have you *tried* to help it?" he asked, eagerly. "Mrs. Munroe, your husband is not a Christian, but he has a Christian wife. God has put a powerful weapon into your hands; do you use it to the utmost?"

"I suppose you mean do I pray for him?" she said, coldly. "Why, yes; of course I pray for my husband; but you see how much good it has done thus far. There is something besides praying to be done in this world."

"That is painfully true. I wonder if you and I are doing our very utmost. Until we are, we

should not dare lay the unfinished work upon God.
Mrs. Munroe, may I not go for your Cousin
Faith ? "

Mrs. Munroe shivered visibly.

" Not for the world," she said, with energy.
" She is the last person that I want to see tri-
umphing over my downfall.   I will have no one;
and if you please, Mr. Harper, I will not detain
you longer.   Some things are better endured
alone."

" Alone with God," he said, gently ; and then
the bell pealed through the house again.   Mrs.
Munroe roused suddenly to outside life.

" Mr. Harper, I beg you to spare me from
seeing any one.   Say anything — we are sick,
dying, anything you like ; only don't let *any one*
into this house."

More and more bewildered by the strangeness
of his position, Mr. Harper moved promptly to
ward the hall ; but the watchful servant had pre-
ceded him, and was admitting Ermina and Maria
Randolph.

" Good evening," he said, going toward them.
" Miss Randolph, you are fortunately just the
person whom I wish to see in regard to a little
business matter.   Will you both oblige me by
stepping into the parlor a moment?   That will
do," he added to the girl as she turned on a flood
of light.

"Where is Helen?" asked Ermina, wonderingly, as Mr. Harper closed the door after the retreating servant.

He turned toward her.

"She is in trouble," he said, briefly; "and, I am afraid, does not want to see even you."

"That would be an extraordinary state of mind —" Maria began, lightly, but her sister interrupted her.

"Has Horace come home? — is he —" Then she stopped.

Mr. Harper bowed in utter silence.

"Oh, poor Helen!" Ermina said; but Maria's voice had no tenderness.

"She was warned," she said, hoarsely. "She must have known what would come. It is not as hard for her as it is for father, with his only son. Mr. Harper, *do* you know anything about our brother Tom? He and Horace were together."

Mr. Harper did not know,— judging from Mr. Munroe's state, he could only surmise. He sat down on a sofa opposite to the one whereon Ermina had sunken when she made her one exclamation. What a white, frightened face she had! Maria noticed it, and her own seemed to grow harder.

"What a delightful world it is!" she said, in great bitterness. "So much sunshine and happiness. Everything moves along so comfortably. I wonder there *are* any infidels."

"Hush!" said Mr. Harper, with stern dignity. "For the miseries that people bring upon themselves it is weak and wicked to blame God."

She turned toward him.

"Perhaps my father brought *his* troubles upon himself," she said, fiercely. "The best and tenderest man on earth; unselfish, and patient, and long-suffering. Don't you dare to say that my father's trials are of his own making."

Mr. Harper's voice was less severe, but it was still firm.

"Your father is God's own child, and is safe in his hands. I am sure that he trusts *him*, and his daughter should do no less. Your father would not like to hear you call in question his Maker's work."

"I am doing nothing of the sort, Mr. Harper. I am simply enraged at some of his subjects. At you and Ermina, for instance, who profess to have such unbounded faith in prayer. And what do you accomplish by it? Oh, I wish *I* knew how to pray! I would pray this sum of all horrors out of the world."

Something in her earnest words surprised and silenced Mr. Harper; and Ermina said, impulsively,—

"I wish she did; she was always the one to *accomplish* in our family. The rest of us *talk* — Maria *does* it."

"There is great force in what your sister has just said," Mr. Harper answered, addressing Ermina, as she had him. "I do not wonder that people are surprised at our apparent inconsistencies. It is true that we accomplish very little with our mighty weapon; but it is not strange. A weapon cannot be expected to accomplish anything unless it is used. We all desire to do something for your sister and your brothers. Let us do the only thing that we *can* do. Let us pray. Miss Maria, I ask you to begin with us the lesson that you said you wished you knew."

Then the three knelt down, and Mr. Harper prayed. All three of these people had been acting somewhat unlike their usual selves. Both the sisters lived a life of repression, so far as their inner selves were concerned. Both had been moved to speak a sentence or two from their hearts. Mr. Harper was not given to harshness, but his sense of reverence had been rudely shocked, and his voice had responded. Their present position together, kneeling in the parlor of their sister's house, was certainly not an ordinary one, and a less intensely-in-earnest party might have wondered what they would be likely to do next.

They slipped however apparently without jar into their ordinary selves.

" Would we better go in and see Helen ?" Ermina asked her sister as they arose, and Maria answered, in her usual composed tone,—

" No. We can do no good, and of course she don't want to see us. Let's go home."

" Then I will walk over with you," Mr. Harper said. " I am coming back here to make Mr. Munroe comfortable, and if you are needed for anything will let you know."

As he left them at their own door he said,—

" Miss Maria, won't you pray for your brother Tom, to-night ?"

" No," said Maria, with great seriousness. " But I will ask Faith Halsted to do so. That will be much more to the point."

CHAPTER XXI.

A PUZZLING DISCUSSION.

THE kitchen was as usual the scene of conflict. Maria was shelling peas. Faith, in the doorway, tried to help; but everybody who has ever undertaken to "help" at anything, and at the same time look after the movements of a boy a year and a half old, knows just how much such help amounts to. Mrs. Munroe did not even try. She stood leaning against the pillar of the side piazza, her cool blue and white dress fluttering in the summer wind, her head resting just where a bright morning-glory touched her ear. She looked as if trial and pain and care had nothing in common with her. Maria was talking, of course.

"It is a great nuisance, anyway," she was saying. "I'm sorry I joined. I'm sure I don't know why I did, unless it was because father had a notion that my duty lay in that direction. I can't see where duty can consist in making scarlet dogs with square noses and yellow mouths. I always hated worsted dogs, anyway."

Faith laughed merrily. Maria's views of people and things were very funny to her, but Mrs. Munroe looked dignified.

"That is a very silly way to talk," she said, solemnly. "Why *wouldn't* it be your duty to help sustain the church society? You attend church there, and Ermina is a member. Of course part of the work ought to fall on you. I'm sure you needn't make worsted cats and dogs, or worsted *anything*, unless you choose. You can make aprons or night-caps if they suit your taste better; but I think it is manifestly your duty to help sustain the society, especially when its object is to help pay a church debt."

"A church fiddlestick!" said Maria, decisively. "That makes me the maddest of any part of it. If the work was of any *earthly* importance, if they made check aprons for poor children or flannel petticoats for sick old women, I'd tolerate it, and sew all the afternoon, much as I hate it; but this meeting together every other week for a year, to make yellow pincushions and green roses, and every imaginable kind of flummery that comes under the general name of 'fancy work,' and then getting up a great big fair and charging three times as much for a thing as ought to be charged, and having three or four gambling establishments for side shows, and doing it all in the name of the church debt, when each one who works for the concern, by paying in money *half* of what she gives every year for worsted and canvas and beads and cardboard, could wipe the church debt out of existence and have no fuss about it, I don't believe in," and the strong-minded young woman shoveled the shelled peas into her pan, and swept the pods away with energy.

Faith laughed again. Maria's ideas were so queer and so jumbled. Mrs. Munroe still sustained her character for dignity.

"Oh, yes," she said, coldly. "Of *course* you know more about such matters than all the rest of the church combined. I wonder they don't come to you for advice."

"Well, now, haven't I told the truth? What are all the suppers and pin-cushions and grab-bags for? Isn't there a much easier way of raising money, if that is the object? I'll prove it to you. I'm on committee this afternoon. I worked all day yesterday baking cakes. I didn't count *my* time, nor Faith's, nor Pearly's, and they all helped, Pearly especially; but just for fun, or for my own satisfaction, I kept an account of material, eggs, flour, butter, milk, fruit, and hair-oil, as Tom calls the flavoring, and what do you think it amounted to? Just two dollars and ninety-five cents. Now suppose I save my firewood, and my time, and my apron, and give that two dollars and ninety-five cents to the society; and suppose the ones who are to make the biscuit, and furnish meat, and pickles, and cheese, and milk, and coffee, and the land knows what, do the same, wouldn't the church be richer than if we make a dozen cats and dogs this afternoon, and eat my cake and Nettie Thatcher's biscuits in the bargain."

" But you wouldn't do any such thing."

" Wouldn't do what? "

" Why, give your money. There isn't one lady in fifty would take three dollars out of her pocket and give it outright for the church debt; but any of them will make cake."

" Then it must be because we are all poor mathematicians, or fools," said Maria, with increased energy. " If our object is to pay the church debt, we can certainly do it quicker in *my* way; but if our object is to meet in the chapel and eat cake and pickles, I say let the object be distinctly stated, and don't let us make ourselves think that we are a benevolent institution when we are actually eating up money."

Faith had listened and laughed through this talk, keeping silence herself. As she brought Pearly back from a raid after the gray cat, and tied his shoes, she took up the conversation.

"That's a dreadfully one-sided argument, Maria. Mrs. Munroe, why don't you present the other side of the question?"

"Oh, I never argue with *her*," said Mrs. Munroe, with strong emphasis on the "her." "There's no sort of use in it. She has views of her own about everything earthly, and she will maintain them in spite of fate."

"That isn't so," said Maria, good-humoredly. "I am willing to be convinced, if any one will take the trouble; but you see Helen doesn't, she just says 'nonsense,' or something of that sort. Now I appeal to you, Faith. Haven't I told the truth?"

"Only part of it," Faith said. "*I* believe in sewing societies, but not for any of the reasons which you have mentioned. If they were only intended for the purpose of raising money, I should, like yourself, consider them very ludicrous inventions."

"What on earth *are* they for?"

"*I* think for the cultivation of our social qualities, for the purpose of mingling together as a church socially. There are those in every society, who would never meet, never know

each other, if it were not for the social gath-
erings."

"Then why don't they call them social tea-
parties, and not sewing societies?"

"Oh, because it is human nature — and a
very nice, commendable nature, too, I think,
to like to be doing something pleasant and
something useful at the same time. Give us
a mutual object in which to be interested;
and what is more likely to interest us than
sewing for our own church? — unless indeed
we have risen to a higher plane than that,
and are sewing for the Church of Christ. Besides, there is another point, as Helen says.
You won't give the money out-and-out, but
you are willing to give the work. People
need to be educated to systematic giving, even
if the giving is only some loaves of cake; so
that they are given regularly, at set times, a
point has been gained. Now, Maria, you said
you were ready to be convinced. Have you
been?"

"Partly and partly not," said Maria, as she
added more water to the peas. "The social
idea is a good one, and I'll think better of
the institutions hereafter for its sake; but
there's a flaw in them, as you would see if
you were going to ours this afternoon."

"Aren't you going?" asked Mrs. Munroe.

Faith shook her head.

"Pearly doesn't approve of sewing societies," she said. "I'm sorry, because I want to see Maria hunt for the flaws."

"I'll find them," Maria said, positively.

"Oh, I know you will. Flaws are the easiest things to find in the world, if you only look for them."

So Ermina and Maria went to society. Maria, as she had said, rarely went, unless she was on committee and had the work to do. Ermina rarely during these days had opportunity to go, but this chanced to be a time of less haste than usual in the sewing-room.

In the course of the afternoon Maria and Carrie Hartley sat together. Carrie was making a tidy, a pretty thing of wreaths and leaves, creations of split zephyr.

"Isn't it lovely?" she said, holding it up to view. "I am perfectly wild over fancy work; they do have such a poky old society over at the Willard Street Church. I went there yesterday with Nellie Thayer. They are making calico aprons and horrid sacks, and knitting stockings — and, oh, dear! I don't know what. They are filling a stupid box for some old fogy missionary. Shouldn't you think such a society as that would be horrid?"

"Perfectly," said Maria, solemnly. "Why

should old fogy home missionaries be sewed
for, such worthless and useless beings as they
are? Tidies and mats and cushions are what
we need in this world. Who cares for missionaries?"

Miss Carrie stared incredulously at her companion.

"Of course missionaries are useful, and all
that," she said, after a little, "and ought to
be sewed for; but then I think charity begins
at home, don't you? Now our church needs
a new carpet. I am really ashamed of the
old one, it is faded and worn considerably;
and I think we need new chairs for the pulpit.
I hate red chairs, they're in bad taste. We
ought to fix up our own church."

"Of course," Maria assented. "The idea
of supposing that those wretched home missionaries, with their stockingless feet and their
arms out at the elbows, are of more importance than our red chairs, when we ought to
have green ones, is an utter absurdity. I
don't know why we should care whether the
gospel is preached to the prairie heathens or
not, so long as we need a new carpet."

Miss Carrie laughed faintly.

"What a funny girl you are!" she said;
and presently she went to her particular friend,
Addie Wilson, and said, "You ought to have

heard the berating that Maria Randolph gave me because I said we needed a new church carpet! Isn't she a queer girl?"

That is about as correctly as things are reported in this world.

Mrs. Wheeler, the President of the society, was absent. Little Mrs. Clay, the Vice-President, was to fill her place. At five o'clock she went from one lady to another in considerable flurry, and apparently what she said to each produced some consternation.

"Oh, I can't," one lady said. "My dear Mrs. Clay, you must excuse me." "I never did such a thing in my life," murmured another. "It is quite impossible — utterly impossible. I couldn't if it were to save my life," said another.

"What in the world does she want them to do?" questioned Maria of her neighbor. "It must be something terrific; they are getting up quite a commotion."

"Why," said the neighbor, "she wants some one to read in the Bible and pray. Such an idea! Mrs. Wheeler always does it."

Maria laughed outright.

"What an excitement," she said, in mirthful sarcasm. "Every one of those ladies members of the church. I declare, I don't see but one individual besides myself who is not;

18

and they won't one of them pray for the success of their undertaking. What is the use of their knowing how? They must be dreadfully out of practice, or they wouldn't be thrown into such confusion."

And the next sentence was addressed to Maria herself by the flurried Mrs. Clay.

"My dear Miss Randolph, won't you be so kind as to lead our devotional exercises this afternoon? Mrs. Wheeler cannot be present, and it devolves upon me to supply her place. I should be *so* much obliged if you would."

"I presume you mean my sister," said Maria, coolly, inclining her head toward Ermina, who sat at her left. "She is Miss Randolph, and she is a church-member, and so is supposed to know how to pray; for myself I have never learned."

Mrs. Clay turned quickly.

"O Miss Randolph, *would* you be so kind?"

Ermina's lips were opened for a refusal. Maria's eyes were dancing with fun. Mrs. Munroe was regarding her with a vexed air; she herself had just given a somewhat ungracious refusal. Ermina had never tried to pray before any one in her life. Judging from what you know of her daily living, perhaps you can tell how much she was accustomed to daily, searching private prayers. Of course she would refuse. But there came just then, strangely enough, to her mind a sentence that Mr. Harper had let drop in her hearing but a few days before. "One reason why our friends are not converted is because we, their leaders, walk so crookedly that we keep them all the time stumbling over us." Was Maria stumbling over her? "I don't know whether I am a Christian or not," said Ermina to herself; "but I profess to be one; and whether I am or not, it can't hurt me to pray. Now I'm not naturally timid, why should I be afraid to try?" All this in a second of time; then she said to Mrs. Clay, with great composure in her voice, "I never did such a thing in my life; but I presume it won't hurt me. I'll do it." And she moved forward to where the formidable pulpit Bible awaited her. Opening it at random, and beginning to read in haste to cover her confusion, she presently found herself in the midst of words like these: "He hath not dealt with us after our sins, nor rewarded us according to our iniquities." An almost overpowering sense of the truth of this sentence came upon her. What if God *had* dealt with *her* according to her sins! "As far as the east is from the west, so far hath he removed our transgressions from us." How tender and precious and patient were the words!

She had never noticed them closely before; her heart melted over them. "Like as a father pitieth his children, so the Lord pitieth them that fear him." To one who had a father like Ermina Randolph's that verse meant a great deal. She stopped with that, feeling that *she* at least had had enough. She said, with a quiet voice, but with a tumultuous heart, "Let us pray," and felt rather than saw that the ladies were kneeling around her. On her tenth birthday Ermina had learned and recited to her father certain verses. They came back to her now. Very slowly, very solemnly, she repeated them: "Create in me a clean heart, O God; and renew a right spirit within me. Cast me not away from thy presence, and take not thy Holy Spirit from me. Restore unto me the joy of thy salvation; and uphold me with thy free spirit: *then* will I teach transgressors thy ways; and sinners shall be converted unto thee. Deliver me from bloodguiltiness, O God; thou God of my salvation; and my tongue shall sing aloud of thy righteousness." Just here she stopped. What wonderful things she had asked! What solemn things she had promised! Did she really mean them? How *dare* she say more? A solemn silence filled the house for a moment, and then with one more sentence from lips that quivered, "God forgive me and help me for Jesus' sake," she arose. Every word of her prayer had been personal. She did not notice it; she did not even take time to think of the singularity of her position; it seemed to her at the moment that there were but two beings in existence, herself and God. The buzz of conversation commenced again, but she stood apart, as one dazed. It seemed to her that she could not go back and hem the strings for that white apron; she felt as if she must go away alone and repeat those words, "Cast me not away from thy presence; and take not thy Holy Spirit from me." "If only I knew whether I had any *right* to pray at all," she said, pushing the hair back from her throbbing temples. "I surely thought I was a Christian; but I don't know, I really don't know *anything*. How fearfully solemn those sentences were!"

There had been an arrival during the Bible-reading, a tall, fair lady, in a plain black suit. She was evidently a person of some importance, for respectful and curious glances followed her as she moved to and fro. Something about her face attracted Ermina. She leaned down to her friend Nettie Thatcher and said,—

"Who is that woman with eyes?"

"With eyes!" said Nettie, laughing. "Is

there only one person in the room meriting that description?"

"*I* don't see but one. If you want anything more descriptive, she is talking with Mis. Colonel Hitchcock."

" Oh, that is Mr. Harper's sister."

About that time the lady in question said, abruptly,—

"I beg your pardon, Mrs. Hitchcock, but tell me the name of the lady who offered prayer."

CHAPTER XXII.

LIGHT.

THERE is one young lady in that society that I attended yesterday, Warren, who needs my help," said Mrs. Laport, as she stirred her coffee slowly and thoughtfully.

"Only one!" answered Mr. Harper, laughing. "I expected you to find at least a dozen."

"There were interesting faces; but this one is in trouble."

"Who is she?"

"Her name is Randolph. I did not learn much more about her. Mrs. Hitchcock, with whom I was sitting, seemed to know very little about her."

"Which of the Randolphs is she?"

"Are there two of them? I saw only this one. She led the devotional exercises."

Mr. Harper opened his eyes very wide.

"I do not know which of them it can be," he said, quickly. "Grace and Maria are neither of them Christians, and Miss Ermina — Ah, I know; it was probably their cousin, Miss Faith."

"It was Ermina," Mrs. Laport said, positively. "I remember hearing some one speak her name."

"I don't think it *could* have been," her brother answered, quite as positively. "I am sure she would never have led in devotional exercises. You have mixed the people up. It was some other young lady."

"Warren, I never mix up a face that looks just as hers did; and I want to meet her. You must take me to call."

"In the evening?"

"Why, no; you know I don't go out evenings just now."

"She is engaged during the day. She is a sewing girl."

"Is she? Then she must come to me. She can come to tea, and have a quiet little evening with me afterward; and you'll see that she gets home. Won't you, Warren?"

"I could," said Mr. Harper, quietly. "But, Louise, there are people who will think it very strange in you to single out one young lady, and invite her to tea, while you ignore all the others."

" Warren," said Mrs. Laport, as she pushed away her empty coffee cup, " I don't mean to ignore anybody; and you know I don't care for what ' they ' think about my doings. You will manage this matter for me, will you not? "

" Why, I'll try," replied Mr. Harper, as he arose. " But, Louise, you keep me in perpetual wonderment as to what out-of-the-way thing you will require of me next."

Mrs. Laport smiled as she responded, " An effort to help any one who needs help ought not to be an out-of-the-way matter."

So it came about that Ermina Randolph, standing before her mirror — the same in which Helen had so complacently surveyed herself in the lavender silk,— combed out the dark hair, while Mrs. Munroe sat by the window, with a discontented expression on her fair face. Presently she asked,—

" Ermina, how in the world did she come to invite you to tea? "

" She didn't come. It was Mr. Harper who came."

" Well — Mr. Harper, then? "

" He came on foot, I think," said Ermina, provokingly.

" Don't talk nonsense," was Mrs. Munroe's impatient remark. " You understand what I mean. How happened she to single you out for the favor? "

"I have not the honor of the lady's confidence to the degree that enables me to answer that question. All I know is that Mr. Harper invited me, in his sister's name, and I'm going if I ever get ready."

"Well, all I have to say is, don't be too sure of a good time. The old aunt will take you in from head to foot."

"Oh, didn't I tell you Mrs. Laport is boarding at the Sage House. Mr. Harper said that his sister was unwilling to add to her household."

Mrs. Munroe toyed listlessly with the curtain tassel, admiring the dainty fingers set off with brilliant jewels, but the dissatisfied expression still lingered.

"How do you happen to know so much about her affairs? Who told you?"

"Mr. Harper did."

"He seems to be very communicative. He must think you are immensely interested in what concerns them."

"It was a remarkable thing that he should tell me to come to the Sage House to tea, instead of going a mile out to his aunt's, and then add to it that his sister wouldn't allow their aunt to have any more company, and so boarded in town."

"She isn't his sister at all. She is only a half sister."

"I can't help it. He told me where she boards, if she isn't his sister. And they think as much of each other as if they were double brother and sister instead of half. Pin this ribbon, won't you, Helen? I am late, but I told them I couldn't come from my sewing until six."

"You must drag in your sewing at every possible moment. What *was* the use of saying that?"

Ermina laughed.

"I don't drag it in," she said, good humoredly. "It drags me. There is no getting away from it, either physically or mentally."

"We'll go down to the hotel table, shall we not?" Mrs. Laport asked, as the gong sounded. "Would you like it better than tea in my room?"

"Yes," said Ermina, speaking out her mind as usual. "I never took tea at a splendid hotel. I should like it."

"Everything is very pleasant about the house, and there are some very pretty ladies among the boarders. Do you like to look at pretty faces?"

"Yes," said Ermina, smiling, "I like to; but I didn't suppose it was proper to say so."

"Why in the world shouldn't you?"

"Oh, I don't know. I thought **we must**

be indifferent to beauty — superior to it, you know "

" I hope never to become so," Mrs. Laport said, laughing. " Why, dear friend, don't you suppose there will be wonderful beauty in heaven ? "

" I don't know," Ermina said, her face suddenly clouding. " I know precious little about heaven, and what I *do* know has extremely little to do with beauty. But your question in some way reminds me of what your brother said we must ask you."

" What is that ? I hope he isn't trying to puzzle me. He is very fond of that occupation."

" It is we who are puzzled — my cousin Faith and I. You were to enlighten us. It is the old question of expenditure — where necessities end and luxuries commence, and how far tastes are to be gratified ? Whether starving bodies and souls, or æsthetic tastes, are to be uppermost ? "

Mrs. Laport drew a long breath.

" It is an immense question," she said. " I don't wonder you were bewildered. I know I often am. I hardly know why Warren should have sent you to me. It is one of my puzzles. In fact, I'm right in the midst of it. I struggled over it terribly, until I suddenly discovered that what made it so strangely

Tom laughed, and sat down on a stick of wood.

complicated was, I was trying to solve it for everybody. When I stopped that, and went to work in my own little corner of it, it was still sufficiently confusing, but not nearly so bad."

Ermina looked with a steady, earnest gaze at the earnest face before her.

"I wish," she said, speaking with intense energy, "I wish I could ask you ever so many questions."

"You may. I like to ask questions myself. I'm always doing so. I give you the right to ask me any question you please."

"Then I don't think you understand what I mean. It is like this — for instance, you have a silk dress on?"

"I understand you perfectly — why don't I wear a calico instead? That is one of my bewilderments. In the first place, then, I have to go to places where people would think that I insulted them if I came in so simple a dress."

"But why *should* they? If *everybody* wore them, think of the saving!"

"I know it; but now you see you are trying to straighten other people's tangles. Everybody *won't*, and you and I can't make them. We have to take the world as we find it. So you must grant me that I thought I ought to have a nice dress. Now for the rest of the story. I made my dress something of a study. I paid a great deal for it. In the first place, I got it of Mr. Hampton. It is not fashionable to trade there. Mr. Hampton is a young man. He cannot buy largely. He hasn't an immense variety. He is struggling to do business on perfectly strict principles, which makes his progress much slower. I buy my dresses there for all these reasons. I know I have helped Mr. Hampton more in buying silk than in buying calico. Then I had it made at Kate Morgan's. She is a quiet little sewing girl, who has nice taste and conscientious principles. Nobody would trust her with their silk dresses to make. They gave her their calicoes, and calicoes are not profitable dresses to make, for the reason that being only calico, people will not pay much for having them made. I give her my silks. She does them well, and others are discovering it."

"I see," said Ermina, gravely. "There is a principle underlying it all. It is the first time I ever imagined that there could be any principle in silk dresses."

"Then there is another view of it, you know. My silk dress costs much more than a pretty cambric, but it will last much longer."

"I know. But if such expensive materials *could* be utterly banished, wouldn't there be a saving of money?"

"I don't feel quite sure, even of that, because as soon as you make it fashionable *not*
to wear silk and poplin, and take up cambrics
and muslins, *they* immediately become the fashionable, and so the expensive goods. *That*
belongs to other people's part of the confusion,
the part which we cannot control. And now,
my dear, the second gong is sounding. We
must go down to tea. I shall be ready for
the other questions when we return."

"I don't need to ask them," Ermina said,
smiling. "I can pick it out for myself. I
see it is a regular geometrical problem, but
based on a real foundation, and I can study
it out. Only this — is there — or do you arrange all your expenses in the same way?"

"I try to. Bonnets are to be bought of
those who are trying to make honest, honor-
able bonnets, and who are meeting with difficulties and reverses. There are such people
everywhere, if only you will take the trouble
to look for them."

"But, Mrs. Laport, I couldn't work from your
standpoint. I haven't the money."

"It is not my standpoint that you *ought* to
work from, my friend. You have a foothold,
and should have an outlook of your own. Two
persons hardly ever commenced at the same
point to work out an intricate pattern in em-

broidery, but the work is the same when completed. Your motto and mine, and the motto of all Christ's followers, is alike, 'Whatsoever ye do, do all to the glory of God.' "

"I don't see how my long and short seams that I am perpetually making on a sewing machine can glorify God, I'm sure," Ermina said, somewhat moodily, as she followed her hostess down the long winding stairs.

"Don't you?" Mrs. Laport said, smiling back at her from the first landing. "If you are careful that the machine skips no stitches, leaves no treacherous ends of thread, and is, in short, as perfect in its work as you can make it, do you not prove that you are a conscientious worker, and is not a *proven*, conscientious Christian glorifying God in the spot where he has placed her?"

Ermina laughed.

"That would make glorified work of the very sweeping and dusting and dish-washing of life, if only one could feel it," she said, trying to speak lightly; but her eyes shone a little as she added, in a softened voice, "It is beautiful theory, anyhow."

"It is *more* than theory," Mrs. Laport said, emphatically. "It is *Bible*. 'Do *all* to the glory of God.' There *must* be a way to make the glory."

This was not the most important conversation that occurred during that evening. The talk which had the most to do with Ermina's life during all her future, had its summing up in a few sentences which Mr. Harper spoke as he walked with her down the brightly lighted streets of the city.

"Did you receive any enlightenment in regard to the question which puzzled you when I met you down town?" he asked; and Ermina was prompt with her answer.

"On that and on many other questions. Yes, there is light, but it doesn't light me. Such talk is utterly new to me. I never knew that Christianity meant so much. I know it means nothing of the kind to me, so I cannot be a Christian at all."

Unconsciously to herself, perhaps, Ermina had been hiding behind this shadow, feeling that somehow it lessened the weight of pain and responsibility. If such living was Christianity, why, then it could not be that she was a Christian; if she were *not*, why, then she could not be expected to live according to the Christian rule; but she had been a professor of religion for ten years; people thought of *course* she was a Christian. She expected Mr. Harper to say something of the sort, and she was prepared to combat his words, to prove to him that such living as hers

19

could not be called by that honored name; and then she hoped and believed that he would assure her that there were different degrees of attainment in the Christian life, that all could not be expected to live alike, and so soothe the pain and unrest of her weary life. She was not prepared for the quiet, gentle, penetrating question,—

"Do you *not* wish to be?"

How simple the question was, and yet how strangely solemn! *Did she?* She felt the thrill of her own repeated query in every nerve. Oh, she certainly *did*—wished it so much that she wanted the privilege of clinging to the miserable little rag of hope that she had.

"You know if you do," he said, not waiting for her audible answer, "the way is *so* simple and plain before you; in one sense it is of very little consequence whether you were a Christian yesterday or not; the important point is, will you be one to-night?"

"To-night?" she repeated. How strangely that narrowed one down. Why didn't he say to-morrow?—that was so near at hand, and yet it gave one a breathing space. He answered the thought embodied in the tones of her voice.

"Yes, to-night, because to-morrow is not yours. It is a very commonplace expression, yet did you ever think how true it was? Did you ever think of the many commonplace, apparent trifles around you, either of which might cause your death in a moment? I sometimes think of them, and try to calculate their number, until I am amazed that we escape them and live on. Now if you really are uncertain as to whether the question between you and God is unsettled, it is folly in you to be unafraid of death. You are a reasonable being, you have perceptive faculties, therefore with the momentous question of life unsettled, of course you are afraid to go away from life. If there were no other motive to prompt you, this reasonable fear of being called before you are ready to answer should lead you to determine the question to-night. Will you?"

They stood on the doorstep now, and Ermina Randolph will never forget the throbs of her heart as she waited trying to answer the question to her own heart. Her intense, positive nature shrank from committals of any sort. He varied the question a little.

"Will you tell me your decision the next time I meet you?—and neither of us are able to tell so simple a thing about our lives as when or where that will be."

The question seemed almost as hard to answer as the other; but she answered it after a little with a steady, resolute ring in her voice,—

"Yes, I will."

CHAPTER XXIII.

A DISCUSSION CLOSED.

HERE is no use in continuing this discussion, Mr. Munroe. I am quite decided as to my views."

"Discussion!" repeated Mr. Munroe,
speaking a little crossly; his fine temper
was being somewhat injured by the atmosphere
of his home life. "It might as well be continued on that subject as any other. We live in
a state of discussion from week to week."

"I am quite willing to discontinue it whenever it shall please you to give me a chance;
but as for living in this disgusting fashion any
longer I simply am not going to do it. I did
not promise to marry a drunkard, and I have
no intention of being a drunkard's wife."

They were at the tea-table, and Mr. Munroe set down his cup with a ring, and spoke
sternly,—

"It would puzzle me, Helen, to tell what you *did* marry me for. It couldn't have been for love, though your promises were solemn enough; but I suppose they amount to about as much as other promises made in church. I'll be hanged if you ever gave me reason to think you wasted such a commodity as *love* on me. If you wanted my money instead of me, why, I'm sure I give you enough of that. Now why can't you be content and let a fellow alone?"

"Because, as I said before, whatever other foolish thing I may have done, I did not marry a drunkard, and I *will not* be a drunkard's wife. I hope you understand me."

"I have heard you talk often enough to understand you. You certainly do not obscure your meaning with tender words. I'm not sure but it would be policy to be a drunkard out-and-out; at least I couldn't be expected to listen to discussions."

"Suppose you try it," Mrs. Munroe said, with flashing eyes, but perfect composure in her voice. "Try it *twice* more, and see how quickly I will leave your establishment to take care of itself. I'm thankful that I have a home and a father."

Mr. Munroe arose suddenly; his wife's composed words seemed to sting his heart.

"Perhaps *you* would like to try it," he said, angrily. "I'm not sure that you would care, provided I had to keep your purse full. I don't know but we would both be happier. This is a villainous sort of life to live anyhow."

"I'll move across the street to live, if you think you will find it more agreeable; and I shall in any case if you come home once more in the state that you were last night."

"Oh, come, Helen, don't talk to a fellow that way. It was mean treatment, and I'm ashamed of it. I told you so at the time. I'm trying hard enough to keep away from the cursed temptation, but I need your help. I married *you*, Helen, because I loved you, and I need you. This is my time of trial. You needn't think I am not struggling, for I am. You will help me?"

A very pleading sound his voice had, but the world had gone awry with his wife that day; the dressmaker had failed in making a good fit, and so injured an elegant dress which couldn't be matched; so she answered the pleading voice still coldly.

"I can only say that it is a very strange sort of love that exhibits itself in coming home in an idiotic, disgusting condition of mind and body. I would advise you not to repeat an experiment of that kind — it might be once too often."

"Then I'll go and try it." He spoke angrily, all the gentleness, all the pleading, gone out of his voice; and immediately he went out, banging the door after him.

It might have been two hours afterward, it might have been longer — Mrs. Munroe never knew quite what time it was,— that there was a sound of subdued voices in the hall, a kind of suppressed confusion. She stepped at once to the door and met Mr. Harper; behind him were men and a burden. Mr. Harper pressed forward to intercept her step and words, but she had nursed herself into still greater rage during the intervening hours, and Mr. Harper's presence only served to anger her still more.

"You need not bring him here," she said, losing all self-control. "As long as I am mistress of this house, it shall not harbor drunken men. I warned him of the consequences. Carry him around the corner to his father's; let him see the beautiful son he has brought up."

Her eyes were blazing with excitement, and her whole manner was indicative of one who had lost all self-control. To Mr. Harper it was evident that prompt and decisive measures were necessary. His voice sounded almost stern in his effort at self-control.

"Mrs. Munroe, you mistake. Your husband is dead."

What a sudden, *terrible* sentence! She reeled, and would have fallen but for his supporting arm. He pushed open the parlor door, and helped her in, motioning at the same time to the men to move forward with their burden.

Once in the parlor Mrs. Munroe neither screamed nor fainted. She looked frightened and shocked, but not, as Mr. Harper had expected, utterly overwhelmed. She sank down in the nearest chair, and spoke quickly.

"What do you mean? Is he really dead? What is the matter? What happened?"

"It is quite hopeless," Mr. Harper said, averting his eyes that he might not intrude upon her grief. "He went into Harter's about an hour ago. Your brother said he was in a state of great excitement, had been drinking, and drank again. From there he went back to his own store, and Thomson, feeling alarmed about him, accompanied him. He acted strangely, put his hands to his head, said he guessed he had done it this time, and more, too, referring, your brother thought, to some transaction that troubled him. Suddenly, in passing from the store to the office, he fell in what we thought was a fainting fit, but it proved to be congestion, caused by some unknown excitement and — and liquor."

Mr. Harper judged it right to speak the whole truth even then. He added but a sentence. "He breathed but a few times, and did not speak at all; before a physician reached us he was dead."

"Dead!" Mrs. Munroe repeated, as if in bewilderment. "Why, that isn't possible! It is only a little while since he went out perfectly well, and I said — O God, forgive me! I wish I had said anything but that."

Mr. Harper stood in silence, doubtful what next to do or say.

Mrs. Munroe sat silent. If he could have looked at her thoughts they would have read thus: "How dreadful it is! Then I am a widow, and I have been married so short a time. I wonder what I shall do? I suppose I shall have to go home; that's what I said to him. I wish I hadn't said that. I *won't* go home. I couldn't leave all my nice things and live in that wretched, poky old house again. I'm Mrs. Munroe, and I belong here. I shall stay, and have some one live with me; but how strange it will seem, and how dreadful! I'm young to be a widow. I shall have to put on black again, and I've had it off so short a time. Widows wear very deep mourning; black is very becoming to me, but it is very sad to have to wear it."

And this was all that Mrs. Munroe knew about being a widow. Do you think that Mr. Harper would have stood regarding her with such pitiful eyes if he could have read those thoughts? I tell you the pity would have been doubled, yea, trebled. To be a widow, when that word expresses all the unutterable, voiceless agony of a soul to whom life seems to have gone out in the blackness of darkness, is pitiful. But to be a widow, and to have the widowed heart know absolutely nothing of the blessed love that brightens all the past, and lights up the gloom of the future, that is bitterness indeed. But Mrs. Munroe did not know it; perhaps this but increased the weight of pity that a strong, true heart would feel for her. She broke the silence suddenly, looking up at Mr. Harper as she spoke,—

"How strangely *you* are mixed up with my life."

It seemed such a strange thing to say at this time; it embarrassed him, he hardly knew why.

"I was in the store at the time," he answered, in a low, constrained voice. "Mrs. Munroe what are your commands? What can I do first?"

Actually the worst part of this widow's trial was yet to come. It was revealed to her by Tom, who seemed to be her evil genius; she sat crouched among the pillows of her lounge, a light shawl thrown around her, and occasionally she shivered, not from cold, but with excitement and pain. In the next room her husband lay in his coffin.

"How do you know all this?" she said to Tom, suppressed excitement in her voice.

"From excellent authority; your respected father-in-law took the trouble to enlighten me."

"And he said everything was gone?"

"Everything belonging to Horace, and a great deal that belonged to his father. You know the business was left very much to Horace, and his father says that he has not been in a condition to attend to business for some time."

"Thanks to you," she said, with flashing eyes. "Horace was always running down to take a social glass with *you*."

But that his heart was really pitiful for her, Tom could have laughed; the idea of him leading Horace Munroe astray!

"Helen, that is pretty hard on a fellow," he said, half beseechingly. "I could tell you some solemn truths, if it would do any good."

"I don't want to hear your truths, nor anything else. I don't believe a word of all this. I'm not going to give up my house, and go to live with *them*, and be ordered about by Mrs. Munroe; they needn't expect it."

"They don't; that was part of my express direction to explain to you that the family were so situated it would be impossible to receive you

there, and as it was equally impossible for you to
stay here, your only alternative would be to go
home."

" And what am I to live on, I should like to
know ? "

" I ventured to make a similar inquiry, and he
assured me he would do all that he could for
you, but it would be ⁃   ⁃ necessary for you, as
well as for themselve⁃   practise the most rigid
economy." If there ⁃   ⁃ two words in the
English language that   ⁃ Munroe *hated,* they
were those two, " rigi⁃   omy."

" I don't believe a word of it," she said again,
more sharply than before. " Why need you come
here with your croaking? You might at least
have waited until my husband was buried ; he
was *so* good to me ; he was the only friend I
ever had."

Part of this sentence angered Tom, part of it
touched him ; his answer was prompted by a
mixture of both feelings.

" It was not a task I coveted, that of coming
to you with my croaking ; but Mr. Munroe foolishly enough imagined me to be the proper person
to break the tidings to you, and he was particular
enough in having it done before he met you ; he
said he considered it wiser for all parties. He is
not much like our father, and, Helen, the trouble
is heavy enough, but you have friends left and a
home to go to."

"Such a home as that is!" and Mrs. Munroe's lip curled scornfully. "There is a great contrast between that home and this one. I wonder if you think I can ever be content to come down to that sort of life again?"

"It is better than nothing," Tom said, vexed again. "I should prefer it to starvation, and I shouldn't wonder if you would be prevailed upon to take up with it."

Mrs. Munroe turned her head wearily toward the wall.

"I shall have to take up with anything or nothing," she said, in a heavy, dreary tone. "I have lost my friend, my one friend." And then Tom's heart ached for her again; he had a great longing to comfort her.

"There are other things beside this life," he began, awkwardly. "Other hopes and friendships, I suppose. I should think they might be a comfort at such a time."

His sister moved restlessly on her couch.

"*Don't* talk of what you know nothing about," she said, impatiently. "I don't believe in that sort of talk, anyway."

"What sort *do* you believe in?" he asked, coolly, his sympathy fast oozing away.

"No sort that comes from you. I wish you would go home."

"I'm going. I'm glad to have been able to

see how beautifully religion sustains and upholds
people in time of trial. I've heard considerable
about it, but I never realized it as forcibly as I
do now," and Tom Randolph actually went
down the stairs whistling! Maria appeared to
him from one of the rooms below, looking re-
proving volumes.

"It's not quite the thing, I admit," he said, in
answer to her look. "But a fellow sometimes
whistles when, but for education and principle
and all that, he might swear. Maria, Helen has
got to come home to live. Now, you whistle if
you can."

"Home!" Maria said, in undisguised dismay.
"What for?"

"The Munroe property has gone up — Horace's
part of it, anyway; and old Munroe says the
whole is going. That is all moonshine, though.
But they don't feel any too comfortable toward
her. They think it is her fault that he went to
the mischief so fast."

"O Tom! you didn't tell Helen they said so?"

"It's not very likely; though I'll admit that I
was horribly tempted."

"Tom, what in the world shall we do?" Maria
said, going back to the astounding and painful
revelation. "I thought she would live on here,
and perhaps take Grace to live with her. Grace
is the only one of us who can't *possibly* earn her

own living. If worse comes to worse, *I could* hoe
potatoes, but what Grace could do puzzles me;
and now that planning is over with. What shall
we do?"

"Whistle," said Tom, philosophically. "That
is all there is left to do. She's *got* to come, anyhow. Don't you feel the force of the elevating
and consolatory influences of religion that they
tell about? I realize it more and more."

"There's Faith," Maria said, thoughtfully.

"Bah! life goes as smooth with her as a
summer day. What has she to be consoled
about?"

"But she has lost all her friends, you know.
No one left but Pearly."

"Yes, and she had hysterics every day for a
month, I presume; they are just the sort to get
over it quickly."

"Well, there's father.

"Yes," he said, "there's father — that's true.
It's a puzzling world."

All the proprieties were observed in Mr. Munroe's funeral. No one certainly would have
imagined that the firm were on the eve of failure,
from the amount of money lavished on the quiet,
senseless clay and its belongings. His widow
was shrouded in bombazine and crape of the
finest texture, and everything was becomingly
solemn and sombre.

Ermina stood on the doorstep, waiting her turn to enter the carriage. There was some delay. Their father had been the one on whom the widow was to depend for support; but his strength at the last moment had proved too slight for the occasion — Mr. Randolph was fast dropping into invalidism — and Tom had been summoned hurriedly from Ermina's side to attend his eldest sister. During the delay occasioned by the change of programme, Mr. Harper came from the hall and stood for a moment beside Ermina. Instantly she remembered what his last words had been to her. How little either had imagined where they might meet. She wondered if he remembered it. Even as she wondered he bent slightly toward her, and spoke low

"Is the decision made?"

"It is," she said, firmly. "It is *body* and soul this time."

CHAPTER XXIV.

THEOLOGY IN THE KITCHEN.

ERMINA RANDOLPH curled herself into as much of a heap as she could, and placed a cushion for her head. It was Ermina's nature to make herself comfortable, if the thing were possible. She was in Faith's room, making her and baby a little visit. It was one of those cool evenings when grown-up people consider it their duty to shiver around the house with little shawls over their shoulders, and feel it a positive luxury to have a baby in the house, to furnish an excuse for making up a cheery blaze of fire. Pearly, on the floor, was cooing over the firelight shadows, and Faith sat very near the stove to shield the grasping hands from snatching at the brightness.

"Doesn't it go right?" she said, in answer to Ermina's long-drawn sigh.

"Not very," Ermina said, ending the sigh with a little laugh. "Things look mixed, and life seems bewildering."

"It has its bewildering side, I'll admit," Faith said; "but, after all, that is generally because we want to admire the design before it is finished. What is the superlative of your troubles?"

"Why," Ermina said, laughing, "it has none, I guess. That is one of my troubles. A real, definite, tangible superlative would be encouraging; but pin pricks and mosquito bites seem so insignificant in themselves; yet, after all, no one enjoys being pricked or bitten."

"Considering myself the pin that does the pricking, who or what is the mosquito?"

"You a pin! I fancy you might prick, though, if you really wanted to. I don't think you are one of the softly people; but Helen, now, is a real mosquito. Did you really ever see any one who had more talent than she has for making herself miserable?"

"I should think it would require a great deal of grace to endure some things."

"Which is what I haven't," Ermina said, gravely and sadly. "My trouble *has* a superlative after all. I'm just a baby in the Christian life· just groping and feeling my way, when I might be walking firmly on high ground. I've wasted years and years."

"I know. The thought is a sad one, and a solemn one; yet I think perhaps Paul meant that, too, when he said, "Forgetting the things that are behind." I suppose he made failures, but he thought that Christ's blood was powerful enough to atone for even failures, and his love strong enough to forgive them. I don't imagine that Paul kept looking back and sighing over them after Christ had forgiven them. Do you?"

"I suppose not. Yet, after all, it doesn't seem quite the thing to do — I mean for me. I suppose it was all right enough in Paul — it was of course — for he was inspired; but for me, I don't know but past shortcomings ought to be kept before me to keep me humble."

"But not to hinder you," Faith said, quickly. "When Satan begins to use past shortcomings as a chain by which to fetter our thoughts to ourselves, then it is time to forget them. Do you think Paul's inspiration was only for himself? I think God looked ahead and said, 'There are Faith Halstead and Ermina Randolph, they will need the same kind of warning, or explanation, or comfort that Paul does. I will have it written out for them."

Ermina sat erect, letting the cushions drop heedlessly to the floor.

"*Does* the Bible seem like that to you?" she said, with eager eyes. "I wish it did to me. I mean to make it read so. Actually written for me! It is pleasant, but very queer."

"I don't see why," Faith said, stoutly. "Of course it was written for you. Why, the very hairs of your head are numbered, the least little event in life planned for your good. Is that any less wonderful than that God thought of your needs when he directed certain words to be handed down to you?"

Ermina looked thoughtfully at her cousin and spoke absently, "Your Bible is like Mr. Harper's!"

"I dare say, and like yours and Helen's and every one's, if only we will not try to make it read Hebrew when it wants to read plain English. Is there anything unusual about his Bible?"

Only that, as you say, it seems to read for *him*, and not for Paul and Peter only; he has strange ideas; he was speaking of his friends in heaven, and I ventured to ask him a question that has puzzled me ever so much, as to how a husband, for instance, could be entirely blissfully happy in heaven, while his wife was waiting in loneliness and weariness on earth."

" What did he say ? " Faith asked, speaking in lower tones and shading her eyes with her hand, for here was her weak spot in the chain; this seemed hard to her who had all her friends in heaven and missed them sorely and sadly.

" He said I had forgotten the force of that one word ' eternity;' that we measured time by comparison. If my friend were to spend a month with me, an hour given to some one else would seem a very trifle; the nearest and dearest friends you know can be separated for several months, and while they, of course, miss each other, they can still enjoy the life around them and be happy in the thought of the coming together; he spoke of that; he told me of his sister going to Europe; of how much she missed him, yet of how much she enjoyed her journey, and what delightful letters she wrote him concerning it; then he said his mother had been twenty years in heaven, but he thought that eternity was so long, *so long*, in comparison with twenty years; that the years dwindled into hours, and that she, looking forward over perhaps twenty years more of separation, said, ' Only a day or two more and my son will come.' "

" I see," Faith said, still with shaded eyes, and a voice a little husky. " A year is only a half hour in heaven. I had not thought of it in just that light."

Ermina rose up from her cushions. " Well," she said, " I've had my crumb of help and comfort; I'll go now to my sewing. I brought Mrs. Elwood's dress home to baste eleven ruffles on the front breadth."

"I got my crumb, too," Faith said, looking up brightly. "So you see we had an exchange of loaves."

Maria was the next caller. She sat on the floor, squarely before the fire. Maria never took the time to put herself into places of great comfort.

"What a solemn face!" Faith said, gayly. " Was the cake heavy?"

" No, but the biscuit was sour."

" Why, I didn't discover it."

" They were; just a trifle, but enough to evidence their relationship to this totally depraved world. I wonder that any one has difficulty in accepting the doctrine of total depravity. Housekeepers certainly ought to believe in it; the way apple sauce works, and bread molds, and milk sours, and butter grows strong, is bewildering and distracting, to say nothing of the way in which the ants march into the sugar, and wretched big and little flies pounce upon and devour everything they can touch their feet to, and dust and cobwebs poke themselves in everywhere. I'm sick of the world."

Faith's laugh rang out merrily. "What a solemn procession of troubles! that is kitchen depravity, I think, flies and bugs and cobwebs and mold, but no humanity."

"Humanity! plenty of it. There is evidence enough of humanity in Helen to convince me that we all belong to that miserable old Eve who had to please herself, whatever the consequences. I hope I shan't have to be on friendly terms with her, for I know I should twit her about that apple, if it *was* an apple; it is quite as likely to have been a lemon for all I know to the contrary. Things and people everywhere seem awry, and that is the whole of it. I can't help thinking I could have made a better world myself."

"That *isn't* the whole of it, and that is just where you and I make mistakes; it is only a little tiny corner, and the rest of it we can't see at all. Take care, Pearly! No, no, Pearly musn't touch. You can see how wise he thinks he is; the blaze of the fire is beautiful, and he is determined to have it in his hand. He thinks I am a cruel old ogre, keeping him from happiness. I have tried all the evening to convince him that I knew more about it than he did, and I have been wondering whether I shouldn't have to let him burn his poor precious little hand, just a tiny bit, to convince him that there is danger there."

"I see the application in part," Maria said, gloomily. "Only I was talking about flies and bugs—not a sign of a bright blaze do I see."

"And I was talking of the ignorance of both of you," Faith answered, merrily. "You neither of you see but an inch ahead, and you think you see and know all about it. You both think you could manage things better for yourself if you could be let alone."

"What do you suppose is to become of Tom?" Maria asked the question in the same half-petulant, half-gloomy tone in which she had all the time been talking. The transition evidently did not seem so striking to her as it did to Faith. "Do you really suppose he is going to be a drunkard? He is pretty nearly that now by spells; but I mean do you actually think he is going to sink down to that hopelessly?"

Faith's face grew grave and her voice was serious.

"No," she said, firmly, "I don't. I can't think any such thing. I believe he is to be rescued."

"How?"

"I don,t know; God knows, and I have no doubt is preparing the way. Maria, I don't know but he sees that he will have to let Tom burn his hand."

Maria looked up quickly.

"You mean some heavy pain. Through whom could it come? through father?" and she shivered. "I don't want that; it seems to to me that God might make him learn some other way."

"I can't make Pearly learn," Faith said, gently. "I have to sit between him and the fire, and I can't always do that; sometimes I shall have to be moving about the room; it will be necessary for him to learn that there is danger."

"But, Faith, *you* are not God. He surely has ways."

"I think so, and warning of danger is one of his ways."

"Horace's death might have served for the warning one would think. It was sudden and sad enough; but then Tom doesn't attribute that so much to liquor as he does to Helen. Well, I don't know how it will end; but it *does* seem hard that when father has but one son he must be a terror and a misery to him instead of a comfort."

They sat in silence for a little, except for the soft cooing between Faith and Pearly as she changed his white robe for his "sleepy dress," and cuddled the loving little head on her shoulder. When his night-lullaby had been sung and she had laid him among the pillows, she came back to the girl sitting bolt upright, with folded arms, staring into the firelight.

"I should think you would want to pray for him," she said, slipping down beside her.

"What's the use?" Maria answered, coldly. "I never could see that praying did any good. Father has been praying for him ever since he was born. I hear him sometimes at night. You and I couldn't resist such prayers, but God can. What does it all amount to?"

"I don't know, nor do you," Faith said, speaking almost sternly. "And if I were you I wouldn't dare to estimate what he might have been without those prayers."

"But what are you going to do about the *answer?* I tell you, he prays half the night sometimes for Tom's conversion, whatever *that* may mean. Anyway it means something that he *isn't.* What can you say to that?"

"Why, there is plenty to say. In the first place, Tom is still living. There is no proof that God doesn't intend to answer that prayer; and there *will not* be until he dies unconverted."

"Why doesn't he answer it then?"

"I don't know. Suppose you ask him?"

In spite of the daring way in which she had herself been talking, Maria looked a little startled over this sentence.

" I'm sure I don't see why you shouldn't," Faith said. " You like consistency, and you are quick to detect inconsistencies in other people. Does it never occur to you as strange, that one who professes so great interest in Tom, and anxiety for him, should never make any attempt to interest the Saviour in his behalf? It *might* do good, you know, and you must be certain that it could do no harm."

" There wouldn't be much faith about that kind of praying I should think. I thought faith was an important item in prayer? "

" There would be as much faith as you seem to possess, and it is possible that the attempt at prayer might increase your faith."

" I don't see *how* praying can do any good, and never did see. When things are pre-arranged for ages, what difference does it make whether I pray or not? How *can* it make any difference? "

" *I* don't know; but my idea of God is that he is wiser than I am. I presume he knows, indeed I may say I am *sure* of it, else he never would have made prayer not only a privilege, but a duty."

" Well, but, Faith, *are* people called upon to believe absurdities? Take Tom, for instance. If God knows anything, he knows that Tom will either be a drunkard or he will *not* be; and whichever way his knowledge reaches, settles the question. Now what difference will it make whether I pray for him or not?"

"Why don't you reason in that way about other matters?"

"I do. I think in just that way about a thousand things. They will be, or they will *not* be, in spite of me, and I might as well sit down and await their development."

"Then why *don't* you? If there is to be bread made in this house to-morrow, there *will* be, whether I set the sponge to-night or not, so I will just sit down and await its development."

"Because," said Maria, laughing a little, "there *wouldn't* be — not a loaf of bread made in this house from one year's end to another if I didn't do it."

"Not if it were determined upon ages ago?"

"Well," — and then she picked up a stick and poked at the coals — "it doesn't seem the same when we talk about our bread-making and our sweeping."

"I know it doesn't; and it is just here that we make our greatest blunders, I think. We invest everything pertaining to religion in a hopeless kind of mist, and then we sneer at it because it can not be judged according to the rules of common sense."

"Well, just tell me how you explain any of

it — the bread-making, too, if you will. If it is really ordered that I am to make bread to-morrow, why, I shall make it, whether I want to or not, or, rather, whether I set myself about it or not."

Faith laughed.

"You may judge for yourself whether that sounds like your favorite word, common sense," she said, pleasantly. "But I understand your meaning. *I* don't pretend to explain it. If it were ten times more enveloped with mystery than it is, I should still believe it all, for God my Father has put his seal to it; but when I want to speculate, I find no difficulty in thinking that he could have foreseen, and therefore predestinated, if you will, your ability and your willingness to make bread for us, and that your reason and your common sense would show you the need for doing so."

"Then why should not my reason and common sense force me into doing other things that I ought to?"

"I'm sure I don't know," Faith answered, gravely. "It is a question over which I have often puzzled."

Maria laughed, a slightly constrained laugh; her common sense showed her plainly that she had shut herself into a very narrow corner. She arose suddenly from her low seat.

"You may not think it," she said, speaking earnestly, "but I *am* very anxious about Tom — more anxious than I can tell you. If I knew how to do anything earthly or *unearthly* to help him, I would. The great trouble is, I don't know how. I'm sure I hope, if anything *is* to be done for him, it *will* be done promptly. I don't see what it will be, though. Meantime I'll go and set that sponge. I know how to ao that, at least."

And that which was to touch Tom was coming swiftly all the time.

CHAPTER XXV.

GOD'S MYSTERY OF GRACE.

E was tucked into the carriage; his blue wrap thrown loosely about him, for the morning was cool; his blue afghan covered his feet, a blue plume nodded in his white hat, and he looked a very prince among his subjects, for they all came out to see him off — Maria with her broom at her side, Grace bringing the knife with which she was peeling apples; even Helen left her sewing and came out to say good-by to the baby.

"Isn't he lovely this morning?" Grace said, kissing him energetically. "Where are you going, Faith?"

"We are going to rove according to our own wild wills. Where we will go is all unknown to me, and when or how we will return is equally involved in mystery."

"I hope I shall have my sweeping done before you are moved to come back. Don't get sleepy, Prince Pearly, until the house is in order."

"Wish us joy and good speed," Faith said, merrily. "Perhaps something to remember all our lives will happen to us before we return."

"There are two kinds of things to remember,' Helen said, grimly; and Faith had to carry those away with her for last words.

Down the sunny side of the street, trundling along in a flutter of life and joy, went Pearly. Not a bird escaped his notice, not a leaf rustled that he did not hear. Faith, pushing her lovely, canopied carriage before her, chattering in sweet baby fashion to her darling, felt not less happy than he. A still happiness, such as those feel who have given up many of their treasures to the Saviour's keeping, and have grace left to be unutterably thankful for some darling still left in their care. As they turned the corner of Vesey Street, and trundled along on the smooth flagging, Faith suddenly paused. Should she go down Vesey Street? Splendid as the flagging was, it was a street of many children and much whooping cough. She turned her carriage and retraced her steps. She would go back and go down the further end of their own street — that was smooth and broad and pleasant. As they walked Tom Randolph came, with rather unsteady steps, towards them. Tom's step was getting to be unsteady, even in the early morning. It took but little poison to fire his excitable brain. Pearly held up a smooth stone in one hand and a stick in the other, and greeted him with a chuckle of delight. Long before this Tom had given over his dislike for babyhood and surrendered completely to the charms of his little pearl. So now he stopped for the usual frolic; but his breath was odorous with liquor, and his talk rapid and excited.

"What a stupid old ride that auntie of yours is taking, Prince Pearly; creeping along at snail pace when he ought to be running, rushing, *flying!* on this wild morning. Here, give me the helm. I'll give him such a ride as he seldom gets."

"Not too fast," Faith said, anxiously, as he courteously but peremptorily possessed himself of the carriage. No one could be gentler than Tom Randolph when he was himself; but she distrusted him in these excited moods, and yet she did not like to refuse him, so she repeated her gentle caution.

"Not *too* fast, please. Oh, Tom, *do* be careful! He isn't used to it; you will frighten him."

"He acts like it! Hear him laugh! Never fear for him. He's a *man*, and not so easily

21

frightened as the ladies are. Here we go; up, up!" and he swung the carriage suddenly around the corner, one wheel on the stone, the other in the gully below.

Faith shrieked a little.

"Tom, O Tom, don't. Let me have him. Wait for me."

"No waiting for laggards. This is the lightning express. Here we go," and at that instant the carriage struck violently against a projecting stone and overturned. Pearly, thrown forward by the suddenness of the jolt, fell out, striking his head on the pavement. In an instant Faith had him in her arms, and Tom, beside her, spoke in a hurried but thoroughly sobered tone.

"He is not hurt. I am sure he isn't. The fright has made him faint. Please let me take him. I will run home with him and have a doctor in three minutes."

"Don't *touch* him," Faith said, in a low, stern voice. Then she went with swift steps down the street, bearing her still burden into the pretty yard which she had so lately left. Maria was there sweeping the piazza.

"Hi!" she said, gayly, "what is the matter with Prince Pearly? Did he rebel at his carriage? Why, Faith, is he hurt?"

This last in an altered tone, seeing Faith's face. Then she went swiftly in, not waiting for an answer, opened the door of Faith's room, and brought his own little pillow. How swiftly and silently they worked, bathing the poor blue-veined temple where the stone had struck, holding a cloth wet in ammonia to his nose, rubbing the tiny feet and limbs.

Almost immediately the doctor had arrived, for Tom had gone with swift steps to his call. He made very few suggestions, and what he did seemed almost mechanical. Gradually the eagerness of their efforts slackened, and one and another of them looked with frightened, appealing faces at the doctor,— looks which he studiously avoided answering. Finally they stood back, all but Faith, and looked at the beautiful little face, white and still. There had been no quiver of the eyelids, no motion of the little hand, from the very first. As for Faith, she did not even glance at any of them, but went steadily, silently on, rubbing the cold limbs, bathing the blue temple, until suddenly she dropped the cloth from her hand, and gathering her baby in her arms, while she showered hot, burning kisses on his white lips, sank down on her knees. Then they went swiftly and quietly out, leaving her alone with her terrible sorrow.

"Isn't there a *shadow* of hope?" Grace asked, piteously, catching the doctor's hand in her eagerness.

"He must have died instantly. Evidently he struck his temple violently, and it produced immediate death."

The doctor's voice trembled; he had stood that very morning, shading his eyes from the sun, and watching that triumphal little chariot; he knew what a treasure it contained.

"How *did* it happen? Who knows anything about it?" Maria questioned, eagerly.

"*I* know all about it;" and Tom's voice was so hard it startled her even then.

"I ought to know; I killed him. Now you have the whole story; enjoy it."

"Tom! O Tom!" Grace cried, piteously, "don't speak so, don't look so. What *can* you mean?"

"I mean just *that;* I killed him. I had been drinking, and I didn't know what I was about."

Every one but Helen saw that Tom's excitement was so intense that he hardly knew what he was saying; but she exclaimed in horror, "And you care as little about it as that! Tom Randolph, I don't know what you *can* be made of! If I were Faith, I could never endure to look at you again. I should think — "

He interrupted her, in a voice which startled even her.

"Helen, stop! You are the last one on

earth to reproach me. I have not *your* sin on my conscience even yet. The baby was ready to go, and that can not be said of every one." And then Tom dashed away from them out of the house, down the street, like a madman.

The intensity of his excitement had been apparent in his words. It was the first time since Helen's home-coming that he had given her reason to think that he knew one cause of her husband's death lay at her own door.

You could not have found a more beautiful picture than the baby made lying in his white casket, with flowers of every hue and shape scattered with lavish hand about him — not white flowers only, but brilliant red and yellow blossoms.

"He loved them," said Maria, in answer to Helen's protest that colored flowers were in bad taste at a funeral. "He loved the brightest ones best — why shouldn't I put them around him?"

Faith had dressed him herself, in his fairest and daintiest white dress, and buttoned the kid slippers about his ankle, and combed the rings of golden hair about her finger, just as she was wont to do, and said, through blinding tears, "He is going to find his papa and mamma. I have made him beautiful, just as mamma would like to see him, and told him good-bye."

Faith, from first to last, had astonished the Randolph family. None had known better than they how entirely the love and devotion of her life had centered in the beautiful baby, the only one left to her bearing the family name. They had expected her to lie crushed and helpless and hopeless at the foot of that little coffin. But in less than an hour she had come out from that closed room, saying, with a faint smile, "Mamma wanted him very much; she said she *could not* go and leave him. She has him now." And then she had taken up the work of life again — or perhaps I might better say the *enduring* of life. Her *work* had been to dress Pearly in the morning; to watch his footsteps as they tottered from one mischief to another; to hush him for his morning nap; to prepare his simple dinner; to take him on his many rides and walks; to dress him in long, loose night-robes; to watch over him at night; to dress him again in the morning — her *work* was gone.

Happy for those who can feel that duties many and important are pressing upon them, and that they have no time to sit down to grief. During the two days that had intervened since death had come among them, Tom had not been seen at home; his meals, if he had any, were taken elsewhere. They had feared that he was trying to find relief from his remorse in liquor, but a chance word with Mr. Harper revealed that he had not drank a drop since the dreadful morning.

It was the day for the funeral. At four o'clock, Faith's darling was to be put away from her. She had spent the morning in the closed room where he lay sleeping. It was nearly noon when she came out to Maria, and said, " Where is Tom ? "

" I wish any of us knew," Maria answered, sadly. " I have not seen him since — none of us have. I don't know what he is doing, nor what he means to do."

" Has any one been here to offer help of any kind ? "

" Nearly every one; people are coming all the time. Mr. Harper calls every morning; he passed a few moments ago; I presume he will stop when he returns."

" If he does, will you tell him from me that I want him to find Tom, and ask him to come home right away; I want to see him."

" O Faith! I wouldn't try to do that; it will be too hard."

" Nothing that is left to my life *can* be very hard," Faith said, with a quiet smile. " Be sure to tell him."

In accordance with this message, repeated with earnest persistence by Mr. Harper, Tom came just after dinner.

What a young man with a nature like Tom Randolph's had suffered, during the two days past, can hardly be imagined, much less described. Sensitive and sympathetic to an unusual degree, loving little Pearly with an affection not often bestowed by a young man upon a baby, feeling, oh! how keenly, that the precious little life was lost through gross and inexcusable carelessness on his part, knowing that the story, with many enlargements and additions, was in everybody's mouth, he had felt at times as if life was not to be endured for another hour, as if he must put an end to it all. Prominent among his terrors had been the thought of meeting Faith again. Helen's words, almost unconsciously to himself, hovered around him in various forms. "How could she endure ever to see his face again? How could he best dispose of himself so as to wound her in the least?" These were questions which haunted him. Feeling thus, it had seemed at first an impossibility to obey her summons, and but for Mr. Harper's persistence it would not have been obeyed.

Faith was in that closed room when Grace tapped gently at the door, and whispered, "Tom is here."

Faith went forward and opened the door.

"Will you ask him to come to me here?" she said, quietly; and Tom came.

She was startled at the change two days had
wrought. There were heavy dark rings under
his sunken eyes, and his mouth was set firmly,
as one in actual bodily pain. Faith came over
to him, as he stood at the closed door, and laid
her hand gently on his arm.

"Poor Tom!" she said, speaking softly.
"Poor Tom! I wish I could tell you how very,
very sorry I am for you. Your trouble is
heavier than mine, but I wanted to see you
while my darling lay here; I wanted you to see
how very sweet he looks, and I wanted to tell
you that I do not feel hard to you, not any at
all. I know you would not intentionally have
hurt one hair of his precious head. I want you
to forgive yourself, Tom, as entirely as I forgive
you."

For a moment Tom stood, with folded arms,
and that set look about his mouth — then he
strode forward to the side of that little coffin,
and kneeling there, bowed his head and wept
out his agony — such tears as only men shed who
are very rarely moved to tears. Groan after
groan escaped him, shaking the tiny casket
against which he leaned; while Faith stood
aside and looked on in awe at a grief the bitterness of which she had never realized. After a
little he spoke, but his voice was the voice of
prayer.

"O God," he said — and there was solemn, intense meaning in his voice — "O God of mercy and of forgiveness, grant to me that spirit so divine, so like thine that it can forgive even such a sin as mine has been. For the first time in my life I realize what the Christian spirit is. I want to be a Christian — I *will* be one. Give me thy pardon, even as one who follows close after thee has done — that she can forgive me, can endure to look upon me, emboldens me to believe that thy mercy is great enough even for me. God be merciful to me a sinner. Help me for Christ's sake. An hour ago I was eager to die: now I am ready to live. There are things that I can never undo, but I beg for Christ in my heart, shining forth in my life. I have seen it to-day as never before. God of love, take my poor sinful soul into thy keeping."

"Amen," said Faith's low, gentle voice. "Saviour, I thank thee that here at my darling's coffin has blossomed so precious a flower — the new life of a soul — even my blessed baby was not too much to give for this. My Father, I thank thee that thou hast given me so sweet a balm in this sad hour."

There had come a strange change over Tom Randolph's face during this little time. Grave it was, and deeply sad, yet the sorrow was not despair, and the gravity was not desperation.

" Tom, you will come this afternoon ? " This
was what Faith said to him as they arose.

" Can you bear to have me ? " he asked her
piteously.

" Not only that, but I want you to be here."

Then he went for the first time and looked at
the sweet little face that had grown so dear to
him, and that was so full of calm and beauty.
" It is a heavy, heavy price to pay," he said,
tremulously. " My poor soul was not worth it,
but I had well-nigh lost it. I think I was very
near the end."

" Your soul, remember, was worth the death
of the Son of God," she said, solemnly. " See
that you make your life worthy such a sacrifice
as that."

Great was the astonishment of the Randolph
family, and, indeed, of the friends who knew the
sad story, when Faith followed her darling to his
resting-place, attended by her cousin Tom.

" It could not have been true," said the
lookers on. " That story we heard must have
been nothing but a story. Tom Randolph is
with her, and she does not shrink from him at
all."

" Faith hasn't the spirit of a mouse." So said
her cousin, Helen Munroe. " One would think
she would have banished Tom to-day, for
appearance' sake, if for nothing else."

"She is incomprehensible to me," said Maria to Grace. "I can't understand how one who is so intense in her feelings as she is can control herself so as to be patient with Tom."

"She is a rare Christian," said Mr. Harper to Ermina. And the latter assented with a little sigh — it was so very far beyond what she felt that she could have done.

"She has proved the truth of the religion of Jesus Christ as I *never* felt it before. God bless her. God bless and comfort and keep her." So said Tom Randolph, in the silence and loneliness of his own room, just as he bowed himself to consecrate to Jesus Christ his life, body and soul, from henceforth.

Who shall say that the sweet baby, so early gone home to heaven, lived his little life in vain?

CHAPTER XXVI.

LACES AND DUTY.

TOM RANDOLPH sat in the dining-room, with his chair tipped back, his hat drawn over his eyes, and his feet on the rounds of another chair. Contrary to Mrs. Munroe's code of morals, Tom's new start in life had not yet made him a careful observer of all the rules of propriety. The less religion does for a person's own life and habits, the more certain is that person to expect it to work a sudden and complete transformation in the habits of one who has very recently professed to be governed by its precepts. Tom was deep in thought, which, to judge by the expression on his face, was not very pleasant. Mrs. Munroe was plaiting a crepe ruffle, and Maria was setting the table for the next morning's breakfast. The household had narrowed down, the summer and early autumn had gone from them, so also had Faith. Contrary to the opinions of some good people, she held it to be her privilege to make life as endurable as she could, and to stay among the rooms that had echoed to the constant patter of Pearly's little feet made the weight of pain seem heavier, so she went away. Maria, as she set the table, sighed a little as she left vacant the end where Faith and Pearly used to sit. Maria missed them sadly. Tom looked up at last, pushed his hat back a little and smiled faintly. Very few smiles had Tom Randolph to bestow. One may rally from a heavy sorrow which God has sent, and smile brightly even between the tears; but a weight of self-remorse over a sin that has brought lifelong sorrow to some one — a sorrow that but for you might not be — such pain to a young man like Tom Randolph cuts deeply and leaves little heart for smiling.

"I'm a gentleman of leisure," he said to Maria; and she gave a little start of dismay at the news. You must forgive Maria; she did not want her brother to sell liquor for a living, but she kept the family purse, and Tom paid his board.

"Couldn't you wait a little?" she said, deprecatingly.

" I didn't see how I could, Maria. I couldn't sell any more liquor."

" I'm sure I don't see why," Helen said, sharply. " You have sold it for some months, and I should think a few days longer would make very little difference; it would be an improvement on coming home to father to be supported."

Now as this was precisely what Helen herself had done, one wouldn't have supposed that she would have condemned it in another. Tom controlled the impulse to tell her so, and answered simply,—

" I felt that I *could not* sell another drop of liquor."

" Well," Maria said, with a long drawn sigh, " I suppose you are right, and I shall be glad enough that you are out of it when you get in somewhere else; but the week's accounts won't match very well now."

" I know," he said, with a gloomy face, " the burden rests heavily. I'm afraid it will be some time before I can find employment. I've met with nothing but failures to-day."

" Of course," Helen said, with a volume of significance in her tones. " You can't expect people to trust you."

Tom's boots came down from the chair so suddenly that Helen said, with a nervous start,

"Dear me! how rough you are!" but he said not a word.

The outside door creaked slowly, and Mr. Randolph came in with weary step. Helen gave him the easy-chair in which she had been sitting, and Maria brought his slippers.

"How tired you look!" she said, anxiously. "And you are late to-night, too. I think it is too bad that you have to do over-work."

"Not often," he said, feebly; and then he coughed sharply.

"Father," said Tom, with the air of one who had something to communicate that was depressing, and the sooner it could be told and put away the better, "I wish you needed an errand boy or porter, or something of that sort, at your store. I've thrown up my work and am an object of charity."

Mr. Randolph put his tired hands on the arm-chair and drew himself up, and came with eager steps toward his son.

"Thank God," he said, with trembling earnestness. "I thank him that this trouble is ended. I have felt it bitterly. I am a temperance man, you know, my son."

Tom Randolph arose and stood beside his father; he towered above him; he rested one hand on his arm, and his voice trembled more than his father's had.

"Father, *I* am a temperance man, too. I have signed a total abstinence pledge to-day. I hope to atone in a measure for the pain I have given you."

"I'm sure I'm very glad," Helen said, when both father and son had left the room. "As glad as any one *can* be,— only one can't help wishing that his repentance had come a little earlier."

Maria slammed the closet door.

"If you ever get to heaven," she said, irritably, "you will say, 'I can't help wishing I had come yesterday, or waited until to-morrow.' Things as they *are*, are never quite right in your estimation."

Helen opened her eyes in wonder.

"Dear me!" she said, plaintively, "what *have* I said now? I seem to be always saying something."

"*That's* true," Maria murmured; and she banged the other closet door a little before she left the room.

Tom came in search of her while she was in the pantry setting the cakes for breakfast.

"Father was pleased with my leaving the saloon," he said, speaking a little wistfully. She turned toward him a bright face.

"Of course he was," she said, heartily. "So am I — only the world, the flesh and the other one got the better of me for a little."

22

" It is gloomy work for you, I know," he said, sadly. " It seems almost hopeless for me to try to get employment ; at the best there is very little doing, and my former experience and reputation are not flattering. If I were only a girl I would have a chance to try at least."

" A girl! Why, I thought it was more difficult for a girl to get work than a boy ? "

" I suppose it is, generally speaking ; but I know of a chance for a girl. Arthur & McAllister advertize for a clerk. I answered the advertisement this morning, but they informed me that they employed none but females at the lace counter."

This conversation sent Maria to bed with wide open eyes, that continued open far into the midnight. The result of which midnight musing was a conversation with Grace over the next morning's breakfast dishes. The conversation opened with her favorite expression,—

" There's no use in talking, Grace. Something has got to be done.

" I know it," Grace said, meekly.

There had been so much talking that she knew quite well what Maria meant, without explanation. That young lady, however, proceeded to explain.

" Here's Helen on our hands to support, and Tom without anything to do, and father looking paler and coughing harder every night. It's time there was a chance."

"Can you think of anything?"

"Yes, a hundred things; it is easier to think than to do. However, I'm going to try doing. Tom says there is a vacancy at Arthur & Mc-Allister's, and I'm going this very morning to' try for it. If I succeed you'll have to keep house. You'll hate it, I know; but so do I hate lace. That's where the vacancy is — at the lace counter. If you can conceive of anything more stupid than puttering over boxes of lace from morning till night, I don't know what it can be I'd rather bake griddle cakes or wash dishes, and I've no particular love for that employment either. However, tastes and feelings, and things of that sort, have all been ground up long ago, in this house, and eaten for daily bread."

"I don't see how the house is ever going to get along without you!" Grace said, dismay in her voice, in her eyes, all about her.

"It is to get along *with you* the best way it can. I'm sure you can get us all something to eat if you try. Anyway, *I* can't much longer, without some money to get it with; and I know no other way but to go and earn some."

There was *one* other way. Grace timidly suggested it.

"If Helen would only apply for the vacant place."

" Helen ! " echoed Maria, in undisguised disdain. " I think I see her doing it. Why, bless
your heart, child, don't you know it isn't genteel
to sell lace ? It is perfectly proper to live on a
sick father. In fact, it is quite genteel to
starve, if you do it gracefully ; but the idea of
one who had been connected with the *Munroe*
family stooping to lace-selling isn't to be thought
of for a moment."

I may as well say, just here, that no sooner
were the dishes dried and marshaled into place,
than Maria put her plans into execution ; and
the firm of Arthur & McAllister being really in
need, and being well acquainted with her father,
she met with prompt success.

Then commenced a series of martyrdom such
as the Randolph family had hitherto not known.
Such breakfasts as were shrinkingly brought before the miserable victims! Such dinners as
they endured! Grace worked from dawn till
dark, and did her very best ; but she really had
no more affinity for cooking than a canary bird ;
and whatever other branches of business may be
carried on successfully without a fair knowledge
of, and general interest in the details, house-
keeping can not. So the steak was burned or
smoked, and the bread was sticky and sour, the
pies were exasperating, and poor Grace came
regularly to the table with cheeks aglow and

three fingers done up in rags, burned or cut as the case might be.

Maria's disgust sent her daily to the lace counter with a frowning face. She was sharp to the customers, and positively crabbed to sister clerks to such a degree that she more than once received a hint from headquarters that she must be more civil or lose her place. Despite all these grievances the week's salary from the lace counter helped considerably in the family puzzle. So each girl stood her ground with the resolution that helps to make martyrs, though Grace retreated nightly under the bedclothes with red eyelids.

One evening Maria plodded home from the store, through mud and rain, without either rubbers or umbrella (waterproof she had not), and the consequence was sneezes and involuntary weeping out of one eye the next day.

"There is no use in trying to thumb over lace to-day," she said to Grace, who was looking gravely at the greasy spider. "You will just have to go in my place."

"What, to the store!" Grace said, dropping the spider in her surprise.

"Yes, of course. I believe you have cracked that. What *is* the use of being so careless? My head spins around like a top, and feels as large as the flour barrel and as empty. Tell

Mr. McAllister, with my compliments, that he won't have the pleasure of growling at me to-day."

"But what will you do about the work?"

"Why, I'll *do* it. Because I can't walk a mile in the rain, it doesn't follow that I can't do a little work in the kitchen; and I'll have a decent dinner once more, I venture to say;"— this last in an undertone; then, louder, "Will you try the store?"

"Why, of course I'll try; but, Maria, I'm not sure that I shall succeed any better than I do at cooking."

Maria tied a handkerchief around her aching head, and mopped the kitchen floor. Grace rarely had time for mopping; then she made some apple sauce for dinner, that stayed in delightful quarters, a thing which Grace's apple sauce was never known to do. The dinner, though it was only baked potatoes and cold meat, was a success; for, be it known, there is a way to make utterly uneatable even baked potatoes and cold meat, and poor Grace knew that way. Then when at tea time Maria had sufficiently subdued eyes and nose, so that she gave herself up to the pleasure of making a delicious creamy johnny cake, the comfort of the Randolph family reached a height unknown for weeks.

As for Grace, the day passed quietly; the lace

was neither greasy nor sticky, two things which she abhorred; the rain prevented much sale, but in the arrangement of the boxes she proved useful, saying, after but a lesson or two, "I can tell the real from the imitation now, I think."

"How do you tell?" Mr. McAllister asked her, looking her through with keen eyes.

"I don't know," she said, with flushing face. "I haven't learned how to tell scientifically, only this *feels* real, and this one *doesn't*."

"Never mind the science," he said, smiling a little, and then he left her to herself.

Three days Maria's cold held sway; the mopping and the johnny cake proved to be not good for it. After that she went back to the store, and Grace, with a little softly sigh, put on her greasy apron — her work apron was always greasy — and took the dish cloth between her thumb and finger.

Mr. Arthur, the senior partner, summoned Maria to the office.

"Is your sister Grace, who has served us in your absence, a young lady of leisure?"

"Not particularly," said Maria, smiling in spite of his dignity, at the thought of poor Grace with her head in the oven, probably, at that moment. "She is housekeeper for a family of five."

"Oh! At your own home?"

" Yes, sir."

Mr. Arthur leaned his chin on his lead pencil, and mused.

" Well, the fact is," he said at last, " if you and Miss Grace could change places, it would perhaps be agreeable to all parties. She gave very general satisfaction in the store, the customers liked her and the clerks like her very much. She is low voiced, and gentle in her movements, and she tells real and imitation laces by instinct, or in some other mysterious way; at least she rarely fails. In short, Miss Randolph, she has an aptitude for the business which, I may as well say, and you will excuse my frankness — I am always frank — you have not. Now, Miss Randolph, we are prepared to engage your sister permanently, and give her the full salary, which is a dollar a week more than you have been receiving, if that will suit you."

" Engage her in my place, you mean ? "

" In your place."

" Personally, Mr. Arthur, I am delighted with the proposition, and I think Grace will approve. I quite agree with you that I have no aptitude for the business. I *hate* lace. I always hated things that could be copied so precisely that you had to feel of them to tell the real from the false."

Nevertheless, after making this emphatic address, Maria went home in a good deal of a maze. Once or twice she laughed outright. It was very funny, certainly. Grace able to earn her own living, and she, Maria, who had been useful and practical ever since she was born, not!

"There are different ways of doing things I suppose," she said aloud, and quite humbly for her. And this little episode did Maria Randolph good. Also, it did Grace good. There *was* a recognized place for her in the world, then, even if it was only behind a lace counter. She felt more self-reliant.

The wild chaotic kind of living that had been in vogue in the Randolph family subsided, the dishes retired to their respective shelves, and comfort reigned once more. And people liked to buy laces at Arthur & McAllister's.

CHAPTER XXVII

STORM AND "MOONSHINE."

HAT a horrid evening!" Mrs. Munroe said, with a shiver, and she drew a little black shawl closer about her shoulders. "It rains all the time nowdays."

They were all in the little dining-room, Mr. Randolph in his easy-chair, in dressing-gown and slippers, feebly trying to look over some accounts, stopping every few minutes to wipe his forehead and his thin hands, for the constant little cough produced a perspiration that was cold and clammy and disagreeable. In some way Mr. Randolph must have relief from that office. In some way he would soon have it. If no other channel opened, the restful grave would come to his aid. Maria felt this, and she chopped her meat for the morning hash, with her face all gathered in a frown. Life was

hard to Maria, and she made it harder than she
need. Why must she persist in carrying all her
burdens for herself? Grace had drawn as near
the light as she could, and held in her lap the
only brightness that the room contained — some
crimson worsteds. They kept a case of fancy
articles in the store, and Grace made pretty
trifles by instinct. She had made the happy dis-
covery that she could help to replenish that case
with great advantage to her own purse. In
short, Grace was in a fair way to earn her own
living; and it was only busy, practical Maria
who was working hard and earning nothing. So
she thought. But who will be kind enough to
estimate how much those people really earn who
spend their lives in skillfully contriving how to
save the earnings of other people? Ermina, on
the other side of the stand, was straining her eyes
over black ruffles. There was no let up to
ruffles that she had to prepare for the next day's
campaign. They were not always black ruffles,
and the light was not always so dim as on this
evening. All the gloom had concentrated itself.
The Randolph expenses were being narrowed to
a low scale. They had actually reached that
pitiful point when an extra kerosene lamp, when
they were all gathered in one room of an evening, was a luxury not to be thought of; so they
sat close and strained their eyes over one.

Helen was the only unoccupied person. She had affected to read the evening paper until she pronounced the light no better than a tallow candle.

"I wonder you don't introduce one into your economy," she said, scornfully, to Maria, and that young lady answered, with a grave face,—

"Do you suppose it would be cheaper?"

Helen vouchsafed no answer, and the silence that seemed to possess them all was renewed. Tom came suddenly in at the side door, letting in with him a gust of wind and rain, and leaving the door open a crack, as men are apt to do, while he rushed through to the kitchen with his dripping umbrella. Helen shivered and drew further into her shawl, and Maria pushed the door to with a bang.

"You always leave doors open after you," she said, a little fretfully, as Tom emerged from his wet overcoat and came back to the dining-room.

"I wanted to give you a taste of outside life, so that you would better appreciate the comforts of your position," he said, cheerily, drawing a chair near his father.

Helen sniffled.

"Comforts!" she said, sarcastically.

"Why, yes, there is a marked difference between this room and the street. It rains in torrents, and is the darkest night I ever saw.

Well, I am ready for congratulations. I have found employment at last."

Maria looked up from her hash with a gleam of satisfaction. Grace said, "Oh, good!" and Ermina asked with interest, "What is it?"

"Before I tell that, I must remind you that I have been for more than three weeks, now, searching right and left for something to do, and the case was really growing desperate."

Mr. Randolph dropped the paper on which he was figuring, and the pencil in his hand trembled as he said, nervously,—

"You have not gone back to that saloon, have you, Thomson?"

"No, sir." There was an emphatic ring in Tom's voice. "It is a respectable business this time. Only Maria, if you board me, you will have to give me very prompt breakfasts. I'm to be on hand for the seven o'clock car."

"In the capacity of driver, I presume." Mrs. Munroe said this for the utmost sarcasm; but Tom's answer was prompt.

"That's it, exactly. How came you to guess so soon?"

"Why, Tom Randolph!" Grace said, looking aghast.

"Nonsense!" said Maria; "you'll believe *anything*, Grace. Do tell us, Tom, what you have to do with the seven o'clock car."

" Drive the horses attached to it," Tom said,
gravely. " Helen has guessed rightly. I am
tired of idleness — *any* work is better than that;
and this is honest and decent."

Up to this time Mrs. Munroe had not fully
taken his meaning. The magnitude of his
crime seemed too great for her mind to compass.
She sat looking at him with absolute disgust in
her face, and her voice was actually tremulous
as she said,—

" Tom Randolph, I should think you had disgraced your father sufficiently. I don't know
what he has done that he should be so utterly
disappointed and disgraced in his son. I hope
this will not break him down utterly."

" Helen !" Mr. Randolph's voice had that peculiar ring in it that they as children had heard
but a few times in their lives. " Helen! I am
proud of him. I am glad when I see any one
sufficiently independent to rise above foolish
grades and distinctions. So far am I from being
disgraced, I think I never was so sure of a suc-
cessful future for my son as I am at this moment.
Moral courage is something that I never had
very much of, but it is something that I admire
and respect."

" There is no accounting for people's tastes,"
Helen said coldly, even haughtily; then she
took up her paper and professed to read. Some-

way no one liked to express an opinion after that, and the sewing and chopping went on quietly.

Tom left them to look after kindlings for the morning fire. Ermina sewed to the end of her ruffle, and looked wearily over at the pile on the lounge waiting to be sewed. Should she, or should she not, try to do more that evening? She was not obliged to sew in the evenings, but they were hurried; they always *are* hurried in dressmaking establishments; there never seems to come a time when the world is clothed; and it expedited matters so much in the next day's rush to have yards and yards of work turned down and basted. But Ermina was unusually tired this evening, body and heart. She pushed her chair back a little from the light, and shaded her weary eyes with her hand. Life looked un-utterably dreary to her. The rain pelting un-ceasingly against the window, and the wind howling around the keyhole, served to deepen her sense of gloom. Through her fingers she could get peeps of her father's face, and she felt not exactly shocked at its pallor; the sight had grown too common to come as a shock, but it hurt her with a new pain. How feeble he looked, and how puzzled he seemed over the miserable figures. What a daily perplexity life must be to him, instead of having the rest and peace about it that a man of his years needed. The miserable lamp that smoked a little, as kerosene lamps frequently do, added to the general sense of discomfort and discouragement which possessed her. They were even too poor to have gaslight; they were growing poorer, she worked hard at her new business and carefully saved her earnings, yet there seemed to be less to live on than there used. There was less. Mr. Randolph's weakness and feebleness had grown upon him to such an extent that he had relinquished of necessity one duty after another, and, of course, his salary had grown proportionately smaller, and the family were coming to know that it was only by courtesy that his place was kept at all. There was certainly enough to justify a feeling of apprehension as to the future, yet Ermina had of late been able to lift herself somewhat above it all, to trust her life and the lives of her kindred in the Father's hand. To-night though it was nearer despair than trust. She felt utterly cast down and forsaken, as if there were no brightness anywhere. Those ruffles over on the lounge waiting for her seemed like so many imps of darkness ready to sting her; she hated them, and the life stretching drearily out before her, filled with ruffles to hem and gather and plait, looked unutterably horrible. I want you to understand that I

don't justify Ermina for being in this state of
mind. Of course it was unreasonable and silly;
it was no more right than it was for you to be
cross all the morning because the steak was
tough and the coffee cold when you came to
breakfast. I have no doubt it was unchristian,
so are one eighth of the things that you have
said and done to-day; but I insist that it was
very human, and Ermina was an intensely
human girl, with like passions and failings with
yourself. Whether she hadn't a very little more
to try her than you have had to-day, judge ye.
The door-bell pealing through the house startled
the family with a sudden sense of a something
breaking rudely in on their quiet, which people
feel when they have allowed themselves to sink
into the depths of gloomy reverie. Helen
dropped the paper with an exclamation.

"Who on earth can be coming here in such a
storm? It must be urgent business."

Tom, who had been heard banging about the
upper hall, now came down to answer the bell.
They heard him show some one into the parlor;
then he came to the dining-room door and put his
head in. "A messenger for you, Ermina."
Then he vanished.

"Some one about those dreadful dresses,"
Ermina said, with a sigh. "They would come
to look after their ruffles if it rained icicles."

23

"Don't keep the poor victim long, whoever it is, or he will freeze." This was Maria's parting sentence.

The dimmest of smoking lamps served to make the darkness of the little parlor visible. The stove had not even been set up yet; it was not late in the season, and people would not expect you to have a fire when there was no stove in which to make it. By dint of close looking, Ermina discovered a shadow in the dimness; it was tall and wore an overcoat. She went toward it with dignity, wondering at its errand. There was no mistaking the sudden light in her eyes as she neared it; and it spoke, though it said simply, "Good evening, Miss Ermina." She knew the voice, and there was pleasure mingling with the surprise with which she said, "Mr. Harper!"

"Now you are wondering why I came out in the storm," he said, when they were comfortably seated. "I see the wonderment in your eyes, and I am not surprised at it. I confess to you that it doesn't look like a sane proceeding. But I had a reason, and it can be explained in a very few words. I wanted to see you."

"That is remarkable," Ermina said, with a little laugh. "I didn't know any one was ever in that state."

"Did you not?" he said, earnestly. "It is

becoming a chronic state with me. I have been thinking about it nearly all this day, thinking about it and praying over it, and to-night I have braved the storm, resolved to tell you the whole story."

A dozen times they wondered in the dining-room who *could* be keeping Ermina so. Then, as Tom did not appear again, they gave over wondering and went their several ways.

Helen had been asleep when Ermina, who shared her room, pushed open the door, and brought her dim little lamp into the darkness. She set it softly down and went to the window; the rain had ceased, and dozens of stars were twinkling. Helen popped up her head from among the pillows.

"Where in the world have you been?" she asked in wonderment.

"I've been nowhere," Ermina answered with shining eyes. "What a change there is in the weather. Do you know, Helen, the stars are shining, and it looks as though it would never rain again."

"Who wanted you?" asked Helen, ignoring the stars. "And whoever it was, why didn't they spend the night?"

"Why, it isn't but a few minutes."

"A few minutes! It was nearly ten o'clock when I came up stairs. It must be eleven now."

"Oh, no," Ermina said, quickly; "it couldn't be."

"Well, who was it?"

Thus pressed, Ermina's reluctant tongue succeeded in forming the words, "Mr. Harper."

Helen echoed them.

"Mr. Harper! What in the name of common sense did he want? Couldn't he have chosen a lovelier night for his errand?"

"He is not afraid of the rain," Ermina said, evasively.

"I should think not, nor of cold, nor of you, either. It is a wonder you did not freeze. His errand must have been very pressing. What did he want?"

"I declare if there isn't the moon," Ermina said, eagerly. "I didn't know it rose so late. I believe I had forgotten that there was one. Oh, how beautiful it is!"

Mrs. Helen Munroe raised herself on one elbow, and spoke impatiently.

"Ermina Randolph, I have asked you three times what Mr. Harper wanted. If you intend to tell me, I wish you would let the stars and the moon alone, and do so."

Ermina dropped the curtain, and went over to the glass and began to take the pins out of her hair. Her cheeks were very glowing.

"He wanted me," she said, slowly, almost reverently.

Mrs. Munroe sat up straight and looked at her.

"You!" she repeated, intense amazement in her voice. "What do you mean?"

"I mean that, with all that it implies. I do not wonder that you are astonished. You can not be as much so as I was. To think that God had that waiting for me, coming to me, all the while; and only this very evening I felt that my life was desolate. I have been a very untrustful child, Helen. I wonder that he has had patience with me."

Mrs. Munroe fixed the pillows under her head and lay down without another word. The lamp had been out for an hour, and Ermina had been turning herself over in the bed for nearly that length of time, when her sister made her first comment on the evening's revelation.

"Well, I think he took a very rainy night for it."

CHAPTER XXVIII.

A NEW START.

VERY soon thereafter there was another wedding in the Randolph family, utterly unlike the first one — so unlike, so ill befitting in Helen's estimation the dignity of Ermina's coming position, that she went around for weeks beforehand with her forehead drawn in a row of wrinkles, and in kitchen and pantry held endless, hopeless discussions with Maria. As for Ermina, she did in many things just what people are not given to doing under the same circumstances. For instance, she kept her place in the sewing-room up to the very last week of her stay at home. Her reasons therefor were simple and conclusive.

"I've nothing very special to do. I'm not going to have sixteen flounced and plaited silk dresses. My wardrobe is to be simple, from

taste partly, from necessity a great deal; and 1
need all the money I can earn."

A morning wedding, no guests, no wedding
cake. Over each of these three movements
Helen exhausted herself and the patience of
those around her with argument.

"An evening wedding was so much more
tasteful and stylish."

"As to taste," Maria said. "That, of course,
was a matter of taste, and tastes differed."

"And as to style," Ermina chimed in. "I'm
not stylish, you know; don't aim to be."

"But Mr. Harper was," Helen said. "Very
stylish, and immensely wealthy. She thought
some little regard ought to be paid to his position."

The mention of Mr. Harper's name always
produced a softened and quieted tone of voice in
Ermina, so while Maria answered with unusual
sharpness that "Mr. Harper's wealth was not
supposed to pay the wedding expenses, and his
position was strong enough to take care of itself,"
Ermina said, gently, that "Mr. Harper entirely
approved of the arrangements; indeed they were
of his own planning."

"Well, I *must* say you are queer creatures,"
Helen said, with lifted eyebrows and vexed
voice. "I don't know after all but you are well
matched. One would suppose that if people *had*

any friends they would like to see them about them on their wedding day. But, as Maria says, there is no accounting for people's tastes."

There was a mixture of sharpness and humility in Ermina's answer,—

"I don't at this moment think of an individual in this town, outside of our own immediate family, that I care particularly ever to see again. It is a mortifying fact, and I don't doubt that it is my own fault; but it is a *fact* nevertheless. I'm sure I hope never to have to own it in regard to any other home of mine."

"No danger," Maria said, grimly, "Mr. Harper's millions would secure plenty of friends."

Maria's was, however, a sort of satisfied grimness. She was very willing to have millions come into the family, especially when in their train they brought every other qualification. Her tussle with poverty had been too long, and her heart was too unselfish not to feel genuine joy that one of the family had emerged into the sunlight, especially when that one was Ermina, decidedly her favorite sister, and more especially when the sunshine was of Mr. Harper's own bringing; she thoroughly believed in Mr. Harper.

"There are two ways of getting married," she said, in a burst of confidence to Grace over their night toilet. "Helen married the handsome house, and the lace curtains, and the silver tea

set, and the diamond ring, and plenty of silk
dresses, and Horace Munroe thrown into the
background, as a kind of awkward necessity.
Ermina now is going to marry Mr. Harper because the houses and the jewels come with him.
I guess she is quietly glad whenever she happens
to think of them, but it's Mr. Harper *anyhow*.
I recommend you to follow the latter example;
it sounds more like the marriage service."

"I'm not going to be married at all," said
sleepy Grace. "I'm going to stay at home and
keep house for father."

Maria shrugged her shoulders.

"My patience! I pity father," she said, significantly; and the next instant was glad that
Grace was too nearly asleep to feel the point of
the sentence. Maria was nearly always sorry for
her sharp points after she had made them.

"But I don't see why you can't have a little
cake, like decent people," said Helen, returning
freshly to the charge after a night's rest. "Who
ever heard of a wedding without any wedding
cake?"

"What is the use of it?" Ermina asked,
briskly. "If it were to be an evening entertainment I suppose we should *have* to have it;
but who wants to munch cake at eight o'clock in
the morning? I'm sure I would rather have a
potato."

"Such an unearthly hour," murmured Helen, in increasing disgust; and Ermina innocently reminded her that it was an hour later than usual. There was little use in discussions; both Mr. Harper and Ermina seemed to be hopelessly set in their determination to ruffle the family life as little as possible. One little sentence escaped Ermina in conversation with Grace, with whom each sister was more apt to be confidential than with each other.

"I would have liked a little more of a commotion, of course. Who wouldn't? It is not in human nature not to want to make a nice time when one is married; but we had such a dreadful time getting over the expenses of Helen's wedding that I am determined to bring no more debts of that kind. I would rather have baked potatoes and salt for the wedding breakfast than to have father harassed with bills."

Tom was dressing for the wedding, though Helen disdainfully said she saw no use in dressing — they might as well wear their calico wrappers; but they didn't — instead they put on their best dresses, and the table looked fresh and pretty, with no cake but doughnuts, but delicious coffee to drink with them. Tom needed assistance in the matter of a button, and was glad to find Maria at liberty for a minute to sew it on. During the operation he laughed outright at his own thoughts, and then proceeded to explain.

"One of my brother drivers came to me last night for a confidential chat. I wish you could have seen his puzzled and important face. He is that Jerry that you think is so good-natured. What do you think he wanted?"

"I'm sure I don't know. This button has split in two, Tom."

"Well, here's another. I couldn't imagine what he was coming at. He called me aside and looked so important. He begged my pardon for troubling me — they are all remarkably polite to me — and he said that four or five of them had been having a time with their washerwoman because she didn't use starch enough. They're wonderfully particular fellows on Sunday. She ironed in wrinkles, too, he said; and then, after considerable stammering, he managed to get out that a number of them had been talking over the immaculateness of my linen, and had decided to get me to negotiate with my washerwoman, whoever she was, to see if she would do their work. The poor fellow was utterly crestfallen when I told him that my laundress was my sister."

"They are letting that coffee boil over. I smell it!" was Maria's lucid reply. "I knew something would happen if I came away. Is that all you want, Tom?"

"All right — much obliged;" and Maria went back to the breakfast.

"A rich brother-in-law is a very fine thing to have, but you can't eat him, nor make clothes out of him; so the summing up of the whole matter is, that I must find something to do that will help support the family; and, Helen, you will have to keep house and do the cooking." Of course it was Maria who said this.

"I'm sure I'm willing." Helen said, drearily. "Only I can't imagine what you will do."

"I'll do *something*," Maria said, determination in her face and voice.

Something besides a wedding had come to the family. Only the day after Ermina left them, Mr. Randolph, going to his office as usual, looking not paler nor more feeble than usual, so far as they could see, came from there an hour afterward in the carriage of his employer; was supported on the arm of a brother clerk to his room; he had fainted at his post. "Nothing serious, I trust," the young man said, reassuringly; and the daughters hoped it wasn't, and told each other that he had been unusually fatigued and excited during the preparation for Ermina's departure; he needed rest; to-morrow he would be better. But to-morrow came, and to-morrow, and after a good many to-morrows had passed they began gradually to realize that he would not go to the old seat in the counting-room again. So there was Grace's salary in the store and Tom's wages as a street-car driver to support the family! No wonder that even Helen awakened to the necessity of doing something. But what was it to be? Several days were spent in fruitless search; and it was after one of those days, when Mr. Randolph's cough had been more distressing than usual, that Maria in a mood half way between apathy and despair, washed the dishes by the light of a smoking kerosene lamp. It needed a new burner, but they were too poor to afford one. She was alone in the kitchen; Grace had returned to the store, and Helen was resting on the lounge in the sitting-room after the wearying duties of the day, for Maria had been out all the afternoon engaged in her unsuccessful search for employment, and Helen had done the kitchen work with what patience and skill she could command for the occasion. Tom, in the woodshed, was whistling softly, and the tune he whistled suggested the familiar words,—

> "Thus far the Lord has led me on,
> Thus far his power prolongs my days,
> And every evening shall make known
> Some fresh memorial of his grace."

Presently the whistling broke into **actual** words, and he sang,—

> "Much of my time has run to waste."

Then he pushed open the kitchen door, with his arms full of kindlings.

"There is no truer line than that," he stopped his singing to say to Maria; "and yet, isn't it a queer world? I'm actually trying now, with all my might, to redeem the time. My work is honest, and I'm trying to be faithful; and I overheard Judge Morris tell his son Charlie — who used to be my chum, you know — that he was afraid I had gone to the dogs; that I was actually a street-car driver!"

"The *rest* of *my* time is likely to 'run to waste,'" Maria said, dwelling moodily on the line quoted. Then she roused herself to respond to his remark. "I shouldn't care what Judge Morris thought, or his son Charlie either. I presume they considered you all right while you were a gentleman of leisure. Tom, how came you ever to decide to take that work to do?"

"Well," said Tom, speaking reflectively, and depositing his kindlings in the box as he spoke, "indirectly, Peter Armstrong had as much to do with it as any one. You don't know, perhaps, what a queer fashion he has of reading the Bible? He discovered that there was a Peter in it, and he 'hunted him up,' as he says, and read about him; sometimes lives a week on an idea of Peter Bible's; sometimes it is a month

before he takes up a new item. I have been
immensely interested in his system. Now you
know it is only a little while since I started out
on a new plan of living, and something suggested to my mind the determination to be a 'whatsoever' Christian."

"A what?" said puzzled Maria.

"A 'whatsoever' Christian. I'm afraid I
should have shrunken from it if I had comprehended in what ways it would lead me. I have
been amazed a good many times already. Well,
one morning the verse proved to be, ' Whatsoever thy hand findeth to do, do it with thy might.'
It was after I had spent some weeks in looking
for work, and that very morning I had not been
away from the house ten minutes when I heard,
in a curious sort of way, that they were having
trouble with the car drivers — dismissed several.
' Whatsoever thy hand findeth,' said I to myself.
' My patience,' said I. Why, I didn't think it
would set me to driving car horses! But it was
the only ' whatsoever' that appeared to me that
day, and by night I had decided it. I have not
been sorry," said Tom, taking off his hat and
brushing the thick hair from his forehead. " In
fact, I think I can say I am glad, though the
position has not been a particularly pleasant
one."

"It's a queer idea," Maria said, with a short,

little laugh; " but I think there is a good deal more energy than religion about it. I like that sort of motto."

" Adopt it," said Tom, eagerly. " I wish you would. I think you would like it; and I'm sure I would like the way in which it would lead me."

" I wouldn't be afraid of that," Maria said, loftily. " I'm no shirk. I wouldn't be a bit afraid to live out all the ' whatsoevers ' in the world."

" Then try it," Tom said, with increasing earnestness. " Will you? I haven't the least doubt of your ultimate success if you undertake it. Come, will you pledge yourself? "

" Why, I presume I've always done it. I know I've done with my might whatsoever I had to do."

" That isn't the first one," Tom said, significantly. Then he went back to get more kindlings. When the dishes were done and the kitchen in order Maria went to the window and looked out into the moonlight, folding her arms on the window seat and staring out without seeing moonlight, or stars, or anything else but her own thoughts.

" Tom," she said, suddenly, as that person came in again, this time with a pail of water. " Have those men — Jerry, and those others you told me of — found a washerwoman to their mind yet?"

"No," said Tom, laughing. "Isn't it queer that they should be so particular? They keep in a continual growl. That Jerry is engaged to be married, they say; and I presume that is why he wants such shining linen. Mine shines beautifully, they say."

"Well, Tom, I'm going to put your 'whatsoever' straight into practice. You tell them, to-morrow morning, that I will do their washing for them. This is Friday evening. I'll begin next week, and you can keep on the lookout for some more people who want washing done."

Tom set his pail down so heedlessly that the water splashed over himself and the floor.

"You can't mean it!" he said, regarding her with an incredulous stare.

"Yes, I can. I'll show you if I don't. I can buy soap and starch, and we are obliged to keep fire; and washing clothes at seventy-five cents a dozen isn't unprofitable business. Besides, I can't find anything else to do. If it isn't a 'whatsoever,' I don't know what you would call it."

"Well," said Tom, after regarding her speechlessly for a few minutes, "I don't know but it is. It is one that requires rather more moral courage than car driving, I believe; and it only goes to prove to me that if you should take up that motto you would carry it out with power. But, Maria, I tell you, you have skipped several. I wish you would begin at the beginning."

"Well, I will," said Maria, energetically. "I'm not afraid of it. I've always believed that genuine religion — that which accomplishes the work in this world — was just doing with energy what was set before one to do. I'm willing to try it. I haven't the least idea what they say; but I'm not afraid of them. Shall I take them as they come?"

"That is the way I am doing," said Tom, with shining eyes.

"Very well. You say you are a 'whatsoever' Christian. I'll be a 'whatsoever' *woman*; and we'll see how far apart we'll keep. I'll look up the first one as soon as I have time."